THE DEVIL'S SCIENCE

BOOK 1

"IN THE BEGINNING"

First Edition

PAGE PUBLISHING, INC.
New York, NY

First originally published by Page Publishing, Inc. 2015

ISBN 978-1-68213-106-0 (pbk)
ISBN 978-1-68213-107-7 (digital)
ISBN 978-1-68213-583-9 (hardcover)

Printed in the United States of America

This book is dedicated to Shawn and Toby

In my life, I was blessed with two friends, who entered in my heart.
They took away my emptiness, and I hoped we would never part.
As time went by, I grew closer to them, each and every day.
The first one's name was Shawn, and we met one night in May.
At first he was a good friend, and grew to be much more.
He stayed with me when homeless, cold, scared and sore.
Shawn became my little brother, the one I never had.
He ended up wanting to stay with me, even over his dad.
We left the town we grew up in, and watched it fade in the mirror.
The future seemed fresh and new, although we were full of fear.
Our voyage brought us to Florida, where the weather was so hot.
Things were tough with money and jobs, but give up....we would not.
Enter my second best friend, a sheltie, cute as he was smart.
He came to live with us, and he immediately stole our heart.
His name was Toby, our little boy, and no one could care for him more.
The three musketeers were created, and we both loved him to his core.

Shawn loved him as much I, and Toby loved us both.

Together we went thru the trials of life, our bond continued its growth.

Years went by, and the three of us. were as happy as can be.

We lived a life of joy and laughter, that everyone could see.

In early morning, one November day, my Shawn, he went to sleep.

Alone in his room, to never wake again, the price he paid was steep.

Like all good things, they must come to an end, and the three of us became two.

I was sad and not myself, while Toby would search for you

I tried my best to keep pushing on, the best that I could do.

But the memory of his face would always come shining through.

Toby also could sense the loss, but selfishness he did not know.

He focused all his attention on me, and all his love he would show.

My Toby would cuddle up to me, closer than he ever did in the past

The sadder I got, the more he loved me, his love continued to last.

Time went on and he began to age, where he eventually lost his sight.

But nothing could dampen this puppy dogs heart, even with no light.

Years go by and he stopped playing ball, which I knew he greatly missed.

But to make up for the lack of things, my face he would constantly kiss.

At age 14, he was getting old, and was really slowing down.

But you could never tell it from his face, he never wore a frown.

One summer he was not doing well, but would never give up the fight.

For me he would stay as long as he can, and hold out with all his might.

But on the 1st day of October, all his fight was gone.

On that day he left me, and went to be with Shawn.

Near the end there will be signs from the stars. People with fear & foreboding of what is coming to our world. Luke 21:25-26

HISTORY OF AUTHOR

I was born in Upstate NY. My father died when I was just ten years old from a Service-related injury serving in the Korean War. My mother raised me and my two brothers and sister. I am the youngest of the four. After graduating from High School, I moved to the closest city and attended Community College. I graduated with a Double Associates Degree. I then worked for a bank as Head of Security. While there I slipped during an Ice Storm and fell, in which I fractured my spine. The injury was severe and I was forced to go on Workers' Compensation.

As with all Insurance companies, they fought my case to the point where it became necessary to hire an attorney. After not showing up multiple times for hearings, I was forced to fire him and represent myself. I won the case and did such a good job that the judge told me he had never seen anyone handle a case so well. He advised me that I should consider handling cases myself for others. While unable to work, I attended an on-line University and got my B.S. and M.A. I took the NYS Workers' Compensation Bar exam and passed on the first attempt. From that point on I represented thousands of Injured Workers', Disabled individuals and many Handicapped people for almost ten years.

With most of my family moved to Florida, I ended up closing my firm and moving down there to help my mother. I worked as a Legal Consultant for a Doctor for several years until I was in a Car-accident. While stopped in traffic someone hit me from behind doing over 50 mph. I was hospitalized and diagnosed with all the disks in my neck herniated (Four severely). I was forced to go on Disability.

The injuries to my neck are so extensive I am forced to see a Doctor and go to Physical Therapy. With these limitations, I decided instead of giving up altogether on life, I would do what has always been a great passion of mine... to write. So that brings us to the current.

A percentage of the profits from this book will be put towards a fund to open a Workers Compensation/Disability/Injury Firm to specialize in helping 9/11 workers/victims, who stayed at ground zero to help others and contracted medical complications and now years later, are being denied treatment.

EPIGRAPH

Thomas was a middle-aged man who lived a troubled life of sadness and grief. He tried to maintain his sanity through the worst events life had to offer. Little did he know that fate had something much more in store for him that would change his life and the world forever.

This story looks at the complexities of religion against the marvels of advanced technology and the many shades of grey in between.

It will challenge the seemingly easy process of determining what is right and wrong and show how there is never a clear path but degrees of lesser evil in all the choices we face.

Is there a God? Is there a devil? Is there a heaven? Is there a hell? Are there aliens? Is there more than one universe? Is there more than one reality?

You are about to take a journey with Thomas into a world that looks at these questions, which have baffled man since the beginning of time.

INTRODUCTION

I have never been someone who was religious or believed in the stories of the Bible. I had completed many years of college and accumulated six degrees. During that time I took many courses on different aspects of religion—introduction, origin, world religion, and several more. In theory, it just seemed to be a way to cope with the trials and tribulations of life and explain the unexplainable.

When my best friend died in front of me one morning and I saw the life leave his eyes, it took a part of me with him. I never fully recovered from that incident. If anything, it just made me realize that we are all just biological machines created by a random act of nature and there is no great power out there—but I could not have been more wrong.

Not only is there a God, but many of the religious events in the Bible are true. There are also great beings of advanced scientific technology that are similar to us. The way I found this out is a story that will challenge your own beliefs, no matter what they are.

CHAPTER 1

It had been over a month now since my best friend died. We were very close, and he knew me better than I knew myself. I met him when he was at his lowest in life. He was homeless and jobless, yet you could never tell that by his attitude and incredible sense of humor.

I was having a party at my rather luxurious apartment. I never looked down on people no matter their status in the world. Young or old, rich or poor, they were all welcome in my castle. It was summertime, and we were all in my barroom, playing darts and drinking. It was an atmosphere of friendship. Everyone was getting along, and conversations were flying back and forth. Each person's recent summer adventures were being told.

Shawn was mostly quiet at first, but as the drinks started to kick in, he began to move from group to group, engaging in each discussion. He made his way to my group, who were closest to the bar and was sort of the lead clique. Being that I was the owner of the apartment (as well as the booze), he came over and sat directly next to me in a very noticeable way that made everyone pause and acknowledge this obvious forward move.

"So you are the owner of this awesome apartment?"

"Yes, I am."

He put his hand out and told me his name. I told him I was glad to meet him.

He then said, "Well, I'm going to sit here next to you."

It was a bit uncomfortable right at that moment, but as he continued to talk, I realized he was well known and liked by everyone in the room. Although he did not use big words, he was quite good at expressing himself and excellent at describing events. In other words, he was not an educated person but very good with his communication skills.

There was just something about Shawn. I knew his background and knew he was practically homeless and broke, but he was still happy as a person could be and was the life of the party. Someone like that you can't help but like and want to be around.

From that night on he would no longer be homeless. A person with that kind of heart and attitude should not be tarnished by the great negativity that life can do to people. So I (by all symbolic standards) adopted him.

We eventually moved from the cold northeast to live in the south. We got jobs, another nice house, and lived happy and content for ten years, until that morning—the morning known to everybody as Black Friday (the Friday right after Thanksgiving). To me it was well named because it turned into the blackest day of my life. It changed me from a happy, enthusiastic, and optimistic person into the exact opposite of every one of those attributes.

Since I was only Shawn's best friend and not a true blood relative, I had no say over his funeral or what was to be done with his body. It was decided that, for cost-efficiency reasons, his body would be cremated and sent back up north. Before he was to be cremated, I went to the funeral parlor and asked if I could get a lock of his hair. I would not be able to attend his funeral due to the fact his father hated me for bringing him to Florida and would certainly not allow me to be a part of any final ceremony.

I was given the lock of his blond hair and thanked the director of the funeral home. For a year that hair stayed on my wall in the original plastic Baggie. I would stare at it for hours as well as talk to it.

That's when I started to think about religion again. Although all those college courses seemed to discredit it, I thought, what if it's real? That would mean Shawn is still around in some form. It's all I had. So I started to research the paranormal and stories of the afterlife. Book after book and site after site. Religion to witchcraft and everything in between was researched in depth.

I became so knowledgeable on the subject that I began to try conjuring spells and communication amulets. Nothing ever showed even the smallest sign of success. While doing all this, for some reason, an event from my past came back to me. When I was very young, in fact, the age where you just start to remember things (four to six years of age), I had a strange ability. I was not sure why I was just now remembering it. It was not anything super incredible, but it was noteworthy enough that my third-grade teacher took me to the side one day and discussed it with me.

I remember her name was Mrs. Stryker, a nice enough older lady about in her sixties. Although very smart and a good teacher, she would have a very hard time controlling a room full of rambunctious seven-year-olds. She would try and teach, and sometimes everyone would just ignore her and/or create havoc.

She lost her temper a few times, but this would only work for the first couple times and eventually fade.

I remember feeling sorry for her. She was good-hearted but just not aggressive enough to put a real scare into the kids in order to keep them in line. I was very popular. I was the class clown and made everyone laugh and was looked up to by just about every student. I guess one major reason I failed to remember this later in life was this attention and praise did not last into my teens. As time went by, I became more shy and ordinary.

But back then I was popular. My parents even saw it when they would go to teacher conference meetings. Every kid wanted me to go to their house to stay and would literally fight each other over it. When they would do that, I would step between them and make direct eye contact. I could make them stop fighting and get along. I remember the strangest aspect was I did not use words. In my mind I wanted them to stop fighting and get along, and they would. I would want them to shake hands and apologize to each other. They would do that too, without me saying a word.

Back then I just remember how cool it was, but being young, I thought it was just an ability everyone had and that I just learned to use it before everyone else in my class. It ended up being even more. When a kid would get too wild with Mrs. Stryker, I remember I would call their name, and they would turn to look at me, and as soon as our eyes met, their expression would change, and the hair on the back of my neck would rise. "Just sit back down and relax," I would say in my mind, and as soon as I did, they would return to their seat and often be overly quiet for the rest of the day. They would also be very apologetic and friendly towards me the next few days. When I would do this, the teacher would always be grateful. But the more I did it, the more she changed her look towards me from thankfulness to a look of concern.

I remember her asking me to stay after class just before lunch one day. She smiled with her always pretty face and proper clothing and said, "Thomas, I really appreciate you helping me at times with the class, but I don't like the idea that you are scaring or threatening your classmates."

Being young, I was confused about how she perceived this.

"Mrs. Stryker, I have never hurt or threatened anyone," I said with a look of puzzlement.

"Why do they all listen and obey you so well?"

I tried to explain that I just tell them to stop misbehaving and they just do it.

"But I don't hear you tell them that. You seem to just look at them."

"No, I tell it to them in my mind so you would not hear me."

She smiled and, I believe, just blew it off, as just being a young child who did not understand what she was trying to ask.

Remembering this gave me inspiration into paranormal events. It was also strange I had not thought about it in so many years. But if I did have some kind of telepathy or mind control, maybe I still have it, and maybe I could use it to talk to Shawn.

I tried to recall how I used to do it forty years ago. It was so long ago, and I barely remember doing it at all, let alone how it was done. I know it was not by speaking or, more accurately, not speaking aloud, but saying it in my mind. I also know the eye-contact aspect was important. We had to look into each other's eyes. If that was the case, how was I going to do that with Shawn?

Defeated again after what seemed like a short glimpse of hope, I looked upon my wall at Shawn's lock of hair. Every time I did, I would get this sick feeling rush through my stomach and then in my whole body. I missed him so much. To die at twenty-eight is too young. He had so much more to do. We had way more to accomplish.

Shawn and I were meant to accomplish many other things and have several more adventures before our lives came to a close. It was not fair. If there was a God, how could he allow events like this to occur?

I burst out into tears, as I do three to four times a day. Even after a year, it still hurts that bad. I may never get over it. I remember pounding on his chest and trying to breathe my air into his lungs so his brain would not starve from lack of oxygen. With every compression and each exchange of air, I was getting closer to exhaustion and yet the only result that could be seen was that Shawn would get colder and paler. I remember being exhausted, but I could not give up. He would never give up on me. Between compressions and breaths, I stopped to check to see if his pupils were fixed and dilated. I remember from college first aid that if his pupils were not responding to light, his brain was gone. When I raised his eyelid, that was what I was looking for, but that was not what caught my attention. His eyes were dark. Not that we have lasers or glowing eyes, but when we are alive, our eyes have a light to them. Shawn's eyes were dark and lifeless. That's when I knew my best friend was no longer in the room with me.

I would get so sad that it felt like a knife was plunged deep into my stomach. Other times it was darker—an anger that felt like I was on fire. I would lose my temper and punch holes in the walls and kick things. Why did you let him die God? I thought to myself. There can be no God if this can be allowed to happen. On nights like that, I would get to a point where my hatred would peak. When that would happen, something changes in me. I would not feel like myself. It was like I thought in a completely different way. It also felt like I was not alone.

When the anger maxed out, I could almost hear someone else. I knew I was alone and not insane (yet, at least), but a presence I could not describe.

When I would ask why, I would get an answer, but it was never anything positive. In fact, it was dark, and the responses were from the darkest realms of human thought.

> Me: Why did this happen?
> Voice: Because your god hates you.
> Me: What? Why did I think that?

Voice: Because you did not, I did, and he hates you.

During those events, my heart would race. The anger and the creepy feeling that I'm talking to myself in my head and getting answers were eerie. I decided to rationalize to myself that it was just a safeguard that my brain was utilizing, some sort of coping mechanism. So I would play along. I lay down in my bed and began to see how far this could go.

Me: So who are you?
Voice: You would not believe me if I told you.
Me: Well, I'm a brave guy, I can handle it.
Voice: You did not handle seeing your best friend turn colors. I think at one point he was a pretty shade of blue before he turned pale white.

Wow, that was dark, I thought to myself. This coping mechanism is supposed to be helping me, but saying things like that certainly does not.

Me: I don't think I want to play this game anymore. Good-bye.
Voice: Think you can turn me off so easily?
Me: Yes, I do, you are me and just my own subconscious, and I have had enough of playing this game. Good-bye.
Voice: Oh not so fast. I'm not you or your subconscious. That fucking Freud thought he had it all figured out. Glad I shut his lights off in 1939. He loved spring. It was his favorite time of the year, so I pushed him to the limit two days after spring began to put an end to him.
Me: What the hell!

This was getting too weird. The answers were too specific, and the voice was no longer sounding like me. I have no idea when Freud died.

I sat up from bed thinking I might have been in that state where your eyes are closed and you are starting to fall asleep. The comment about Shawn turning blue hurt. Flashes of that image kept going through my mind. I looked over at the wall to his lock of hair. "I think I'm starting to go nuts, Shawn. Should I be worried?" Just then the tack that kept the Baggie fastened to the wall popped and flew across the room, and the Baggie with his hair fell to the floor.

What the fuck! I jumped up and grabbed the Baggie from the floor. It was warm, in fact, very warm. I set it down on the stand and went looking for the tack on the other side of the room. I can understand the tack not being secure and coming loose and dropping to the floor. But how did it shoot across the room? I searched and searched but with no luck. I pulled my bed away from the wall and moved the furniture. I searched for over an hour and did not find it anywhere.

I have six college degrees. There is always a scientific explanation. The coincidence of it happening while the other me's voice was replying to my questions was strange. I was going to lie down and ask about the tack and try to get some more information to see if it would still work, but something made me decide that was not a good idea.

I went out to the living room and started talking to my nephew, who moved in with me after Shawn died. He and I were all the family each of us had. I told him about the tack event but decided not to talk about the answering voices in my head. Justin (my nephew) just laughed and only partially even listened to the story, as was normal. He was fifteen years younger than me and was in his late twenties, so his mind was full of all kinds of things other than my situation.

Justin was almost the same age as Shawn (two years younger), so they both got along extremely well. Shawn's death took its toll on Justin too. They quickly became close friends from the beginning. Shawn was like the big brother Justin never had.

Days turned to weeks, weeks to years, but the healing process did not seem to move with time. Some days it even seemed as though it was getting worse. I would see something that would remind me, and it would dawn on me Shawn is dead, like it had just happened, and that feeling would come over me so strongly it could drop me to my knees.

The voice I had heard in my room was not an everyday event or constant by any means. But I still heard it. It now sounded meaner and deeper each time. The things it would say would be darker and crueler each time. I began to believe that this voice was not any coping mechanism that was helping me through this grief but a warped part of me that was just getting worse.

I decided it was time I saw someone about it. The fact that it's been years and his death still hurts this bad is more than enough reason to seek counsel. I also have to discuss this voice. So I searched the Internet. There were many to pick from, but as I went to click on the very first one listed, a pop-up came on my screen. It took over the whole page, and it showed a very impressive list of credentials. The ad said he was a specialist in grief therapy. He was close-by and took my insurance. He seemed like the perfect choice. So I called and made an appointment.

The morning I went to see my newfound shrink, I was having a good day—not a great and happy day; those type seem to no longer exist. I was in a "dealing with it" frame of mind. I was optimistic that this doctor was going to be able to put me on the right track.

His office waiting room was noticeably bland. Everything was an antiseptic white. There were very few pictures on the wall except for one, an ink blot, which to me looked like two horns and the shape of the devil. I made a mental note to *not* mention that observation to him. I was the only one there and no receptionist to be seen, which I thought was odd. How good could this guy be if he has no clients? I thought to myself. Then I heard…

> Voice: Maybe he cures psychotic people like you quickly so he does not have to hear all the crying and whining for any prolonged period of time. Maybe best you just go home and not bother with all this. Maybe he will even make it all worse.

I was not expecting the voice. It took me off guard and away from my semipleasant day. I started to feel a major anxiety attack coming on. I immediately reminded myself. "Just ignore it. The Doctor will find a way to put an end to this crap."

Voice: Oh is that what you think? This guy is going to kick me out and put me in a jar. Would not be the first time that has been attempted and by far smarter and more powerful entities.

Now I was unhinged and shaking. This guy is not going to be able to help me at all if I go in there all stressed and nervous from the start. Maybe I can reason with my subconscious and get control over it long enough to get through the session.

Me: Listen, who wants to go through life scared and sad? That's no life at all. Let's try to keep a positive thought, shall we.

Voice: How positive do you think Shawn was when he was on the floor, choking? Or when they put him in that oven to turn him into ash? Think he was positive at that moment in time?

The laughter of this voice was roaring. It was so loud I could hear nothing else around me, until I finally did hear something else—a crackling sound, searing and snapping. Then I saw the image of Shawn's body being burnt and the skin popping and falling off, images so sharp that I could only describe them as some form of high-definition. Then the smell began, an odor that was so foul it made me gag.

I put my hands over my ears, but that seemed to make it louder. I then put my hands over my nose to stop the smell that was about to make me vomit. That made me smell it even stronger. I then put my hands over my eyes to stop from seeing this waking nightmare.

Once again, that only made it more vivid. This was something I had never experienced. This was worse than any symptom I had ever had. My heart was racing, and I was reaching a point where I was unable to tolerate it anymore. Then in the middle of this event, I saw Shawn, blackened and burnt, open his eyes and say, "Why didn't you help me?"

It was like a whistle had gone off, that my mind had reached the maximum it could tolerate. "Stop this!" I yelled in my mind. But it was not just in my mind. I had screamed this out loud—very loud. But suddenly it all stopped, and I could hear a different voice. "Mr. Williams, are you okay?" It was the doctor standing over me with a cell phone in one hand, like he was about to make a call, and a clip-board in the other. I looked up at him. All sounds, smells, and other stimuli from this event were gone.

There was a silence as we looked at each other.

He reiterated his question, "Are you okay? Do you need an ambulance?"

It took me a couple seconds to gather myself. "No, Doctor. I'm sorry."

"No need to be sorry, Mr. Williams. Let's bring you back to my office and get you a glass of water."

With that I followed him to a very nice-looking room with light blue walls, a waterfall (a small artificial water) and soft, relaxing music in the background. He got a paper cup and filled it with water from a dispenser and handed it to me.

"Please have a seat."

There was a couch like I had never seen before. It had the look of extreme comfort, like if you lay down on it you would have to fight to stay awake. I sat down and looked over at him.

"Basing on what I just witnessed in the waiting room, I have a feeling we have a lot to talk about."

His name was Dr. Olcult. He was middle-aged, around midfor-ties. He had very dark hair, almost jet-black, with no signs of thin-ning. He was average height, weight—everything was just average. He spoke slowly and articulated every word. His eyes were a dark brown that was so dark it was almost hard to differentiate the color with his pupil. He sat in an equally plush-looking chair with posture that was beyond perfect, almost to the point of looking uncomfortable.

Doctor: Now normally I would start with having you fill out a bunch of paperwork, but with what I just saw, I think we need to get right to it. Would you like to explain what was hap-pening in the waiting room?

Me: Well, I guess that looked pretty bad. That was the first time that has ever happened. I came here for events far less drastic. I mean, that was—

Doctor: Let me interrupt you. Let's not start with you feeling the need to make excuses or rationalize to me reasons for events that happen to you. If it's new or old, constant or periodic, it does not matter. What is important is that you tell me everything and not hold back and not feel reluctant or scared to tell me something. I don't do this with all my patients, but I have decided to do this with you. I am going to tell you about something that happened to me. It's farfetched and unbelievable, but it did happen, and I will tell you about it so you can feel free to describe your own wildest or scariest things and not feel like you are telling me about events that are too incredible. Okay?

Although I was a little annoyed at being interrupted on my first words spoken to him, he did have a way that put me at ease. So I nodded my head in agreement.

Doctor: When I was young, about seven to eight years old, I was abducted by aliens. They contacted me while I was alone in my bed.

I stared at him blankly as he looked at me, scanning for my response. We both sat there for what felt like forever—until he broke the silence.

Doctor: Most people have a little more input when I tell them that.

Me: I'm not sure how to respond to that, Doc. I'm here for help and you say something like that.

Doctor: As I said, I don't tell all my patients this, but I looked over your online application and saw you hold six college degrees. Two of which are in psychology? You were/are an attorney?

To me that gives you something many of my patients do not have. You are well educated and probably see and think in terms of logic and scientific fact beyond that of the norm.

Me: Yes, all the more reason that might not be a story to tell me, especially on my first visit.

Doctor: All the more reason I *should* tell you. I'm not going to go into detail about it other than to say to me it was as real as you sitting in front of me right now. It was hard to shake, and sometimes it still bothers me, but I have put the event in its place in my mind, a place where it is not forgotten, but it can do the least damage to me.

Me: And that's what you would like to do with my trauma, put it in a place where it can do the least damage?

Doctor: Possibly. But before we do that, I have to understand it, analyze it, and find out its who, what, where, and how. Know it like you know it. Only then can I decide how to best proceed and deal with it. Do you understand? As far as my abduction, I am not going to say any more about it until we have discussed what happened to you. Then, if you want, I will tell you everything that happened to me. Agreed?

Me: Sounds like a pitch to me, Doc, a story to just get me to feel that nothing is too outrageous to tell you. But that's okay. Sounds logical to me.

Doctor: See, that's that education I was talking about. I think we will get along fine and get these issues under control in no time.

After an hour of describing what happened to Shawn, we concluded the appointment. He said that we will talk about what was going on in the waiting room next time. We made an appointment for my next visit; he shook my hand and told me to hang in there.

Driving home, I was reviewing my conversation with him and started to think about what happened before the appointment.

That event was serious. What if that happens while I am driving or doing something else that takes all my attention? The images, the smell, not sure how much more of that I could take. That voice was so deep and scary now. It no longer sounded or represented me at all. I would have done anything to save Shawn, and subconscious or not, I would not think like that. It's just not me. But even the voice made that claim. But if it's not me, who is it?

I started to think of the other stuff the voice said too, the things about Freud and when he died. I did not even come close to discussing that in this session with the doctor. But we will need to—and soon. What is certain is that I need to get a handle on this problem.

CHAPTER 2

Back at home it was the usual empty house. My nephew was at work, and the house had that empty feeling that was created by the loss of Shawn. Every place I would look in any part of the house was a memory of something we had done.

I sat in my chair and turned on the TV to try and get this depression out of my head. Of course, TV was the same thing. Every show and commercial reminded me one way or another of the tragedy I witnessed.

It was starting to get dark, so I decided to take my Toby outside, my loving dog that Shawn and I raised, to let him walk around and do his business. Toby understood the loss of Shawn. He loved Shawn as I did. When Shawn died, Toby would search the house for him. That went on for over a year, and he still did it sometimes. He would go to Shawn's old room and look around. If the door was closed, he would scratch on it and whine. I would open the door for him, and he would run in as if he would find him lying there on the bed and wake him with kisses like he had done so many times in the past.

For the first several times, that was very hard and would always dissolve me to tears. I would talk to Toby as a human would do and try to explain, "He is not here and will never be here again," to which I would burst into tears and completely lose it for an hour or more.

It was a clear, hot Florida night, and the stars filled the sky, this night especially, because there were no clouds, and it was a new moon, so there was full clarity of the night sky. While staring up at them, I started to think about the doctor's opening line about being abducted by aliens as a child.

My scientific mind just kept returning to that admission as a way he could let me feel free to say anything without reservations. With so many stars just in our own galaxy and with the numerous galaxies in our known universe, it is just common sense and shear mathematics that so many possibilities would logically have to add up to other life somewhere in space. To believe that we are the only intelligent beings in the cosmos is naive and if they are centuries ahead of us technologically, their abilities would be nothing short of "God-like" to us.

Look how far we have come in just a hundred years. From cowboy days with horses and wagons to cell phones and space shuttles.

With that logic, if they were a couple thousand years more advanced, the things they could do would be incomprehensible to us. All the things in the Bible, which seem so farfetched, could easily have scientific explanations and suddenly not seem so unbelievable.

That night I lay in bed and watched TV. Many times the TV would be on, and I would be looking at it but not really watching it. It's more like not being alone. Having people talking on the shows felt like I had company and made the nights easier to bare.

The reception on this night was poor. Normally that was because of adverse weather, but I was just outside, and there was not a cloud in the sky. The screen would get fuzzy. The sound would get muffled. Great, my only enjoyable outlet and it can't even help me out tonight. Then it suddenly went to pure statistic. As I was about to grab for the remote and shut it off, I could hear something within the hiss. At first it sounded like someone with a CB radio was bleeding over onto the television set. It sounded like words and even sentences. I turned it up, and the screen went black, and the hiss lowered but was still audible.

Guess it's time for a new lamp for the TV. These new flat-screen TVs had a great picture but need a lot more upkeep. That's when I heard my name as clear as day. "We need to talk with you, Thomas." It said with only a slight hiss in the background. Then the TV went from black to an unusual colorful design. It was hard to describe, but my best analogy would be, if a rainbow was like talking with someone with two Dixie cups and a string, this was a cell phone, an unbelievable mix of high-definition colors making incredible designs. Then again I heard something, "Can you hear us?" Still convinced it was just a bleed-over from another device, I was about to shut it off, and then it said out loud, "Let's try turning up the gain." This reminded me of the lingo from back in my days of talking to the truckers on CB Radio. Then the TV went to a deep metallic blue color, and the hiss stopped completely, and I heard, "How is this, Mr. Williams?" I stopped and glared at the TV for a second. A feeling of uncertainty came over me. But it still could be bleed-over and maybe just a coincidence with my name. So I gave it a test.

> Me: Are you talking to me?
> TV: Yes, Mr. Williams.

What the hell. Voices in my head and now the television is talking to me. I guess Shawn's death really did put me over the edge. Hallucinations and severe depression was obviously symptoms that I had finally "cracked". Almost joking halfheartedly, I said out loud, "Talking to me through my head is not enough, you got to ruin TV for me too?"

> TV: We are not the one who talks to you in your head.

Then as quickly as all this happened, the TV went black and then went to the previous show with full sound and no sign of the audio or colors it had just displayed.

"Wait, then who are you? Who is the one in my head?" I yelled at the screen.

Seconds later my nephew Justin came running in.

"What's going on? Who are you yelling at?"

I looked at him and held back bursting into tears.

"Nothing, just a bad dream."

Justin knew I was not in good shape and did not take my best friend's death very well at all.

He shook his head and said, "Just try not to think about him."

And he shut door and went back to his room.

The next morning, I awoke refreshed. I slept well and had no bad dreams or any dreams at all that I could remember. Within a couple minutes of being awake, I started to think about the TV incident last night. I had enough psychology degrees to know voices in my head, and now voices on the television were not a good prognosis. I knew I had post-traumatic stress disorder, and it was causing me to have serious depression issues, but auditory hallucinations were a much more serious symptom. If I was to try and stay sane, I would need to know that these voices are not real. I must accept and acknowledge that my mind is manufacturing these events, and when they happen, I need to just ignore them and repeat to myself that they are not real, that it is just my injured mind creating them.

As I got out of bed, I looked at the wall that had the Baggie of Shawn's hair in it. It was not there. Then I remembered the tack flying across the room. That was not my mind playing tricks. I saw that happen. But I remembered what a college professor once told me, "There is always a scientific explanation." The paint on the wall heated and cooled, expanded and retracted, then, *pop*, it flew across the room. There, a scientific explanation.

So this day seemed to hold hope. These mind-created voices were just my broken psyche, and everything else can be explained. The appointment with my shrink was in a couple more days, and chances are, he was going to be able to help me even more—if aliens don't take him away first. That was *not* nice, I thought to myself. With the stuff going on in my mind, I have very little room to criticize anyone else.

I went to the kitchen, ready for breakfast, only to find there was very little food in the fridge or cupboards. My nephew was a big guy, like 230 lb. and 6' 2" and had an appetite to match. I guess it's time to do some shopping. So I got ready and made my way to the grocery store.

I was not rich by any means. When I was a lawyer, I had made really good money, but my move with Shawn to Florida never seemed to find me the same kind of job or pay. But the remnants of a time I did have money could still be seen, such as my car: a small two-door sports car with a soft top. I was a big Batman fan, so I had decorated it to look like a small Batmobile. I had even paid some guy from a garage who did work out of his home to add some cool gizmos. I had a lever that I could pull that would release roofing nails from underneath and behind the car. When roofing nails land, they all tend to be in an upward position and are fairly long. It would easily flatten the thickest tires of anyone pursuing me. Another cool thing was a reverse CB radio.

It was not capable of being used as a regular CB anymore; instead, it could transmit radio waves that could overtake and distort any wireless device within a mile. Police radios, CBs, even cell phones and TVs would be distorted. I, of course, was never in a situation to use the roofing nails or the air-wave distorter (as I called it). It turned out to be my A.W.D was just a fun way to mess with people if I got bored. I never really used either gizmos because of how highly illegal they both were.

The car itself would turn heads. It just stuck out, and I can't remember a day where I took it out when someone did not mention or compliment it some way. It was my pride and joy and was kept in mint condition, almost ten years old and not even ten thousand miles on it. It also had many added engine extras too that made it faster than I would ever need. It was my baby, and I loved that car.

As I pulled into the store, I was lucky and got a second-row parking spot. This was rare because where I lived it was very populated and a continuous madhouse. It was very different from where I grew up in my little town in Upstate New York.

As I entered the store, there were two guys in their mid-twenties having what appeared to be a very heated conversation. It was so intense that I was hesitant to even walk by them, but I had to because they were standing in front of the entrance. I just kept my eyes down and walked by them. Not that I'm a wimp, but two guys in great shape that are half my age were not something I wanted to deal with.

In the store I started shopping for things I needed. Picking up way too much, I thought of the old saying "Never go shopping on an empty stomach" is very true. I got what looked like a cart full of stuff and headed down the last aisle. When I made the turn to proceed, there were the two feuding gentlemen, who still seemed to be in a very poor mood with each other. As I turned the corner, my cart accidentally hit one of the guys right in the hip.

The guy stopped his disagreement with his buddy and set his full attention on me.

"What's up, homie? Watch what you're doing, you fuckin' retard."

I tried to apologize as fast as I could, but nothing I said was being heard by this guy. So I let him cut a few more insults and finish his sentence and again said I was sorry and started to walk away. The guy's friend seemed more interested in not wanting to make a scene and tried to get his buddy to just let it go.

I started pushing my cart down the aisle, looking at things I was not even interested in just to show the appearance that I was not scrambling to leave. Just then I heard, "Hey, asshole, were you that clumsy when you were giving your best friend CPR? No wonder he died. Hahaha!" I stopped in my tracks and just stood there for a couple seconds, not processing how this stranger could know that information and just focusing on how mean and rotten that comment was.

I turned around, and the two were still looking at each other, bickering. That seemed weird since he just yelled directly at me, but rational thought was not my best attribute at that point.

"What did you say to me?"

I glared at the dude. They both stopped and glared back at me.

The one I did not hit with cart said, "Dude, he accepted your apology. Just leave it be and move on."

To which I said, "The comment about my best friend was uncalled for, and how the hell do you even know what happened that day?"

They both looked at me puzzled, and the nicer of the two spoke again, "No one said anything like that. Better go home and take your meds."

"Yeah, I will do that. Try and not spend all your food stamps at once. You might need to trade some for crack," I said in my best smart-ass tone.

The guy I hit with the cart dropped everything he was carrying and headed directly toward me. From the corner of my eye I could see someone who worked at the store, who was stocking shelves, get up and head down the aisle.

The man came right up to me, walking in a weird kind of swaying way, looking down as he approached me. His buddy tried to grab him but was pushed off. The man came up to me and acted like he was going to make a hand gesture and quickly made a fist and punched me right in the chest. This, of course, hurt and took some wind out of me, but it did not do as much damage as I thought it would. He then grabbed me by the shirt and pulled me up close to him. Our noses were less than half an inch apart.

My mind was going a hundred miles an hour, anger, fear, and a multitude of emotions all combining at once.

"I'm gonna fuck your world up, boy."

Then our eyes locked. The hairs on the back of my neck stood up, but the panic was gone. I looked deep into his eyes and could only describe it as being like a combination lock clicking into its final number. I could hear several different shouting voices, but they were all his, yet he was not speaking.

"You need to calm down," I said in my mind.

His face went from anger to a puzzled look.

In my mind I once again said, "You need to let go of me and stop this anger. All your anger has escaped you. All you can feel is the day your mother told you that she would sell the car or house to help you and that she loved you more than she loved anyone or anything else in this world."

He immediately let go of my shirt and took two steps back. By this time his buddy and the store manager were quickly approaching.

Store Manager: Is there a problem here?
Guy 2: No, sir, we were just leaving.

The guy who grabbed me just stood there looking at me but with a glazed look like he was not really seeing me. His buddy grabbed him. This sort of broke the stare, and he shook his head and wiped his face, which had a tear rolling down it.

Store Manager: My stock boy saw it all, sir. Do you want me to call the police?

I was about to respond when the guy who hit me spoke up and said, "No, I am very sorry to this man. I was in the wrong and started it all, and my mother would be ashamed of my behavior in this situation. I am very sorry, sir, for what I did."

Everyone was silent, and we all seemed to look at each other.

The manager looked at me and said, "It's up to you, sir. What would you like to do?"

"Everything is fine, it was just a misunderstanding. I'm sure this gentleman would sell his house or car to make it right."

His buddy was taken aback by this response and said, "What the hell kinda shit is that to say?"

But he was cut off by his friend, who stopped him and stared at me with a look as though he had seen a ghost.

"You're right, sir, very well said. Once again, please accept my apology."

His buddy grabbed him, and they headed down the aisle and out the store. The manager asked once again if I was sure I did not want the police to come. I assured him it was okay and it's all good. I paid for my stuff and went back home.

The ride home had me shaken. I even had to pull over at one point, fearing I would crash or become unconscious, because I was practically hyperventilating. These events were all coming too fast and too close together. Did this store event really happen? If I am hearing voices that are not there, could whole events be occurring only in my mind?

I made it home and put the groceries away. I had not eaten since the night before. I remember hearing, when your blood sugar gets low from lack of eating, people can get sick and even hallucinate. So I had myself a bowl of cereal and a container of fruit—a very healthy meal (I rationalized to myself) that would make my mind as well as my body feel healthier.

I sat down in the living room and turned on the TV. I began to review the store incident. It was not till then I connected what happened at the store with what used to happen in third grade with Mrs. Stryker—the ability to help her keep my classmates in check when they would get rowdy and the essential eye contact for it to work. But that had not worked in over forty years. But I also came to realize, I never tried to do it much after those very young days of my youth.

Then that thought came to me again—my professor's philosophy, "To all things there is a logical explanation." But each day with each new event, that concept began to be harder and harder to use as an explanation. Are all these things related? The tack, the voices, the TV, and now this event at the store, is there a common element that connects them together? Then the sad realization came to me that brought me back. I am losing it. I may not even be able to trust what happens to me even when I see or hear it. My stomach felt like it was going to send my healthy meal right back up to me with that thought. Maybe I died and Shawn did not and this was some afterlife experience. But if things happen in front of you, how do you test if it is real or Memorex.

The thought of not even being able to trust my own senses or perception was enough to trigger a deep depression. I sat in my chair most of the day without the TV even on, worried that it might trigger another hallucination. So I would just stare out the window and try to think of some happy times with Shawn.

Birthdays, Christmases, and Halloweens were all fun and enjoyable because Shawn made them enjoyable. In the darkest of times he would crack a joke and somehow make a dim situation lighter and more manageable.

But instead of this helping, it would start the chain of events in my body—stomach ache, headache, and anxiety. The world is full of rotten people who harm others on a constant basis, but we will let them live and flourish and allow fate to take the good ones. There could be no superbeing who would do that or advanced being that could see any logic in this way of thinking.

All we are is a germ that developed into something bigger, meaner, and more destructive. No miracle, just random events that created us. Anyone who thought otherwise was just grabbing at straws and believing whatever got them through the day. It's all just bullshit created by bullshitters and—

Just then it started to happen. I could hear laughter.

Voice: Hahaha!

It started very low, but I could hear a steady hysterical laughter. I also recognized the voice. It was not the robotic voice I heard on the TV the other night; it was the deep and dark one from my mind.

Me: Think this funny, do you? Think my world outlook is worth a giggle?

With that the laughter got louder and even more hysterical. I shut my eyes and tried to control what I now believe is just me. So if it's just me, I can stop it. But try as I might, the laughter just got louder and louder. Something snapped in me. I suddenly had the most "who gives a fuck" feeling I have ever had.

I jumped up from the chair and went to the kitchen. I opened the drawer and pulled out the biggest and sharpest knife I could find. I took it and put it across my wrist.

> Me: I can stop you from laughing. I can control you one way or another, and on this day, I have had enough.
> Voice: Ooooohhhh! Hehehehehe, hahaha, hahahaha!
> Me: You're right, not fast enough.

So I took the knife and went into the bathroom to look in the mirror so I could be sure to see what I am slicing and get it right. I raised the knife once again to my throat and looked into the mirror, trying to find that big vein that I always see in my neck. I had enough, and I was not even scared or reluctant at that point. I was on a mission, and it was going to happen. When I had the knife lined up just right, I was going to make a last statement to myself, so I looked myself right in the eyes.

At this point the laughter stopped, and what I saw in the mirror was similar to my image but was not me. It was like a twin brother of me that was a biologically perfect version of me but who went through a completely different life—not a life of pain and struggle but pampered and well adjusted, no blemishes or dark circles under the eyes, nothing that showed even one day of stress. Other than that, it was me.

I locked into my reflection's eyes, and the hairs on the back of my neck rose, and before I could make a lock with that final combination click, I was tackled and brought to the ground, the knife pulled from my fingers and thrown away, my hands forced to my sides and pinned.

> Justin: What are you doing, Thomas?

It was my nephew, Justin, who must have just got home from work and walked in during the midst of this.

> Justin: You were going to kill yourself? Do you think Shawn would want that? What would that do to all of us?

He was visibly shaken, where I was just the opposite. I was calm and even a little confident. Something to do with the refection in the mirror. I just stared up at him.

> Me: I'm okay now, Justin.
> Justin: Oh yeah, you're just fine. Screaming nightmares and now ready to slash your own throat. You need help. You need to see someone.
> Me: I am seeing someone—a psychiatrist, a good one. I started last week and will see him again tomorrow. So please let me up. It was not what it looked like.
> Justin: You're holding a twelve-inch knife to your neck, how else should I interpret that?
> Me: I was just testing a theory. I was not going to kill myself.

At that point, he let me go and grabbed the knife off the floor. He gave me his best serious look and shook his head.

> Justin: No more testing theories tonight, okay?

"Deal," I said with a lighthearted warmth that even I noticed was unlike me. He left my room and slammed the door. I got up and sat on my bed. I really did feel different. I felt stronger and confident and even smarter. As I would think, the process seemed fast. Whatever happened was not a negative experience. It was a good thing. It almost felt like a battery in me was recharged or replaced by a top-shelf alkaline brand after always using a store or generic brand.

Justin spent the rest of the night checking in on me by giving me an unfriendly glare. It was his way. Instead of being sympathetic and supportive, he was angry and worried I would try something else.

After way too many of these hourly checkups on me from my nephew, I decided to call it a night and go to my room. I brought in my Toby and lay on the bed. I looked at the TV for a second and decided I was not going to start being afraid of it. I turned it on and started to watch the late news.

There was some special news event in the science world, which was always interesting to me, and I needed a good diversion. So I turned up the volume and let myself be encompassed by it. It was talking about a spacecraft we had sent out many years ago—the *Voyager* space probe. It gave some background about its launch date back in the seventies and how a golden album was put on it with all kinds of information, sounds, and a map of our location. It also explained that after these many years, it is the fastest-moving object mankind has ever made. At this point, it has left our solar system and just now entering the Oort cloud, a cloud that surrounds our solar system, and *Voyager* is now on its way into deep space.

That is truly fascinating we created something that actually has left our little solar system, even if it took almost four decades to achieve.

The final part of the story was what had the scientists and broadcasters puzzled. As it was passing the outer planets, they would keep turning it around and have it send us back images of Earth , which was nothing but a mere dot of light at that distance. They did it again when it went past Neptune and finally entered the Oort cloud. At that point the earth could not be seen, and our sun was barely a dim light. But when it entered the Oort cloud, they turned it around and were puzzled when they could no longer see our sun or anything in our solar system. They could see the proper constellations, but nothing from our solar system. Even stranger, the Oort cloud, which is huge and encompasses our whole solar system, could not be seen. They were explaining that there had to be some kind of malfunction because the Oort cloud is so enormous and the craft just entered it that it was virtually impossible it would not see the cloud or any part of our solar system.

After the hard-core national news finished the story, I was so intrigued by this science anomaly that I switched over to the Science

Channel, where an astronomer was stating that he saw the pictures *Voyager* was sending back, and what it was showing was not only the lack of our solar system and the Oort cloud but it was showing the constellations behind us. In other words, it was a picture of space as if our planets and sun were not even there. Once the Oort cloud was entered, all the stars on the other side of us, which *Voyager* should not be able to see because our solar system would be in the way, were clear and visible.

Once again, I thought back to my college professor. "Must be a logical explanation." The guidance system is off, or it's just not transmitting back properly due to the distance of something we have never had that far out. Either way, it was interesting and a good distraction. I thought to myself how this would make for good small talk to Dr. Olcult tomorrow, who was claiming he was abducted by aliens. Maybe he will have an answer. With that I shut off the TV and quickly found myself falling to sleep.

CHAPTER 3

Waking up is always hard for us humans. The first reaction is, "Let me sleep a few more minutes." Thus the obvious creation of the snooze button on alarm clocks. But for me it was even more difficult than that. Sleep was my escape from this nightmare my life had turned into. Yeah, nightmares would happen (and often did), but many times I got to relive good times of the past or do incredible things that the realities of this world would not permit. But it was a vacation of sorts from the work of life itself—because my waking hours were work. Conversing with people and putting on a fake smile to do small talk when I really no longer wanted to talk to anyone were work to me.

All joy was sucked out of me when I saw Shawn's life leave his body. It made things come into focus. This is what is in store for all of us. No happy endings. Just pain and death were the only certainties for all our futures. If you say that to a group of people, they would think you are mentally ill when, in fact, the ones who walk around with no worries and are smiling over 90 percent of the time are the ones that are truly mentally ill. They are in a state of full denial. Their positive nature, a complete work of fiction used as a coping mechanism to get through to the next day. The only true sanity is to face that we have a limited window of time. During that window, most of it will be filled with sadness and loneliness.

When that window of time is complete, you are either R or R—roasted in an oven till you are ash or rotting in the ground till you are maggot food. Harsh, for sure, but not ignorant—accurate.

"Excellent. Bravo. Bravo. That was outstanding, Thomas. I think you could make the happiest, most well-adjusted person on the planet decide to go on a baby-barbecuing field day. Hahaha! You are just my type of human."

I opened my eyes to see I was sitting at a long Elizabethan dining room table in front of a giant fireplace. As I looked around, I could see I was in a giant room with a ceiling so high it could not be seen and just disappeared into the darkness. There was very expensive art on the walls. Everything just screamed top-of-the-line, high class, high quality, rich, and premium.

I was seated at the head of one side of a long table. I looked down to see I was dressed in a full suit of soft, shiny material. I would guess some kind of Armenta suit. The room was dimly lit, but I could make out there was another person on the other side of the table.

I jumped up and got to my feet. What is this? Where am I? Although I did not know where I was, there was something familiar about it all. The room felt somehow familiar to me. I just could not place it.

"Now, Thomas, please sit back down. I went out of my way to see that all your favorite foods were available to you," said the person at the end of the table. "What this is, it's dinner. As far as where this is, well, that will take a lot more explaining."

I started to walk toward the voice that began to also sound familiar to me. As I got closer, the person stood up. It was a young man, maybe twenty-one to twenty-three. He had fiery red hair, semi-long with an eighties part on the side and feathered back. He was dressed way more casually in a "sharp dressed skater look" ensemble. I hated to admit it to myself, but the guy was good-looking in the "movie star/model/rock star type" way.

I was scared and disoriented, trying to recall my last thoughts and remembering I had just went to sleep. A dream would fit, but of all my dreams, I never had one so detailed or realistic. The smell of the fire and the food were obvious. The brilliant colors of the expensive paintings were vibrant. If it was a dream, it was of a level and quality I had never had before.

> Man at Table: Well, it is but isn't, Thomas.
> Me: What?
> Man: Your question. Is this a dream?

I shut my eyes and took a deep breath. I have had a freaky last couple days, and this is just more of the same. So when I opened my eyes, it will all be gone, and if it has not, I am going to play it cool and go with it.

I opened my eyes to see the room had changed to a living room area. Same fireplace and same person and what appeared to be the same awesome mansion.

Man: It seemed like you were not interested in the fine meal I had gone through so much trouble to create for you, so I thought we could relax in here and talk. I am sure you have some questions.

Me: Okay, I will go along with this dream. Seems pretty cool. A mansion, I'm dressed in an awesome power suit. You're a good-looking young man to talk with. What the hell.

Man: Interesting choice of wording. Of course, that is one of the reasons I picked you. You're no dummy. No genius either, but your ability to think in the abstract is well above average.

Me: Well, thank you. Can I ask your name?

Man: Not at all, Thomas. I'm the devil, Satan, but you can call me Luke. Since we will be working together, that seems less formal.

I tried not to flinch and kept my demeanor. I was convinced at this point it was a dream, so there was no need to get scared.

Me: How is Luke in any way an informal name for Satan?

Devil: Lucifer is what I have always been best known as, and the shortened version—Luke.

Me: I see. Well, that makes sense. You look nothing like what the ages of time have painted you to appear like.

Devil: I look different to everyone. Actually, very few have seen me, and even fewer have had the honor of talking to me.

Me: Well, I guess I should be honored. A privilege indeed.

Devil: Oh sarcasm, one of my favorites, for sure. I appear as I do to you because I am a combination of six of the best-looking young men you have seen in your life all meshed together.

Me: You do look familiar to me in a nonspecific way.

Devil: Yes, you have good taste 'cause I am, in your eyes, of course, a very handsome young man.

Even though it was a dream, the subject matter was getting a little too personal, and I did not want to lose my calm and collective appearance.

Me: So what can I do for you? I have had dreams of you in the past. Other than not looking like you do now, you were also not as pleasant.

Devil: Those dreams were your subconscious creating stories for you. That is not what this is. You must realize the detail and colors are more vivid. But mostly the time lag is gone that dreams have. This is in real time.

Me: And HD or, should we say, IMAX quality. Hehe!

Devil: Amazing, Thomas, you do have a sense of humor. I have observed you throughout the years. I thought you had lost that. It was your incredible negativity that I always enjoyed. Your dark version of life rivals my best work.

Me: Well, glad I have been so entertaining to you. So what is this all about? You say few have seen or talked to you before. Why me?

Devil: Human existence is about to be wiped out. I thought you may want to help me stop that from happening.

Me: Now why would the king of darkness and evil want to save mankind? Sort of a flaw in this dream. It's losing its continuity.

I finally decided to sit down on the other chair that was both identical and sitting by the fire. As I sat close to him, his appearance was hard to ignore. If I was to build the ideal version of a young male, he was it. His fiery red hair shined brightly from the light of the fire. His body was lean and toned. His eyes were a warm dark brown. He was good-looking by any and all standards but designed for my particular tastes. Everything about him was just the way I would want the ideal person to look like.

Even though I was still pretty sure it was a dream, I started to realize this was no normal dream. The time lag he mentioned began to be really obvious. Time was proceeding like real time, not dream time. Every minute felt like a minute, unlike dreams, where events happen quickly and things and details change rapidly.

Devil: Starting to come around, are we, Thomas?

Me: You did not answer my question. The devil is not known for his good deeds or wanting to save us humans, so why?

Devil: Let's put it this way, I would be bored without you beings. I would become as lonely and depressed as you are.

Me: Why doesn't God save us? Is that not more of his thing?

He stood up and walked over to the bar and grabbed what looked like a remote control. When he did, I got a good smell of him. It was not a cologne or body spray of any kind but a naturally pleasant aroma. If I had to guess, it was like my mind was scanned for the perfect pheromone extract that was irresistible to me, and it was hard to shake.

Devil: I don't know the answer to that, Thomas. Why don't you ask him? I have not seen him since the beginning. I'm not sure he still even exists at all anymore.

Me: So he does not watch over us, but you do?

Devil: Some things I can explain to you, other things would take too long, and many things you just would not comprehend. So go easy with those types of questions.

He returned to his chair right next to mine. This was turning more into one of those sensual dreams with a little added "save the world" content to it. But it was not unpleasant at all. In real life, a gorgeous young guy like this would not even give me the time of day. But to be alone and the center of his attention, well, how can I not enjoy this.

Devil: Try to keep focused, Thomas. I did not control how you perceived me, but if it is going to distract you, I can appear in a more devil-like form.

Me: No!

I jumped way too fast in answering that question and quickly regained composure.

He smiled in a very appealing devilish way at my reluctance of him changing his appearance.

Devil: Okay, Thomas, I'm flattered, but back to business, okay?

Me: Of course, saving the world, I'm right there with you, Luke.

Devil: Maybe if you're good, we can do some fun things. See, I am not a homophobe at all. That sort of prejudice is beneath my level of thinking, and we are going to be seeing a lot of each other. But for now, let's keep it clean.

Even in my own dreamworld, I get the cold shoulder. This took me down a couple notches—not that it showed outwardly, but I could feel it. I have not had a lot of love of that kind. I had close friends and best friends, but a very limited amount of intimate relationships since I grew up hiding my sexuality as a "closeted gay kid". Even being able to express seeing someone attractive was never possible, especially during my era of the eighties and nineties.

Devil: I want to make one thing clear right now. I can read every thought you have and feel every inch of your emotion. We are only talking verbally here because it's better for the aspect of translation. To connect with you in a telepathic way may injure your mind. My thoughts and what I have seen throughout the ages would overwhelm you. So we will just communicate the old-fashion way—verbally—okay?
Me: Yes.
Devil: Great, one-word answers. Okay, Mr. Thomas.

At this point he stretched out in the chair and put his really nice DC skater sneakers up onto my lap and made another devilish smile.

Devil: Better, but if my appearance distracts you too much, I will turn into a human-sized dust mite, and we can finish this talk that way. Got it?

My immediate instinct was to act like I was offended at being a human footstool, but in all reality, the contact was nice. So I rolled my eyes and acted like it was no big deal.

"Please proceed, the people of Earth are counting on us," I said in an old black-and-white B-type-movie way.

Devil: You remember watching the news about the *Voyager* spacecraft leaving our solar system and entering the Oort cloud? Well, as much as your all-knowing scientist thinks the Oort cloud is just some natural phenomenon, it is not. Your creator made it to encompass your quaint little star and its planets. It's what you would call a cloaking device. It completely hides your solar system.

Me: Why?

Devil: To hide all his little experiments from outside danger. But now your *Voyager* craft has breached it, and it's been spotted by some very dangerous beings that will likely want to eat the population of the planet.

Me: So there is other life? I knew it.

Devil: Duh!

He turned on the TV with the remote. It showed the *Voyager* craft entering a crowded debris field and then entering the massive blackness of space with an uncountable number of stars. The TV changed to me from the previous night walking in my backyard. It showed me looking up at the night sky thinking about the stars and galaxies, except the TV had the audio of my thoughts being played through the speakers, just as I was thinking them that night.

Me: Talk about breach of security. Do you have all my thoughts and actions on audio?

Devil: Focus, Thomas, the earth destroyed, everyone you know dead and eaten. But to answer your question, yes, I have everything you have ever done or thought. Don't feel too special though. I have it from everyone—everyone alive or who has ever lived.

I sat there silently. This was quite the dream, but if it's not, it's one bad situation. I also noticed, my extremely good-looking host was being less cordial as time went on.

Devil: Yes, that is true too. I am not accustomed to being nice to you mortals. This situation has me in a very unique predicament. So maybe less questions and more cooperation are in order.

Me: So here or in the real world, am I an open book to you? You can just tap into my noggin at any time. Not sure I like that.

Devil: Think I care if you "like that"? You should be honored to be in my presence at all. How would you enjoy talking to a germ or bacteria and explaining algebra to it?

With that I had enough. I pushed his sneakers off my lap.

Me: Okay, beam me back. This dream has taken a turn, and I no longer care for it.

The devil, obviously irritated by my words and pushing off his resting feet abruptly, glared at me.

Devil: Okay, I'll send you back. But how about a little parting gift?

He pushed a button on the remote, and on the screen was Shawn lying on the floor where I found him, but this time he was still alive. He was squirming and holding his throat. He was having trouble breathing, and I could barely make out what he was saying, "Tom, Tom, help me, choking, help, Tom."

I looked at the devil, who was watching the screen with a smile, the same smile that just a little while ago I had found so appealing, but now I wanted to rip it off his face. He pushed another button, and the screen went off.

Devil: Never knew he was calling for you to help him, huh?

Me: Now I see the Satan I have heard about. Low-life piece of shit. You think I'm going to help you do anything now? Wow, and I'm the bacteria? Kind of missed the psychology classes when being a super smart, all-powerful being.

Devil: I did not do this. All I have done is show you what happened in the room when he was alone that day. Truth often hurts. Thought you were used to that by now. Maybe some other footage.

Then he pushed another button, which showed Shawn being put onto a sliding bed in a crematorium. The door slammed shut, and the flames kicked on. But I could not watch it. I closed my eyes and started to scream, "No! No! No!"

I opened my eyes and looked up to see my nephew. I was back in bed in my room. The tears were flowing down my face, and I was covered with sweat.

Justin: That's it. You're going to see someone.

I shook my head and got my bearings.

Me: Yes, I am, and my appointment is today, and I'm getting some answers from this doctor.

While getting ready for the day and my appointment, I began to feel like I was on a constant buzz. The lines between reality and the unknown were beginning to blur. What a messed up dream—if it was a dream. I had to weigh the value of things at this point. Logic would dictate it must not have been real, but there was a lot of weird things happening. If I was losing it, then it's all just me, but if things continued even during my waking hours, I have to consider other options.

Time was getting close to my appointment, but I still had a half hour. With my past obsession to research and all the books I had accumulated, the one I did not look through was the Bible. With my recent conversation with Satan (dream or not), maybe I will take a quick look. I remember I had an old Bible my grandparents had in a box of storage stuff in the garage. After some digging and fights with some huge Florida spiders, I finally found it. It was dusty and dirty and buried in a box that looked like it had not been opened in decades, but in my mind, the older the more reliable, as time corrupts stories and especially religion.

I brought the book to my room. It was a very thick book indeed. I remember from my many religion classes that most of the Satan and evil stuff were in the back with Revelation. So I began to thumb through the pages, and I noticed that there was a bulge in the back of it—possibly a bookmark. As I got to that page, I saw what it was. That all so familiar feeling came across me. The item that was stuck in the pages was a tack. But it was not just any tack; it was the tack that held Shawn's lock of hair in the Baggie to the wall.

There was no way to be positive, but it was the blue tack with an X on the tip, a sort of odd tack as very few were like that.

The tack was stuck into one of the pages buried to its hilt. It was in a verse that stated, "It was the beast." As I read around the spot, it talked about the devil. It was more than just a coincidence. That tack could not have left my room and found its way to a box buried in the garage. It was stuck into a part that was directly referring to the devil, the person I had just dreamed about that night before. Although I was scared, there was a calmness that blended with the fear in me. Maybe I am not going insane. Maybe all the stories and unexplained stuff have an explanation. I would have to be a fool to not consider the flip side to this—that it's real and I am part of something much bigger that is playing out in a scale so large it's hard to take it all in.

Right then I decided I was not going to favor the idea that I was going insane anymore. I will still be skeptical, but even scientists have to give in to evidence they don't like, especially when it becomes overwhelming.

But it may not be a good idea to tell the psychiatrist everything. Telling him I'm talking to the devil and controlling the minds of people might get me a long vacation. So I will temper my wording and edit my experiences. Maybe focus on this Oort cloud aspect.

Back in the waiting room, I found myself staring at that bizarre ink blot picture again. "The devil looks nothing like that," I thought to myself. He looks more like a model on the cover of a *GQ* magazine combined with a surfer/skater. But as I thought more about the devil, as good-looking as he is, I realized what a dick he can be, especially toward the end. That was beyond evil to show Shawn being cremated. If I have that dream again or if it's really him, I'm not sure I would even talk with him. But it did really seem like he wanted me to genuinely help him.

Why would the devil want to help mankind? He said he would be bored without us. Maybe there is something to that. I think it has more to do with the balance of the universe. If every day was happy and great, happy and great would become routine and eventually would become meaningless and inevitably be a nightmare. Under this philosophy, bad (or evil) is needed. The negative events make the good ones better. I always wondered about the great question of why such bad things have to happen, but it seems to make sense now. If this theory is correct, God would need a counterpart to make existence work and have meaning.

As I was deep into these theological and philosophical thoughts, I saw the doctor coming down the hallway. He waved me back into his office. I resumed my seat on the overly comfortable couch, and he sat at his chair. The waterfall and smell seemed to bring me back the feelings of the original visit.

Dr. Olcult: So how are we doing today? Better than the last visit, it would seem. No screaming profanity in the waiting room?

Me: I am sorry about that, not sure I was screaming profanity, but to answer your question, yes, I do feel a bit better.

Dr. Olcult: Good. See, just one visit and you're almost cured. Surprised you even decided you needed to come for a second visit.

The room was silent as I tried to assess if he meant that or not. But after ten seconds of uncomfortable tension in the air, he smiled and said, "That was a joke, Thomas. I do want you to talk, but I would like you to talk about whatever you like."

Me: The Oort cloud?

He looked at me with a puzzled expression.

Dr. Olcult: Be glad to talk about that, it's your dime. What about it? I see you listen to the news.

Me: Yes, incredible we have created something that not only has breached our solar system but has been able to enter the Oort cloud as well.

Dr. Olcult: Yes, we have come a long way. We thought getting to the moon was a—

Before he did more small talk, I interrupted him.

Me: The Oort cloud is a very unique thing, don't you think? Scientists have not seen anything exactly like that surrounding any other systems.

Dr. Olcult: Yes, that's true, but our solar system has many unique properties compared to others. Most gas planets are close to the sun and the solid ones farther out unlike—

Me: Did you hear the *Voyager* craft turned its cameras around to look back at our solar system and could not find it or even our sun?

The doctor did not answer right away. I would gather he was kind of upset about being interrupted and just gave me a blank stare. I really did not care. I was paying to talk to him. "My dime," as he put it.

Me: Sorry, Doc, not trying to break in when you talk. Forty-five minutes go by fast. I want to hear more about your abduction.

Dr. Olcult: For one thing, the *Voyager* probe is almost forty years old, and its onboard computer was never designed to go that far, travel that fast, or last that long. The fact it cannot look backwards properly or send accurate data doesn't surprise me one bit. I think we should talk about you, Thomas, and what appeared to be a two-way conversation you were having in my waiting room last time. That might be a better use of our time.

Me: I don't. So just tell me what they looked like?

Dr. Olcult: Okay, let's split the difference. Tell me what was going on in the waiting room last time, and then I will tell you about my event. Deal?

Me: I sometimes hear a voice. But I now realize it's just my subconscious trying to balance the ups and downs of existence as we age and go through the events of our life. Did they look like us? What was the exact date?

Dr. Olcult: Well, Thomas, that's a very standard, if not sterile, answer. Sounds like one from a textbook. Anyway, I was not a child when I was abducted. I was not even abducted. It was very similar to what you experienced in the waiting room. I hear someone talking to me that seemed to have a different agenda and different education than me.

Me: What do you mean "education"? You have a PhD? What education did this voice have?

Dr. Olcult: And what did this voice say to you that had you so upset you were yelling and on the verge of crying?

Me: He showed me images of my best friend that were not us drinking or having fun but quite the opposite. My question please.

Dr. Olcult: More science orientated. I don't even care for pure science. My studies were that of the science of the mind, not dark matter equations and gravitational orbit projections. I don't even know what that is. That's my point, Thomas. These voices are just us reaching out in a different form. Not aliens, just our own brains trying to adjust.

Me: Talk about generic answers, Doc.

Dr. Olcult: Thomas, I was just using that as an example. Why does that upset you? Do you believe these voices are real? Do they tell you to do things? Like kill people or destroy things?

What? Where was he going with this? My Spidey sense was more than tingling. I was getting some very bad vibes from this guy.

Me: You know, Doc, I suddenly don't feel so well. I think we are going to have to cancel the rest of this session. Please feel free to bill me for the full forty-five minutes.

Dr. Olcult: Please, Thomas, I did not want to upset you. I merely used that as a possible suggestion. The fact that it has got you so unsettled means I have hit a nerve. If you wish to leave, that's fine. Let's set up a time for your next visit.

Me: That's okay, Doc, I don't have my schedule book with me. I will call you and make the next appointment.

Dr. Olcult: You are not working, Thomas, and you don't have a schedule book.

Me: And how do you know that? I never said I was not working, and lots of people have schedule books or even the new smartphones have schedules.

As I was saying that, I pulled out my smartphone and showed him the schedule app, which had nothing listed in it. As I was doing that, I realized I was proving my own point wrong.

Me: Look, I will call you, and we can talk more. I'm not upset, and everything is fine.

As I stood up, I knocked over the stand that had a lamp on it, which fell to the floor and broke.

Me: Sorry, sorry. I will pay for that. Just let me know what everything costs.

Dr. Olcult: Thomas, please relax. It was an accident, and I'm not making you pay for anything. But I must insist you schedule another appointment before you leave this office. The fact that you're hearing voices is very serious and can lead to dangerous things.

I told myself I was not going to tell him about the voices for just this reason. But I blurted it out and now regret it. I was now upset and wanted to leave.

Me: I will call you when and if I decide to come back.

Dr. Olcult: If you do not make an appointment or, further, not show up for that appointment, I will be forced to report to the authorities you hear the voices talking to you and you could be a danger to yourself or the general public.

That really hit me hard with a major combination of anger and nerves. I barely know this guy. This is not a standard or normal way for creating trust in a patient-doctor relationship. He is basically blackmailing me into coming back.

Me: I happen to know there is a patient-doctor confidentiality that prohibits you from discussing what is said during these sessions.

Dr. Olcult: There is, unless, at my discretion, I feel you could be a danger to yourself or others. So what do you say Thursday at the same time?

I glared at him then looked down at the broken lamp. I moved forward and made an obvious step onto the pieces of the broken lamp and crushed one of the big chunks under my sneaker.

Me: That would be fine, Doctor.
Dr. Olcult: Excellent, Thomas, I will see you then. I think we are making excellent progress.

CHAPTER 4

The drive home was not a good one. I went to this guy for help and feel like I'm being blackmailed out of money for his office visits.

Well, I made the appointment, but there is no way he can force me into going to it. As far as his threats go, he can shove those too. I will just deny I said anything of the sort. What a crooked world.

You do what is right, what is preached to us to do—seek counseling if you are having issues—and this is what it comes down to. If he really wants to push this issue, I will just claim I would say anything in order to not see this guy anymore after he told me his abduction story.

I turned on the radio to once again try to focus on something besides these crazy events. All the stations had news, blah blah blah. Even all the music stations had the DJ going off about something. I did not even listen to what was being said. My head was too full of everything else going on. So I just shut it off and made my way home.

As I pulled into the driveway, I noticed Justin was home already and a couple other cars too. Very unusual for him to be home this early but good, I thought to myself. I can tell him about my awesome doctor visit he was pushing for me to have so badly.

When I walked in, Justin and two of his coworker buddies were all fixated on the TV screen, all their eyes wide open and totally connected. They did not even hear me walk in or notice me standing there. The only one who did was my precious little Toby, who always greeted me. He was going blind, but his other senses were super strong as he stood up and put his front paws on me. I picked him up and sat down in my chair.

I looked back at Justin and his crew, which were like zombies. I just shook my head and looked at the screen to try to figure out what was so compelling. Just then the power went out. One of Justin's work buddies jumped up in a major panic and said, "Come on, guys, I'm going home. I want to be with my family." They all got up and said good-bye to Justin and left in a huge hurry. What the hell! Must have blown a fuse! Justin looked at me with a very blank look.

Justin: It's like some kind of movie.
Me: I paid the bill, Justin. Must be a fuse or something.
Justin: Have you not been watching TV?
Me: No, I just came from the shrink you said I needed to see so badly, and he was a total dick and tried to—
Justin: The *Voyager* probe sent back a message.
Me: Yeah, I know all about that. It looked back and could not find our solar system. NASA thinks it's just a glitch.
Justin: No, it sent back a text message, in which they're claiming the probe is not even designed to be able to do.
Me: A text message? I did not hear about that. When did this happen?
Justin: It just came over all the news stations about thirty minutes ago. My boss let everyone go home early.
Me: What did this text message say?
Justin: It said, "Prepare for us and our arrival. Prepare yourself and your families. Prepare for death."

Justin was not one to memorize stuff that well, but these three quotes he said without a second thought or hesitation, as if he had been hearing it over and over again, which I guess he had on the different TV stations.

Just then the power kicked back on with the television. It was the emergency broadcast sign and that annoying loud sound advising people to stay in their homes and not to panic, that a state of emergency and martial law was being imposed until further notice.

Then the news came back on. Apparently this message was received by NASA and authenticated but was picked up by several other individuals and other countries who had been monitoring the probe as well. They released this information first, and it was not considered credible until someone from CNN insisted that NASA allow an interview with them; otherwise they would just release the story with only the information they have.

It was always my belief that if something like this ever happened, the government would never just blurt it out in less than two hours, but with today's twenty-four-hour news cycle and the fact it was picked up by many other independent individuals, the governments of the world decided against trying to hold it back. Of course, as we scanned the channels, some other stations were in doubt about any of it, and others thought it was some form of misinformation.

But the major news companies all were competing with each other on who had the smartest and most credible person to say that this was not a mistake. "Something reprogrammed our probe and sent this message, and its origin was just outside the area of Pluto's orbit in the Oort cloud," stated one of the scientists.

The government, of course, was playing it down, that it was likely a hoax of some of kind and nothing to be worried about. One interview stuck out in my mind and started to get played over and over. It was a lead scientist at NASA who had analyzed the message and source and concluded its authenticity and distance.

He explained the same message was sent in every known language (even dead and obscure languages), and some were not even any known language that the best linguistics could recognize. They all were identical in wording though with the same ominous-type message.

As I sat there, that feeling came across me again. Is this all real? Could this be happening? I started to think about what I kept rationalizing as a dream. The devil said this was going to happen. If it was just a dream, then it ended up being quite accurate. I started to go over the whole conversation that took place. The devil said, "I could stop this." He wanted my help to stop this.

The devil was being put in a unique position to help mankind or have no humans left on Earth to mess with ever again. But why would he need my help? Why not just do his black magic and send these guys off to another galaxy? Furthermore, why did he let this probe be discovered in the first place? Why did he not just blow it up? Then a familiar creepy feeling came across me.

Then there was that familiar voice.

> Devil: Starting to see it's all very real, are we? I will answer all your questions tonight when we meet again. Till then, try not to stroke out. No pressure, but if you die, so does everyone on the planet. No pressure, of course. Hahaha.

I tried to respond to him in my mind and get the questions I wanted answered now. But somehow I could sense he had tuned me out and it was no use. My heart was racing. Justin was in his room. I was going to knock and see if he was okay but could hear him cocking and loading his rifles and guns. That was his way of coping with this, so I decided to let him be. Besides, what was I going to say that would calm him down? My own heart was racing, and I needed to calm down myself.

I looked down at my Toby, who, even mostly blind, still could look at me and acted as if he did not want to leave my side. Dogs are a lot smarter than we give them credit for. They can sense their owner's feelings. It was also well documented that animals could perceive upcoming disasters before they even occur.

In my best calm voice, I asked him if he wanted to go outside. Of course, those words always triggered him to be happy and excited. We went out to the fenced-in backyard. The often quiet neighborhood was eerie, no loud explosions or anything, but a multitude of voices everywhere. It was like the whole world was talking at once. You could also hear squealing tires and cars going very fast. No doubt people wanted to get home or go to the store for supplies. Wait, supplies! We should be doing that too.

As that thought entered my mind, Justin came from his room and said, "We need to go to the store. We may need to hunker down for a while and it might be smart to stock up on supplies."

I could not agree more, so Justin started heading for the garage with his shotgun in hand. I explained that it may not be a good idea to bring something that big and obvious, but the protection factor, I completely agree with. He set down the rifle and showed me his 9mm sidearm pistol.

With that we were off. We were going to take his big Chevy Tahoe but decided that my smaller, faster car might be a better plan if traffic got bad. Off we went to Walmart for not only food but batteries and other stuff, but as we pulled into the store area, we quickly realized everyone else had the same idea. You could not even get into the parking lot of the store.

So we decided to just go to one of the regular chain shopping stores. That would basically be the same. We were able to get in the parking lot, but the doors had a line just to get in. As we were trying to park, we heard gunshots. It appeared two people waiting to get in were having a dispute about their place in the line and started to shoot at each other. Without saying a word, we left there too.

Justin: Well, I am willing to bet they're all going to be this way. This is a full-blown national panic.

Me: What about Rick and Stacy's?

Rick and Stacy's was a little mom-and-pop store that we often went to. It was small but had a good inventory. But we liked it most because of its location. It was on a back road and rarely had customers. We knew the owners pretty well because it was close to our house, and we gave them a lot of business. Their story was they were lottery winners and always wanted to own a store. So with millions from the right pick of numbers, they fulfilled their dream and did not need to worry about advertising, sales, or lots of customers.

So off we went. It was a great idea. No one was there—actually no one at all, not even Rick and Stacy. My best guess was, when they heard the bad news, they headed to their apocalypse cabin they had built, which we had talked with them about on many occasions. Most times they would just use it as a vacation getaway and never really thought it would be used as a place to go when the world actually did fall apart.

We walked up, and Justin pulled out his gun and was ready to shoot the lock, but I pulled on the door, and to our surprise, it was not even locked. We entered slowly and carefully, but it was vacant. This world news just hit only a couple hours ago, so we were in luck to be the first there. We filled bag after bag and box after box—food, batteries, anything and everything practical. We loaded my little two-seater to capacity. Although we wish we could take more, the sounds of the outside world were getting louder and more violent.

> Me: Justin, we need to head home. I don't think we can get any more in my car, and I'm worried about our house and Toby.

So with that we grabbed a couple more items and got in the car. As we were starting to drive away, a pickup truck pulled in. It had a bunch of teens and twenties kids in the back of it, and they just glared at us. It was obvious we were packed in because we had stuff on our laps after the trunk was full. They waved for us to stop and talked in a relatively nice, nonthreatening way.

We stopped and noticed several of them were jumping out of the back, some with baseball bats and other similar blunt weapons.

At that point Justin said, "Tom, let's get the hell out of here now!" He did not have to tell me twice. I put the gas pedal to the floor, which I had never done before, and the tires started to spin and smoke, but we were not really going forward very fast.

I was never put in a situation where I got to put my mini Batmobile in a situation like this. As the wheels began to really smoke, some of the guys jumped back into the truck, and some were just a few steps from the car when the wheels grabbed hold.

The takeoff was whiplash level, and we were zero to eighty-five in about four seconds. The road was a pretty long straightaway back in the woods, and after a few seconds, Justin said, "Damn, Tom, this little car books!" But as he said that, the giant pickup truck could be seen from behind us. So we went from eighty-five to a hundred ten, to which most cars would be shaking apart. My Miata was holding the road as if we were doing fifty. The problem was this truck probably had eight cylinders, and one hundred was not that hard for them either. Although we had the jump and a good lead, they were maintaining a football-field length.

That's when the shooting started. We could hear the bangs, but none had hit us—yet. But if they take out a tire at one hundred miles per hour, they won't need the guns. Justin went for his 9mm and cocked it and was starting to put down the window. I stopped him and said to hold off on that idea. They may have close to the same speed, but I can lose them. The straightaway ended, but we were still in hillbilly country. I took a wicked turn at about seventy that fishtailed us almost completely sideways. Thankfully I am a good to great driver, and my little two-seater sports car was made for maneuverability. I corrected for the drift and got us on to another road. We watched as our pursuers did not slow down that much and attempted the same turn and almost flipped and spun out in a full 360.

We went from a fifty MPH power turn, back to ninety MPH and then made another sharp turn in the other direction. Meantime canned foods and batteries were flying around inside the car, hitting us both in the head and body.

My adrenaline was definitely flowing, but so was my confidence in driving my little Miata, until suddenly in front of us was the first other vehicle we had seen since this chase began. I had to rapidly slow down and started to lay on the horn. But it had no effect on the car in front of us. In fact, it began to slow down more. Now the pickup I had done so well to lose was hauling ass down the road and was closing in fast.

"Shit, shit, shit." I attempted to go around, but the car moved into the outer lane with us. Then we saw the car in front of us had someone hanging out the window, and they had a gun and took a shot that clipped Justin's door. We were in a squeeze-play sandwich and not looking good. Just then, as the car in front of us was in the middle of the road, preventing us from passing to the left, I swung the wheel to the right and punched it. My car's turbo kicked in, and before the car ahead of us could correct and turn back the other way, we were by them.

Now we were cruising at 117 mph, and signs and houses were flying by, also more gunshots. We could see we were coming up on a more populated area. This would eliminate my car's speed and maneuverability properties and our only edge. Both vehicles were clearly seen in the rearview. We were coming up to a sharp turn, which brought us to a traffic light where we could see an open flow of traffic.

> Me: Okay, Justin. Let's hope this thing works after seven years.

I looked down at what looked like an old-fashion emergency brake release but was actually the gizmo I had installed illegally a long time ago. Just before the sharp turn, I pulled it. At first there was no way to tell if it worked or if anything even happened—no noise or confirmation light. I rounded the turn and had to slam the brakes as the light was red, and cars were going by on the upcoming street. I went into the grass and was about to jump into traffic with cars coming or not when we could hear screeching and smashing sounds.

Apparently my roofing nails worked. We could see many of them still on the road, and both the pickup and car did not make the turn. The car had spun around backwards and went down an embankment, and the pickup had rolled several times out of sight.

Just then the light turned green, and we peeled off as quickly as possible back toward home. I looked over at Justin, who always thought I spent way too much ($1,200) on that gizmo. He had an ear-to-ear grin. "That was very awesome, Tom!" I tried my best calm, cool, and collective smile back and continued back home.

I quickly opened the garage door, entered, and then shut and locked it. As much as we packed into my little Miata, all in all it was nothing that would last more than a few weeks—maybe a month if used conservatively. But with what was going on at the big stores, we were very lucky to have cleaned out Rick and Stacy's and managed to get what we did.

CHAPTER 5

The television was not being very optimistic about the situation. More specialists and scientists were being overly blunt that this was no hoax.

The transmission was coming from *Voyager,* and the message itself was also authenticated by several highly qualified people.

Then the news would show the effect this was having on the world and a little taste of what we went through getting our supplies. The world was in turmoil. People were worried and panicking. The newscaster said the president was going to be on tonight and to have radios ready because there might be rolling blackouts. The bottom line was, stay in your homes and hope that this could still be some form of elaborate hoax. Otherwise, pray that our alien friends could be negotiated with because their message of death did not leave a lot of room for hope.

I was going to stay up and listen to the president's announcement but decided it was not worth it. Justin and I had listened to the news for three hours straight, and it was all the same over and over.

Many qualified people were confirming all the data, and then many Joe Nobodies were saying it was all a conspiracy to control the population.

I was wrestling with whether to tell Justin what I knew and what has been happening to me and, most importantly, my dream, which seemed to be "balls on" accurate at this point. But Justin, like the rest of the world, was on overload. I did not feel that telling Justin what I knew would help him or the situation at all. If my dream was real and what the devil told me was the truth, then the best thing I could do was to try and return to that plane of reality and find out more about what is going on.

So I told Justin I was going to sleep and put my hand on his shoulder. I said that we are in good shape with all our supplies, and he should try to get some rest.

I picked up Toby and went to my room. Toby, like many animals, could sense there was something wrong. Strange sounds from outside and on the streets with yelling and squealing car tires was certainly not helping with his nervousness. But beyond that, I could tell he knew something was wrong. I put him on my bed and lay down. He, as always, curled up next to me. I tried to close my eyes and let sleep take over. Unfortunately, it was not that easy. There was too much going on, and with my heart racing, it made relaxing close to impossible, let alone trying to sleep. I lay there and looked up at the wall where Shawn's lock of hair had been for so many years. But now it was just an empty space.

It made me think of where I found the tack. What was unusual is that I found it in the garage in a box that was buried by other junk inside a book that had not be opened for years. But with all that's going on, that did not seem so unbelievable compared with the events of the past week. But why was it pinned to the word *beast*. Was someone trying to tell me something? I remembered *beast* was a common reference to the devil in biblical terms. He is, of course, not the hero of the story and would obviously be given an unflattering name. Yet he seemed to genuinely (in my dream) want to help. He even seemed to be nice to me for the most part—other than at the end when showing me Shawn burn in the oven. But that was because I got lippy. I made a special mental note that I must at all times keep my cool with him. If everything is what it appears, then he may be the only hope we have against beings with technology hundreds or thousands of years ahead of us.

I kept tossing and turning. The harder I would try to make myself sleep, the harder it was to even get close. I finally came to the conclusion that I was going to need some help. I hated to do it with what was going on. With all the chaos, we need to stay on high alert and not be drugged or sleepy. But this is too important. So I took out a bottle of sleeping pills from my drawer. They were unopened because I never usually had sleep problems. I opened them up and took out two then decided to take an extra to ensure I would sleep and stay asleep and not keep waking with all the commotion outside. I swallowed the three pills and then changed all my bedding as I figured that would help too. Nice clean sheets always helped. As I was finishing the last of the pillowcases, I could feel the pills kicking in big time. Wow, they seemed strong.

I lay down and started to look at the bottle. The directions, which I never read before, stated, "These are extra strength. Only take one pill for a full eight hours sleep."

Damn, what the hell. Everything in pill form is always two. I have a low tolerance, so I should have taken a half; instead I have taken three. I lay down and now tried to resist going to sleep, but to no avail. Within seconds, I was asleep and could recognize that familiar smell of the fire and the mansion. I opened my eyes to see I was all dressed again in my full suit back in the living room, sitting right where I was when I left the last dream—the comfortable couch with the huge two-hundred-inch screen that was blank and appeared to be turned off.

I stood up, and just as I did, that familiar voice spoke.

> Devil: Well, hello, Thomas. It's good to have you back.

I turned around, and there he was, sitting in his very throne-like chair. It was red and velvet with a high back. Of course, once again he was dressed very well, not a suit like mine but a classy shirt and fashionable long skater shorts. It looked like a creation right out of my mind's combination of things I find most desirable.

> Me: Hello again, Luke. You're looking very well again.

I stuttered on the word *well* because it was not the word I was going to use; in fact, *handsome* would have been more accurate.

> Devil: Well, thank you. Once again I wish you could restrain your hormones, but it is not your fault that you see me this way, and maybe

it will even be beneficial in helping keep you more calm. As time goes by, you will, no doubt, be less and less calm with the events that are about to take place.

Me: Yes, it seems your alien buddies are on the way, just as you said.

The room in an instant got cold and 30 percent darker. The devil's eyes lit up in a dull red.

Devil: They are not my friends, Thomas, and you would be wise to never refer to them as such again.

I thought back about not getting him upset and staying on his good side and tried to reset.

Me: I am sorry, Luke. It was not my intention to say something that would offend you. As a flawed human, I say things sometimes in a way that is not really how it is meant, particularly with the English language. Sometimes things come out a little too general or generic from what was meant to be expressed. Please accept my apology.

The room resumed back to original temperature and lighting as well as the devil's expression going back to his standard cocky smile.

Devil: Not a problem, Thomas. And that was very well expressed too. I see you have thought over our predicament and made a choice to embrace me and the situation as well. I applaud that. Your open-mindedness is one of the many reasons I picked you.

Me: If you are trying to save us from an invasion, then of course I am on your side. But I have many questions. Are you against me asking some?

Devil: I welcome them. The better you understand, the easier it will be for us to work together and accomplish our goals, so to speak. Since you have well dosed yourself for sleep, we have plenty of undisturbed time to get to those questions.

Me: Yeah, that's true.

The devil laughed, got up, and poured himself a drink from a beautiful, luxurious bar. As he stood, I could see such detail in this dream like no other. Every color in the room was vibrant and every smell was so authentic, from the fire in the fireplace to the smell of a clean, well-kept house. The devil's body was just like his face—flawless. He was not some huge bodybuilder but the perfect toned, slim-to-skinny body with all the right dimensions. He wore my favorite type of clothes by brand and color. His dress shirt was not tucked in and was overlapping his dark shorts, which were worn very low, showing his boxers, which I could make out had little cartoon devils and the number 666 all over it.

Devil: Always checking me out, Thomas.

Me: I'm sorry again. Please don't change to a life-sized dust mite or anything.

He laughed in a quick roar, which gradually turned back to that cocky chuckle.

Devil: No, I have changed my mind on that. I appear as your mind has created me. It's the same with any mortal who has ever seen me throughout time. But I like how you see me—young, fit, and sort of a cross between a skater/surfer or a maybe a model. I also think the distraction does not overbalance the calmness and comfort it creates while you are around me. So from now on, I'm fine with you peeking a look and your dirty thoughts.

Me: So you can read my mind?

Devil: Yes, a little, for now.

Me: Just here or in the real world too?

Devil: Both, but much less when you're conscious. I still can read your thoughts when you're awake, but not with the vivid detail of when we are here together on this plane of existence.

He finished making his drink as I turned around and sat back down on the oversized red-and-black velvet couch. When I did, I looked back up to see he was sitting very close next to me. I jumped in surprise and then tried to return to a calm.

Devil: Okay, let's go, Thomas. You got a lot to ask. Goooo!

Me: You said last time you wanted to save us because you need us.

Devil: No, I said it would be boring without you. I don't need anyone or anything.

Me: Okay, I stand corrected. I also get it. Saving the world is not usually a devil-type thing. The Bible says you wish to destroy it and us.

Devil: The Bible is riddled with errors and statements taken out of context. Not that it is completely fiction either, but remember, it talks of events millenniums ago or longer and translated so many times I have lost track.

Me: And God does not want to save us?

Devil: As I said last time, I don't know what he wants or if he cares or still exists.

Me: So you have never seen him?

Devil: I have seen and talked to him—a long time ago, when this whole adventure began, when he created the universe, reality, and me and you.

Me: So he created you? Always read you were reluctant to say or admit that.

Devil: Why should I? I am a requirement for this all to work. All good and no bad is just a form of unbalance. Without me in the mix, all the balance is gone. He created me so there can be good. He also created me with all his abilities. If he did not, it would not be balanced. As I remember, he was very OCD about that point. But I'm not complaining.

Me: So if you have all his powers, why do you need me? Why not just wipe out the *Voyager* probe before it was detected?

Devil: There are rules I must follow. One of them is I can't interfere with your scientific evolution or stop your technological advancements in any way, which have come along impressively well. From apelike dipshits to sending probes out of your solar system is quite the leap. Even I will concede to that.

Me: So there are limitations?

Devil: Not limitations, Thomas, rules, rules we all must follow. Even God himself must follow. Not that he has anyone to oversee him, but rules that he must follow to maintain his own goals. To deviate from them means things won't happen or turn out the way he wants, so he must maintain those rules.

Me: Okay, so why me? Where do I stand in this? Why do you need a flawed, puny human?

That once again got that cocky grin, which I began to like more and more.

Devil: You, my puny, flawed human, are a necessary factor. By the way, those are your words and not mine. Most humans make me sick, but you are a special breed and special in many ways.

Me: You did not really answer my question.

Devil: How rude of me to not offer you a drink. I fixed myself one and drank it right in front of you and did not ask if you wanted one, not that you would feel any of alcohol's effects while you are here—unless you wanted me to let you.

Me: No, thanks to the drink or the offer of feeling intoxicated. You still did not answer my question though.

Devil: Let's hold on that one.

Me: You are not going to answer me with our little game of questions and answers?

Devil: No, I will answer it, but not yet. You will understand better if you wait on that one, but I promise I will answer it. I will say for now, it's part of another set of rules about me directly intervening with the human equation. But there is a loophole. You can interfere... with my help. Technically, I'm not sure if that's a loophole or not. But these events are bad. This is by far the worst thing that has ever happened to the human race, and I need to find a way to help without breaking the rules.

Me: So you will use me to stop this invasion?

Devil: Yes. As a Lawyer, you know about loopholes. We try to stick to the rule book, but sometimes we must be creative with solutions.

Me: According to the news they said these aliens are on their way. Although right outside our solar system is eons to us, I'm sure it is not to them. Meaning they will be here soon.

Devil: Well, this brings us back to the rules aspect Thomas. God put a speed limit on the universe. Even with their advanced abilities and technologies, they have to abide to the "light speed rule". Now they also have their loopholes and can cheat and create a wormhole, which will speed up their arrival time. But they are a great distance. They are not even in this galaxy. So this gives us some time—not a lot, but a few weeks, maybe less.

Me: You must be monitoring what is going on right now. This news is ripping the people apart. They are going to start tearing each other to shreds.

With this I saw a new evil grin. I did not like this one as much as the other. This one had less of a human quality to it.

Devil: Well, that is expected. In the long run it will reduce the population by 20–25 percent. Acceptable loss.

Me: Well, I have an idea about that. Maybe we can reduce that factor and chain of events, but in the meantime, I have another question.

The devil adjusted how he was sitting and flipped his feet around, which were still on my lap. He took a big drink and then looked at me. His hair was so red. Even red does not describe it. That was puzzling to me. He was culmination of people I found attractive throughout my life, yet I remember very few that had red hair, especially that red. But what I could see was all the faces of the others I noted in my life. His hair was parted to one side and would sometimes allow a bang to fall down and partially cover one eye.

Devil: I'm waiting, Thomas.

Me: Do you have to have your sneakers on me?

Devil: Thomas, let's not waste time with that. You like it. I can read your mind, your every thought, at least for now. So I know it not only does not bother you, you actually like my contact. You have not had a lot of that in your life. So why waste your time putting up a front? What is your next question?

I looked down at the ground. As skilled as I was at debating, it's impossible to do it with someone who knows your every thought.

Me: Of course, you are right, but why not just use this form of telepathy to communicate. Would we not get things done faster?

Devil: As I said last time, it's too much information, and frankly, I like talking in this old-fashion way. I have not done this in a long time. See, Thomas, I am lonely too. I'm the evil deviant. Humans are conditioned to hate me from the beginning of time. I am the outcast. You know a little about how that feels. Why? Because I am doing what God wants and created me to do. Talk about ironic, huh? But to talk to you in this civilized manner and have you not fear me and, in fact, like me in some way is enjoyable to me. But let's not get too mushy. Back to questions.

My years of being a lawyer made me good at assessing if people are lying or trying to con me. But I did not sense that. All I got was a true feeling that he was lonely and *did* like me in some strange way. But this is an entity spoken about as the king of lies and deception. I must try to keep that in mind.

Me: Okay, Luke, why did *Voyager* not see Earth when it turned its cameras around to look back? It did not even see our sun.

Devil: Because God does not want you humans to be changed, injured, or contaminated by other life forms. So what you call the Oort cloud is actually a protective mass that makes your solar system invisible to the rest of the universe. It hides your entire solar system from other life forms. It has worked very well right up to now, when your exploration device entered the cloud and was immediately detected by the Pelusoians.

Me: Pelusoians? That's the name of their race?

Devil: Well, as close to the English pronunciation as possible. They are similar to humans in their curiosity but differ greatly when it comes to feelings of guilt and compassion. They, like you, seek knowledge and ways to better their society. They will do this by consuming most of the living and organic life on Earth.

Me: Consume? You mean they want to eat us?

Devil: Yes, they are overpopulated. Their inhabitants had to move to a second planet and on and on, which only allowed their population to grow exponentially. They consume planets by eating all living organic material. They have done this to many other planets, but Earth is the mother lode because the human race has done so well for itself through the years and prospered greatly.

The emotionless way how he described these beings and what they will do to us was as cold as the information was. It was just like some horrific Hollywood movie about an alien invasion.

Me: How am I going to help or, better question, stop this?

Devil: Because I was given my powers by God, but I can't directly use them to change your fate. You are going to stop them by me helping you. As I said, that's the loophole. But if I am to do this, which is border line breaking the rules, I can't tell you how to proceed. I can get away with giving you the means to stop them, maybe drop some hints, but to give you the power and tell you how to use it would surely be a breach. This is why you were picked Thomas. Your creativity and imagination of being a movie nerd combined with the logic and intelligence of a Lawyer.

Me: So I will have god's powers to do anything? Okay, say I wipe them all out, or better yet, send them to other side of the universe.

Devil: Not quite. First, no matter where you send them, they will find a way back. Their technology is far ahead of mankind's. It's hard to put into words. Second, we can't do anything until they are in our galaxy.

Me: Why our galaxy? No, wait, let me guess, rules!

Devil: Yes, you pick up fast. My realm is this galaxy. But even when they reach here, we can't just wipe them out. We must come up with a way to deter them from wanting to come to Earth.

Me: So there's a "no hurt them" rule too? I mean, they are coming to kill us all, and we can't harm them?

I felt a weird sensation. I have felt anger and even rage before, but the thoughts of slaughtering this race gave me no feeling of remorse. The ideas and images of turning them inside out and melting them to a liquid form started flowing through my mind with no hesitation. No anger I ever felt compared with this and no remorse or guilt to balance it.

Devil: Okay, I need to explain this too. The more you are around me, you will start to connect and relate to my way of being. The thoughts and rage is part of me rubbing off onto you. It's not all a bad thing. You are going to need to shed some of that meekness to get this job done, but it has to be measured and balanced with the Thomas inside you. Once again, balance is the key.

I did not fully believe what he was telling me about transferred anger and resisted his description of my "meekness," but I tried to take everything he said and store it in my mind.

Me: So you won't be guiding me with ideas?
Devil: I cannot tell you what to do. If I do, we jeopardize being penalized and having no abilities, thus you have no abilities. The mission and how you proceed and implement those decisions are all you.

The devil took a remote and clicked it at the huge screen. It showed a map of sorts—our galaxy and where their galaxy was in comparison. It also showed small blips of where they could create wormholes to shorten their way here. All in all, it showed it would take about twenty-five days for them to reach where the *Voyager* craft was inside the Oort cloud.

Devil: So you need to start thinking of how you would like to proceed. What you would like to do? Keep in mind you can and will need to be aggressive, but you cannot just snap your fingers and make them all go away. The Pelusoians are technologically advanced, but they lack the human touch. Think more like robots, even though they are not. They are living organic beings but have a very narrow train of thought. They only think in terms of what benefits them and how to acquire it.
Me: So how will it work? How do I get things done or wheel your forces?
Devil: Actually, I have not thought this fully through myself. Do you have any ideas on that?
Me: Is it true the human brain only uses 10 percent of its ability?
Devil: More accurately would be like 15.2 percent.

Me: Let's boost me up to 100 percent. That would be a good start.

The devil stood up and did one of those deep belly laughs and went to get another drink.

Devil: I don't think so. Then you would not be the Thomas I picked. You would be something completely different and not have the same qualities that make you the perfect candidate for this. But maybe we can do something along those lines. When you awake, I will give you the brain you had at seventeen years old. That should put back many of the brain cells you killed off back in college. You will have all your memories. I will just transport the brain of when you were seventeen into your head now.

Me: That's good, but not great, not "stop an alien army" good.

Devil: I will also tune it up and make your neurons three times faster than normal and boost your brain's ability from 15.2 percent to 30 percent.

Me: Like 14 percent more? Why so little?

Devil: Listen, idiot stick, the 14.8 percent extra is in some key areas that no other human has ever utilized. The parts of the brain I am activating will be very helpful. So your brain will be new, faster, and have some extras. That's the best I can do with your idea without changing you into someone or something completely different who will be of no help.

I noticed that, as the devil finished making his drink and walked back to the couch, he was a little unsteady in his walking, and his last couple words were slurring just a little bit.

Me: I know you said I can't get drunk in this realm, but does that apply to you as well?

This got me a glare that I could feel right down my spine.

Me: Hey, go easy, that was not sarcasm. It was just a question. Remember, we are working together, learning from each other.

His evil look subsided back to the evil grin.

Devil: I can feel the effects of alcohol. This is not your normal realm. You're a fish out of water. I am at home. But keep in mind, I have been drinking for thousands of millennia, so my tolerance is off the charts. Besides, I need to keep myself calm too. I have never faced a situation quite like this.

He stopped abruptly and sat down next to me and, in an overly exaggerated way, lightly slammed his sneakered feet on my lap then stared at nothing in particular. I wanted to say something light, maybe even reassuring after that little admission. I could sense his frustration and reluctance. How difficult it must be to be an entity who has lived so long and always have been so sure of yourself to suddenly face this situation. It had to be difficult, to say the least. I tried to leave the direct subject matter and gave him a chance to vent.

Me: You must have seen your share of incredible things throughout that much amount of time. But nothing quite like this, huh?

Devil: You fools never had the ability to put yourself in this level of danger before. But of course, I can't stop your scientific advancements. Otherwise, this whole event would never even be happening.

Me: Can I ask you about some stuff unrelated to the aliens?

Devil: Sure, we're in this together.
Me: Cancer, car accidents, and things like that—your creation?
Devil: No, I can't take credit for those things. That's all part of the creator and the great design. Years ago an earthquake killed thousands. Of course, everyone blamed me. I've never killed anyone. I do not directly make anything happen. I can whisper in an ear or two, but no direct intervention.
Me: And what about?

I went silent for several seconds and looked at the floor.

Devil: I had nothing to do with Shawn.
Me: What if I told you I need him? He could help me with this. Back in the day, he used to—
Devil: Sorry, Thomas, you have reached another rule. No bringing back the dead and no using these abilities on anything that's just for your benefit or has nothing to do with saving the planet or stopping the invasion.
Me: Is he in heaven or hell? Are there such places?
Devil: I tell you what, those questions are deep and would take a long time to explain. If we are successful, I will answer all your questions, no matter how long it takes for you to comprehend them.

I did not want to push that topic any further. So far he had been accurate and, as far as I could tell, truthful.

Me: Okay, back to the main topic. When I go back, I will have a young beefed-up brain, but I doubt that will stop an invading race of advanced aliens. What am I going to use to stop all this from happening?

Devil: That is up to you, Thomas, but may I suggest one step at a time. Make decisions one by one, and as things happen, come up with countermeasures. Don't try to have an all-encompassing solution before they even occur. You may need to base each choice on their moves, so try not to overthink it.

Me: The world is in a panic. That will not help the situation. I want you to override the *Voyager* probe to transmit something for me. They have already taken it under control, so I don't think you will be violating the scientific interference rule.

Devil: I concur. What do you want me to do with it?

Me: I want it to seem like the message it transmitted was an error, an explainable malfunction that can be wrote off and make the world believe they are safe again, that the guys at NASA mistook the transmission and the craft was damaged while entering the Oort cloud.

Devil: How does this help stop them? Seems like a waste of effort and resources.

Me: Keeping the world calm makes things easier for me to get things done and move about. I may need to go places and eat food. Is it not logical to make things as easy and less stressful as possible for me so I can pursue our goal?

The devil once again made that same grin. He took his sneakers off me and got up and sat very close to me, almost shoulder to shoulder.

Devil: You must know, Thomas, in all my existence, I have never been in a situation like this, one where I must have a comrade and keep my negative or evil side, if you will, in check. I thought it would be harder to do. But you have a deviousness to you that I can relate to and even like.

Me: Thank you, I guess. I also am not used to this. You probably know my life rather well and all my experiences. The only one I was ever close to was Shawn. That relationship was only platonic. I loved him like a brother. He knew me better than I knew myself, and the same was true in the opposite. But as far as physical attraction or contact, my life has had little of that.

At that the devil pushed an inch closer to me. I'm not sure if he was in my head or just knew everything about me, but his scent or pheromones were extreme to me—not a cologne or designer body spray, more of a natural combination of a human scent at its most pleasant. Knowing his looks were designed in connection with my likes, I am sure this pertained to all my senses.

Devil: It must be tough for you too. You see me as your mind has created me. I am the exact person of your dreams, so to say. I myself have lived a similar life. Watching over you humans throughout time, I have seen more than a few that were beautiful. See, I'm not straight or gay or anything as you humans like to label each other. I can appreciate the human figure and natural beauty, but to me it's the mind that attracts, the cunning and logic, the rationale and intelligence. Male or female does not matter to me. As for looks, I can make you appear any way I wish to perceive you. But I can't create personality, not really.

Me: Well, I know I'm no looker. Slightly overweight, out of shape, and scarred face from bad acne in my teens. So I doubt I am.

Devil: I know all about your self-doubts. It's too bad you feel that way, but having survived the life you were given, let's just say you may not be a ten, but the tough life you endured made you a strong-willed person, which I find as equally attractive as you do my appearance.

Me: As for the *Voyager* probe, can you do what I ask?

Devil: I can do it, but I cannot guarantee how many will believe it or question the change, and I can't force people to believe one way or another. That must be for them to decide. But it's already been done. Garbled miscommunication due to transmission error due to damage in the Oort cloud.

Me: That's perfect. Not everyone will believe it, but depending on how authentic you created this ruse, most will.

Devil: And how good do you think I am at creating a ruse?

Me: Quite good, I suspect, Luke. Will I ever see Shawn again?

Devil: The thing about the future is, it's not fixed. My answer to your question can change the outcome. To tell someone their future is a paradox. If you tell someone what will happen, you have changed the way the outcome will unfold. With that said, I can't tell the future. No one can. The past is fixed. The future is a chain of a googolplex of possible outcomes.

Me: You're talking about alternate realities?

Devil: Well, yes, sorta.

Me: I think I saw another timeline or reality in my mirror. It was me but a much more perfect, well-adjusted, flawless version of myself.

Devil: Yes, that interesting ability you have when you make eye contact. Another reason you were picked. It's quite a trick. No other human has ever had that ability.

Me: I hope you did not mess with that when you did my brain tune-up.

Devil: Thomas, now think, why would I not be able to do that?

Me: Because it's a form of scientific or evolutionary advancement, thus breaking the rules?

Devil: Yes, very good, Thomas. You do pick up quickly. By the way, if you ever try to use that little trick on me, I will make you regret it beyond anything you can imagine. Are we clear?

Me: Yes, I never even considered that fact.

Devil: Good, make sure it stays that way, otherwise—

As he was saying this he reached for the remote to the big TV.

Me: That is not necessary, Luke. If you read me, you can tell I already believe you, and there is no reason to prove to me how serious you are about that.

He grinned and set the remote back down.

Devil: I really do enjoy this, and you, Thomas. You are not my equal or even close, but you are one of a kind. I think we need a break from this. What do you say, since we still have a while before you awake, we have some fun?

His smile was so alluring. My overwhelming physical attraction toward him made every questionable remark he made (like "having some fun") seem like a sexual innuendo to me.

Devil: No, Thomas, get your mind out of the gutter. I was thinking more in the lines of something you would consider if you had your own holodeck or controlled dream.

Me: Wow, that does sound like fun.

Devil: Plus at the same time we can try some practice scenarios too. Kill two birds with one stone.

As he said that, he set down his drink and snapped his fingers. Instantly we were in Times Square in New York City.

Me: Wow, cool trick! Are we really in New York City?

Devil: No, as I said, it's like a hologram. It's a simulation. Let's go have a drink.

CHAPTER 6

Once again the realism of the dream was indecipherable from real life—all the people, sounds, and smells. I had been to NYC once but never Times Square. It was exhilarating, to say the least. While we were walking, people were bumping into me, and you could hear arguments. It was just like being there. The devil walked with a fast pace and seemed to know exactly where he was going. I noticed a difference though. As I tried to keep up with him, people were constantly in my way. I had to dodge and maneuver to not have collisions with other pedestrians. Not the case with the devil, whether timing or just some form of control, he never even came close to any collisions.

We finally made it to a club, a really nice one. The sign said Club 54. I remember Club 54; it was from back in the seventies or eighties and no longer existed. Back in its time it was the place to be. There was a long line, which the devil paid no attention to. He walked straight up to doorman, who immediately let us in. You could hear comments and complaints from the others in line, but we just walked by them and directly in.

I had never been in a club, and this one was historically one of the best ever. Once again I marveled at the colors and lasers. Even if it was a dream, it was awesome from the sound and visual experience alone.

The devil continued to walk with determination as if he knew right where he wanted to go, which ultimately was a VIP booth that overlooked the entire place. As we sat down, we were immediately waited on by a very attractive young man. The devil told the good-looking young man, "The usual," and then looked at me. I decided, since alcohol had no effect on me in this place (and being in NYC), I would go big with a Long Island iced tea.

I noticed at that point our clothes had changed from when we were at his mansion. My three-piece suit was more casual yet no less classy, and the devil's was the same high class skater look.

Devil: So what do you think of this, Thomas?
Me: Very real. But it's not… right?
Devil: No this is just a facsimile of one of my favorite places.
Me: I remember this place from history. Was noted for its sex, drugs and Rock and Roll.

As I looked around, there was not an ugly or even average-looking person in the place. Men and women were of the highest quality. All were model types, all from eighteen to twenty-three. I had to admit I was enjoying myself tremendously.

The server came back with our drinks. He set mine down and gave me a wink and set down the devil's, which had fog coming out of it, like that dry-ice effect.

Waiter: I see you brought a very handsome young man with you this time, Luke. Maybe you could let me borrow him?
Devil: That's up to him. We are here on a business meeting, Jason, but come back in a little bit.

Jason was very handsome. He had very blond hair and was thin but fit. As someone in their late forties, I also enjoyed the compliment and the attention from such a young, polite, and handsome guy. But as good-looking as he was, he still did not compare with the devil, and as much as I knew that, I know he did too.

Waiter: Well, if you two need anything, you just let me know, and I will be here to serve you.
Devil: Thank you, Jason, we will do that.

I still was having a hard time adapting to how nice the devil was. Years of research and all the classes, but this was nothing like he was always described, and it was difficult trying to adjust to that.

Devil: I like your class ring.
Me: Yeah, it looks nice, but it's nothing special. Not made of gold or even silver, just some cheap metal, but I have had it for over thirty years, and it's like a part of me. I have lost it a half dozen times, but it always seems to find its way back to me.

As I was saying that, I was looking down at it. The blue diamond-like rock started to emit a light and got very bright then dimmed back to normal.

Me: What was that all about?
Devil: I just enchanted your ring. Of course, the one here is just part of this fake world, but I have done the same thing to the one in your reality as well.
Me: And what exactly does enchant mean?
Devil: It will give you abilities. We need a way for you to use my powers, and now you have it. Look at it more as a good-luck charm. It mostly will keep you protected in the beginning.
Me: Look, not that I don't appreciate it, but you keep giving me these trinket abilities. If I or we are going to stop an advanced alien race that's leaps above us technologically, I will need more than a young brain and good-luck charm.
Devil: We barely know each other, but I am trying to build trust, Thomas. You know I want mankind to survive, so when I do something to help you, just know it has been thought out completely. You know how a granddad is clever because he has had years of life expe-

rience? Well, I have lived millions of lives of experience.

Me: Okay, I got ya, and I do trust you, Luke.

Devil: Well, that warms my heart (*said very sarcastically*). Also, keep in mind, this is a process. We have to take it slow. Although you were picked because you are a decently smart hairless ape, you are going to need to gradually get used to not only using this power but the best way to use it.

Me: Understood, and thank you for being patient with me.

Devil: Well, I am going to go use the little devils' room. I will be right back. Enjoy the area and mingle if you like. It's not like you will lose me.

At that he stood up and scooted around the giant corner table we were sitting at. Before he left, he put his hand on my head and whispered in my ear, "Don't flirt too much. I may get jealous." I looked up and smiled, expecting that evil grin; instead I saw a stone-cold-serious face.

Then he made his way through the crowd with more than half the room packed with people, both men and women checking him out as he walked by them.

I watched him until he was out of sight and looked down at my drink. I just realized I had not eaten or drank anything in this dream state. So I picked up my Long Island iced tea and smelled and tasted it. It certainly had that strong alcohol smell, same as the real world. So I took a big gulp. Yes, it also had the same strong taste too. In fact, it was so strong and real I choked a little on it. As I did, I noticed Jason, our server, was standing right next to me.

Jason: Oh, sir, I am so sorry. Did the bartender make it too strong for you? I will bring it back and get you another.

Me: No, no, that won't be necessary. It's just that I have not drank in a long time. I'm sort of out of practice. Jason, could I ask you a question?

Jason: Certainly, sir, I just got done work. If it would be okay with you, may I sit down at your table?

Me: I would like that a lot. Please do.

Jason scooted into the rounded table and got right up close to me, not like he was on my lap but certainly closer than a person would most likely sit next to you with a booth that size. I once again noticed his hair—as blond as blond can be. He also had such a young face and a perfect nose. He looked to be early twenties and, once again, fit, not muscleman fit but had a swimmer's body. He was tall, like 6' 3", and probably not an ounce of fat on him. He was a beautiful specimen by all standards—dreamworld or reality.

Jason: What did you want to ask me, Thomas?

Me: Do you know the associate I came in here with?

Jason: Well, of course, sir (*with a boyish giggle*).

Me: And who is he?

Jason: He is Lucas Dark, the richest, most powerful man on the planet, but I'm sure you know that, sir.

Me: Please don't call me sir, makes me feel old. Thomas or Tom will do nicely. Is that cool with you, Jason?

Jason: Oh yes, I am very sorry, sir—ehr—I mean Thomas. I did not mean to offend you. That was not my intension.

I could see he was visibly shook up and nervous, like he had just called me the most offensive name created. I even noticed his hands were shaking.

Me: Whoa, whoa, Jason. No harm at all. Why so nervous, guy? You are like a model. You have nothing to fear from me.

Jason: It's not you I am worried about.

Me: Then who?

Jason: I do not want to say anymore.

Me: Please, Jason, feel free to safely tell me what you are afraid of.

Jason: There is not much to say. Your friend is a powerful person, and I do not wish to talk about him.

Me: Okay, that's understandable. How long have you been working here?

Jason: I have lost track. Many years.

Just then the music stopped, and houselights came on. A voice came over the loudspeaker. At first you could not hear him well with all the people talking in the club. But as he continued to speak, the people began to quiet down.

Voice on intercom: We are sorry to interrupt your fun, but there has been an event of global proportions. We are unfortunately going to have to close for the night. It appears there is a national emergency, and the US government has announced martial law has been put into effect. We are unclear of what the actual problem is, but all televisions and radios are on an "emergency broadcast" mode. You are advised to go home and wait for further instructions. Please leave in an orderly fashion.

I sat there as people all started to gather their belongings and head out. Jason stayed seated and was just watching the people leave.

Jason: Are you not going to get ready to leave too?

Me: No, I think I will wait for Luke to return.

Jason: This is kind of scary. I wonder what is going on. I have never seen the owner clear this place. He would not care if it was the end of the world. He would keep the party going.
Me: I would not worry, Jason. Just stay here with me. When the place clears out and Luke comes back, you can go with us.
Jason: I can go with you and Mr. Black?
Me: Sure.
Jason: Where are you guys staying?

That was an interesting question. As this was all a simulation, I'm sure the devil would end this soon enough. As far as this "emergency," I'm sure it's something he has cooked up, as he did say this was a test of some sort. My plan would be to wait there with Jason until the devil returned and take it from that point.

We waited at least twenty minutes until the place was just about empty. No sign of my evil grinning associate anywhere. Jason got more and more nervous. He was not a coward or anything like that. But you could tell this situation concerned him greatly.

Jason: Do you think he left you here?
Me: I seriously doubt that. But let's go see if we can find him.

CHAPTER 7

We left the booth and started to roam through the place. It was a huge club. The dance floor alone was like a football field. I remember this place from history. I think I even watched a movie or two about it. It had many layers and secret rooms to it. After another twenty minutes of searching, we were met by security guards that informed us we would have to leave. At this point I started to panic a little. Where was he? What the hell kind of test was this?

I tried to explain to the security guard my friend was still here, and I needed to find him before I went anywhere, but they began to get physical. Jason was doing his best to try to explain he worked there and I was with *the* Mr. Lucas Black, but it seemed to have no effect.

At this point they were grabbing us by the wrists and arms and were forcibly dragging us both to the door. I started to get that feeling I got back with the devil in his mansion, that primal anger. As my arm was being twisted, I looked down at my hand, which began to hurt, and saw my class ring starting to have a dim glow.

Okay, this was a test of how I would handle things and use this so-called power I was given, so it was time to give it a try. I had no idea how this even worked. I remembered back to the devil telling me to make a plan then use the power. Well, first thing was to get these guys to stop pushing us around.

I looked down at my ring and said, "Strength." The ring's glow got brighter. I could feel a boost of exhilaration. As these two six-foot-plus guards who looked like linebackers were pushing us towards the door, I stopped walking. As I did that, I noticed their momentum stopped, and we came to a complete halt, which gave everyone a surprise.

The guard tried to regrip my arm and make another push, but it did nothing. I was immovable. I then grabbed the guard's arm and twisted it, which made a very loud cracking sound. As I looked, I had twisted his arm all the way around the opposite way in some unnatural-looking position. I had obviously broken his hand and arm. This was not what I wanted at all. With this, the other guard saw what happened and let Jason go and lunged at me, knocking me down to the ground.

The second guard went to grab me as I sat on my ass on the floor of this place, I got one foot up onto his chest to keep him at bay. But instead it catapulted him backwards and slammed him into the wall, which splattered the whole back of his head over the wall. Now the first guard grabbed some form of billy club with his good arm and went to hit me with it. As he swung it at me, I grabbed it and yanked at it to get it away from him. When I did, his whole arm came out of place. It did not completely detach but was obviously not fully connected anymore.

He let out a bloodcurdling scream, and Jason turned as white as a ghost and was looking at the wall with splattered blood and brains all over it and the other guard with both arms looking like something from a horror movie.

This is not what I wanted. This had not turned out well at all. These guys were just doing their jobs, and I virtually destroyed them both.

Jason looked at the surroundings and then, with a blank, cold look, turned to me and was about to speak when the room went dark, and suddenly I was back in the living room with the devil sitting in front of the fireplace on the couch where it all started. The devil was sitting next to me with his sneakered feet on my lap.

Devil: Not quite the outcome you expected, huh?

Me: No. Did you enjoy doing that to me? You want me to help and then you pull that shit?

Devil: Me? Always me, huh, Thomas? Love to hear how you rationalize this as my mistake.

Me: I asked for strength, and you went all bionic on me. You overdid it. I had no idea I was going to have that kind of strength.
Devil: I gave you a ring that can help you, and you used it with the most general terminology possible, *strength*. Not how much or of what kind. This is not a game. I can give you the tools to help you, but I cannot supervise your use of them.

What felt like an hour of silence as we looked at each other was just a few seconds. He was right. I was careless and nonspecific. He gets these powers from God. I need to use them with more thought.

Me: You're right. I'm sorry to be blaming you.
Devil: Good answer. That's why we had that little practice session. It's not easy, as one may think, to be given powers and use them in just the right way and in just the right measure.
Me: I'd be grateful for your input.
Devil: Well, think about the situation. They were trying to get you to do something you did not want to do and were using physical force. So you wanted them to stop in order to do what you needed to do. So to stop them you used physical force back, and that turned out rather, well, gruesome. What would be another way to get them to stop?
Me: I guess just say stop or take over their minds.
Devil: Or think even more general. When trying to resolve problems, always think simplistic.
Me: Yeah, duh, just put them to sleep.

I put my head down in my hands. How simple that solution was and how easily I dropped the ball on my first test. Maybe I'm not the one for this. I could not handle the death of one person, my best friend. How well am I going to handle the stress of all human existence?

Devil: Wrong, Thomas. Don't doubt yourself like that. It was more than just one person. It was the person you were closer to than anyone you ever met or ever knew. You saw him die as you were trying to resuscitate him. Although in the history of humans, there has been far worse, that is still rated pretty high on the shitty scale. I have been around since close to the beginning of time. I know every human whoever lived and every experience they have gone through and what they are capable of. Through all that, I have picked you, and I don't have the slightest doubt. I'm not wrong.

Me: Wow, good pep talk. But this reading my unspoken thoughts is hard to get used to.

Devil: Do you want me to stop reading your thoughts?

Me: No, I need you to understand me. I need you to know my doubts and strengths. I find it hard to believe that, of all the seven billion on the planet and the countless number that existed through time, I am your choice.

Devil: Well, you are, and quit trying to milk me for more compliments. This is very unlike me. I am supposed to be the rotten, evil prince of darkness, not your confidence-building boyfriend.

Although his face showed no smile or evil grin, I was getting a sense for him too. He was a sarcastic dick. But that was his way of drilling a point home.

Devil: Well, your sleeping pills will be wearing off soon. We don't have time for another bout in the simulator. Any questions you want to cover?

Me: Are these Pelusoians as strong as us? Do they look like us?

Devil: Easier to just show you.

He reached for his trustee remote and clicked it. The huge screen came on and showed a planet that at first glance looked like Earth, a big blue marble, but with a closer look, the land masses did not make the same shapes as our North America and Europe and so forth. There seemed to be more land and less water. Earth is like one-fourth land to three-fourths water. This looked more like one-third land to two-thirds water.

Me: This planet, it's not in the Milky Way galaxy?
Devil: No, it's not even in a galaxy your human scientist buddies have discovered or even charted yet.

He pushed another button on the remote, and it showed a spaceship of enormous size, like the size of the United States. Then he pushed another button, and it showed a city with buildings and incredible architecture. The cities and buildings spanned the size of a state.

Me: They are very advanced, it appears, far ahead of us.
Devil: Not in all things. Yes, technologically, but they are just as ruthless and warlike as you, maybe more. No diplomacy or compromise. There are no weighing factors or voting. Things are done by logic and pure necessity. In that way, humanity is more advanced, but that is my opinion. It could be argued that your political system has failed and stalemated itself, but that's another discussion.

I started to feel strange. The room, which was already dimly lit, seemed to get even dimmer. My mind even felt cloudy and sluggish.

Devil: Yes, you have been here quite some time now. You will need to go back soon. So let's review. When you awake, your brain is replaced with a younger version of itself. It has also been upgraded for speed and given a percentage more to use. Those abilities you may not feel right away. No other human has ever had that. Also, your class ring is enchanted. Need to use that with great caution and respect. Remember the club and the two security guards, except that was not real. You do something similar in your realm, well, I think you get the picture. Any last questions?

Me: When will I see you again?

Devil: We will meet every time you go to sleep. There will be no further voice in your head from me now that we have met and talked. Do me a favor and think through every decision and choice from this point on.

Me: What about the probe's message back to Earth that it was all a mistake?

Devil: Already done. You will be hearing about it on the news as soon as you get back. Remember, not everyone will believe. It's the nature of your species. The evidence will be very strong though, very thorough. In time, most will believe it. But in time, the Pelusoians will be spotted entering your system. At that point, nothing will be able to fool them.

Me: I see.

The Devil stood up and gave me a very serious look.

Devil: Although it is my expert super intelligent opinion that you are the best person for this, that does not mean you will do everything perfect without error. My last advice is to use the abilities as minimally and least conspicuously as possible. Giant, grand events will always work against you. Your decisions on how you use this power are more important than the power itself. Till next time.

CHAPTER 8

I woke abruptly to my nephew shaking me. He seemed all out of breath and super hyper. I was back in my room in my bed. As I began to wake up, I immediately noticed my vision was different. Everything was in super high-definition. This became instantly obvious even with the normal blurry wake-up effect.

Me: What's going on?

Justin: On the news all morning they have been talking about the probe. It was all just a mistake. They think it glitched and transmitted a false message. Three top-level scientists have confirmed it, and even NASA is putting out a worldwide apology.

Me: Wow, that's awesome. I knew it was all too strange. Well, I guess we will have enough food for a while. Haha.

Justin: Well, we are still under national guard, and they want everyone to remain at home for at least two days until things can get back to normal.

Me: Well, I guess you get two more days off from work.

Justin: Damn right. (*He took a big swig of a beer he had in his hand.*)

Me: A little early for alcohol, don't you think?

Justin: Early? Its two thirty in the afternoon. You slept for like thirteen hours. I guess those new sleeping pills work well, huh?
Me: Yeah, I think I may have taken too many, but yeah.

Justin then took another swig of his beer and happily went back out to the living room. Wow, thirteen hours sleep and I sure did not feel rested. I guess when I am asleep and in the realm with the devil talking, it's not like real restful sleep.

I got up and hopped in the shower. Once again the aspect of my vision was incredible. Not only was it HD, but it was like when I focused on something I could zoom in with super clarity. Also, the sound of the water in the shower was louder. But what I really noticed was that I could hear the TV in the living room on the other side of the house. When I tried, I could block out all noise except what I wanted to hear. It was like I was in the room with the TV and all other sounds around me, the shower and CD player, I could block out.

When I finished showering, I got dressed and went out to the living room. Justin was outside, talking to the neighbor. I started to listen to all the reports that were on every channel. Some were slightly different than others, but all of them were based on the new premise that it was all a technical error created by the probe, and expert after expert was confirming this. Charts and graphs and video simulations with all kinds of people with tons of letters after their name (MD, JD, PhD , etc.) described how this mistake happened.

There were still a couple interviews with people saying how it was hard to imagine how a probe could send such a specific message back that was by complete accident and the message to make such sense. Otherwise, it was reporters and other people with obvious relief that the world was not going to end.

Well, the devil certainly kept his word on changing the situation with the probe's dire message. I also could feel a difference in myself. The constant low-level headache you get when in your late forties was gone. My sight, hearing, and all my senses seemed to be enhanced. I could think clearer, faster, and with more detail. I was still me, but just a sharper version of me. The speed and clarity of my thoughts reminded me of my youth, but it surpassed even that.

I looked down at my school ring, which I rarely took off (even before the devil's enchantment of it). Although I had college rings too from all the universities and graduations throughout my life, nothing was as important as that high school ring. I barely made it through those years and so many times I almost quit after turning sixteen. If I had, there would be no other degrees or college rings. That high school ring was the foundation of all education that followed. Most kids had their school rings made of gold or silver and were worth a lot. I did not have much money back then, so the ring was made of some unremarkable metal that was worth very little. It did not take away from its appearance though. It was a sharp-looking ring; even over thirty years after its purchase, it still looked like new.

But now it was going to be much more—a power source that would help me to save the world. But as the demonstration with the devil showed in his simulation, it needed to be used with great thought and in the most common and simplistic way; otherwise it could cause more damage than good.

Reviewing the events the devil had simulated to me made me feel stupid. I needed to neutralize the guards so I could follow through with the task that was at hand. The use of brute strength to fight them was not what was required. All I needed to do was just put them to sleep. Keep it simple and small was what the devil said and I need to embrace that concept. I liked that phrase: "Keep it simple and small." I made a mental note to keep that quote handy whenever I was going to use the ring again.

Justin came in and was explaining that he was talking to the neighbor about the new events and what a relief it was. He also said how it was noticeably less noisy outside compared to yesterday. It was almost back to normal. With that I decided to take my car out for a drive. I needed some fresh air, and driving my awesome car always made me feel better and somehow gave me a calmness to think.

As I went out to the garage, the first thing I noticed was the bullet holes in the door and what appeared to me some near misses on the trunk. That car was my baby, so this was upsetting to me. This car has been in mint, showroom shape for many years, and now it had bullet holes in it. As I walked toward it to take a closer look at the holes in the doors, I rubbed my hand over the two distinct bullet penetrations, trying to feel if they felt as bad as they looked. When I waved my hands over the holes, I noticed that, when my hand reached the other side, they were gone. The hand I used was my right, which is the one with my class ring. I noticed the ring gave a very light glow when this happened. The bullet holes were gone like they were never there. I walked around the car to the only other place that had damage at the trunk. I did the same thing and softly touched the surface and waved my hand over the scratches, and the same thing happened. There was a slight glow from the ring once again as my hand passed over them; all blemishes were gone.

The first feeling was excitement. I healed my baby. Then a second feeling came over me, confidence, then the third and least liked, guilt. I'm sure the devil would not be happy of this use of the power. It was meant to save the world, not fix my car.

"But I did not try to do that or even think about the repairs. It just happened as I waved my ringed hand over the damage," I said out loud to myself in the garage. It's true. I was not abusing this ability. I was feeling the marks, and the ring did the fixing.

Maybe the ring has a mind of its own. Maybe I wanted it fixed and the ring felt that and did it. Either way, I did not make an outward effort or say, "Fix my car." It happened without even trying.

I did a good job of convincing myself it was not an abuse of my power and left the guilt of the event behind me. As I pulled out of the driveway, I could also tell (as Justin did say) that things seemed a lot calmer. I still could hear the occasional cars speeding and wheels screeching but much less disorder and panic than there was just the day before.

I drove to Walmart, where we were just at yesterday. Today it was still full of cars and people. This time a third of the vehicles were cop cars and army jeeps. I drove around the parking lot and took a look inside the front doors from my car, and I could see the shelves were being restocked, and there were armed soldiers at every aisle.

Since we really did not need any supplies or food for the next month, I decided to not even go in. I drove around to other stores and saw the same thing—lots of cops and soldiers but also order and calmness returning too. The devil really did a good job with capping this event. As he said, there were still some doubters, but overall, things had come back from the brink. I actually had to remind myself that things really were not back from the brink and that the ominous situation still exists, that these advanced beings I now know as Pelusoians were ruthless, uncompassionate alien beings that only saw our planet as a place to invade and the inhabitants as food to eat.

After an hour of driving around, I decided to make sure my car was filled with gas. I made yet another mental note that, from this point on, I should always have the car full of gas and ready to go. I stopped at a small gas station that did not look to be too busy (although it was by normal standards). I noticed as I made my way to the pumps that there were basically two types of people. The first were the happy, relieved ones who were smiling and would say hi and converse about the last twenty-four hours with anyone. The others were the ones with blank looks on their faces. They seemed to still be in shock and had not yet recovered.

As I got to the pump, I went to put my debit card in and noticed the sign, "Cash only till further notice." So I walked into the store.

This little convenience store looked like it was hit pretty hard yesterday. Most of the shelves were empty. I went to the clerk, who seemed in a good enough mood, and said, "Twenty-dollar ultra." He smiled and took my money. I decided to be one of the happy, talkative people.

Me: Hey, looks like you got cleaned out pretty good.

Clerk: Yeah, but it's all insured, and hey, looks like we are not going to be turned into slaves of an incoming alien race. Haha!

"Yeah, that's true," I said with multiple ironic thoughts in my head. "Guess gas is all you got to sell for a while."

Clerk: Well, that and my case of lottery tickets. I grabbed them when I locked up. I was in such a rush, it was the only thing I could think of at the time. Want to buy one? It seems no one is interested in playing the lotto after these past events.

Me: Wow, you would think it would be just the opposite.
Clerk: Well, the tickets are worth a lot, especially when it's something the insurance won't cover.

I went to hand him my twenty for the gas, and he ripped off a $20-dollar ticket.

Me: No, this is for my gas, can't really be spending money on lottery right now.

As I said that, the ticket he was trying to hand me was close to my hand, the hand with the class ring. When the ticket got close, it lit up, and I mean quite a bit more than when it fixed the car holes. In fact, it lit up so much the clerk even caught a glimpse.

Clerk: Cool ring. It glows up like a flashlight. Never seen one quite like that.

In a sort of panic, I pulled my hand back and put it in my pocket. The clerk was giving me a curious look, so I tried to make things go smoother.

Me: Well, here is the twenty for gas and another twenty for the ticket. What the hell, it's been such a crazy couple days I might as well.

The clerk immediately smiled and took the money hungrily and seemed to instantly forget about the ring. There was quite a line forming, so I said my pleasantries and quickly headed back to the car. Since I had just filled the tank a couple days ago, I could only get $17. 20 jammed into the tank. I decided to not even bother with the change and just took off back home.

As I pulled into the driveway, I noticed Justin's truck was gone. I guess he must have had the same idea that I had. It was unusually hot even for Florida that day, so I was relieved to get inside and into the pleasant air-conditioning. Of course, my loving dog, Toby, met me at the door. His eyes were so white with cataracts, he could barely see, but he still managed to remember and maneuver around the house and furniture to always find his way to me.

I sat down and turned on the TV, and it was the same thing it had been all day. Some different scientists were saying the radiation inside the Oort cloud could be considered the major cause of the malfunction. One guy was very skeptical though. Some professor from New Zealand made a point that had most others stomped. "The craft was designed to send back pictures and data. When did it learn to spell and send back messages, especially in all languages known to man?" You can tell, when he said this, it made a dent in many of the ongoing theories. Some other scientist from NASA had some rationalization that it was just a glitch caused by the radiation, and when it thought it was sending pictures, it was sending a garbled form of alphabetized rambling.

The debate kept going back and forth, and I listened to it for a few more minutes and tried to find a movie or something other than this news topic. In the age of cable and two hundred plus channels, you would think there would be something else on. But as I clicked, each channel was the same, so I gave up and shut it off.

As I sat there, I got the keys out of my pocket and went to put them on the table when the lottery ticket fell out of my pocket. I had almost forgotten about it for a while. As I looked at it, I thought back to the poor gas-station owner trying to push its sale on me and how easy I caved in. I better start to get a stronger will when it comes to things, I thought to myself. But I did buy it, so I might as well scratch it off. I was never lucky at such things, especially the lottery. As I read it, it explained that three matches and you win that prize, and at the bottom there was a special box that could multiply the winnings up five times the amount won.

As I was reading the ticket instructions and payouts, the phone rang. I was so distracted reading the ticket I did not even look at the caller ID.

Me: Hello!

Psychiatrist: Hello, Mr. Williams, this is Dr. Olcult. I wanted to remind you of our appointment tomorrow. With all that was going on with this alien hoax and all, I wanted to make sure you remembered to be here.

Me: Doctor, with all that's going on in the world, I think it's best we suspend our scheduled appointments. It seems there is—

Dr. Olcult: Mr. Williams, I thought I was clear about the importance of continuing your counseling at this point.

Me: The more I talk to you, Doc, the more our conversations sound like threats than anything else.

Dr. Olcult: Well, see them as you like, but please be here on time tomorrow.

Me: And if I don't, with the world on lockdown and the national guard at emergency status, you are going to get the police to take the time out for a patient who has missed their appointment. I don't think so, and I think you realize that as well.

Dr. Olcult: You're right, of course, but things are very quickly returning to normal, and it would not be long before they would have to follow through with my professional request. Look, Mr. Williams, I will make a deal with you. Show up for tomorrow's appointment, and if after that you no longer wish to see me, I will agree to terminate our sessions and leave you alone forever. Do we have an agreement?

Me: Fine, Dr. Olcult, I will see you tomorrow morning as scheduled.

Dr. Olcult: Thank you, Thomas. In the meantime, don't do anything major.

What did that mean? I thought to myself. What a strange thing to say. Did he think I was going to kill myself or something? I will be glad to be done with this guy.

"Okay, Doc, no major things," I said with an overly obvious sarcasm, "until after I see you tomorrow."

> Dr. Olcult: Very good, Thomas. Until then, have a good rest of your day.

He then hung up, and I sat there for a second, taking in the conversation. I walked into my room and went to lie down and remembered I had the ticket in my hand. Not wanting to even deal with it at the moment, I opened my dresser drawer and put it into a box I had in there with some other papers. I can scratch it off later.

CHAPTER 9

As I lay down, I once again noticed how sharp my eyesight was. There was a housefly buzzing around my room and landed on the ceiling. As I locked on to him, I started to really stare at him. As I did, my vision began to zoom in like a lens on a camera, 2×, 3×, 4×, and more. It got to a point where I could see him rubbing his two legs together from my bed all the way to the ceiling. Once again, it was not just the zoom but the clarity. It seemed my new super High-Definition vision gave me an incredible enhanced view of my surroundings. It seemed like it could go even further too. The focus, clarity, and zoom felt almost limitless.

I finally stopped and shut my eyes and then reopened them. The zoom aspect went back to normal. It appears that was how I could control this newfound ability. I could zoom at will, and when I wanted to reset, I would just close my eyes hard for a couple seconds, and the zoom vision would end.

I began to think that this must be part of my brain upgrade the devil had spoken of. If that was one aspect, what were some of the others? I remember my hearing was far improved too. On that basis, probably all my senses were souped-up.

The devil certainly has come through with everything he has claimed right down to every detail, not just some twisted version that in the end was just a trick or play on words, which has been a classic devil move in literature throughout time. Everything was just as he said, if not better.

I should continue to try and test my senses and any part of the brain upgrade, but I was still kind of scared about the ring. With what happened in the simulation, I was not ready for anything like that again. Actually, I began to worry a little bit about the car's bullet holes. Is he going to be mad at me for that? I honestly did not try to do that, and he is not someone I can lie to. He knows my thoughts, so he will know I did not abuse the power. It was more like the ring had decided what it wanted to do. Not that I was against it, just more of a separate decision-making process seemed to be at work.

Either way I am sure to ask about that once I see him again. The more I thought about it and the things the devil had told me, the more I realized how much it seemed the devil's hands are tied by all these sets of rules. Although he acts and makes it seem like he has no boss and is in control, it sure does seem like he walks a tight rope of strict guidelines. I mean, it would seem to me he must have his own plan to stop or get rid of these Pelusoians. Combine that with unlimited power (or as he says it, the same power as God), it seems like he could take control of this situation and deal with it himself with no problem. It appears he does need someone else to do the actual work as well as the ideas of how it's to be done.

It seems that I am the one this responsibility has been given to. That's not a lot of pressure, I thought to myself in a very sarcastic way.

Even my new young turbo brain was getting overloaded. So much has been happening in such a short time. The more I thought about the last couple days' events, I started to feel myself become overwhelmed with nervousness and uncertainty. What if I screw this all up? The world and all life on Earth will be gone. Everyone will be dead including me.

Take that even a step further, now there apparently is a God and devil, meaning there is an afterlife. How is God going to feel about me working with the devil? How will the devil treat my failure to resolve this situation if I fail? Yup, my anxiety was now hitting a level I had never experienced before. My heart was pounding, and I began to sweat profusely. What if I have a heart attack and then the earth has no chance at all?

I needed to stop this line of thinking and the road it was taking me down. I had always been a nervous person. Right after Shawn's death, I was prescribed Xanax and tried to only take them as needed. This seemed like the ideal time for that. So I went to bathroom and took out the container and quickly swallowed one.

I returned to bed and looked at my beautiful dog, Toby. Although old at thirteen and blind with white eyes, he was a show dog by all standards. He was mine and Shawn's dog for years. We both loved him, and he loved both of us. When I was upset or nervous, Toby could always tell. He would do his best to comfort me by pushing up close or licking my face. I would in return pet him, and this was also very therapeutic and calming to me.

As I lay there with Toby at my side, I could feel the nerve pills begin to kick in. They were not completely like sleeping pills but similar. I slowly began to relax and felt the stress of my thoughts start to lessen and fade. Then, before I knew it, my eyes started to feel heavy, and then I gave in and shut them. But as I did, I thought about turning on the air conditioner, so I reopened my eyes. But when I did, I realized I was not in my room anymore. I was back in that familiar living room with the smell of the fire in the fireplace the smell of a clean but not antiseptic house—more like the perfect room deodorizers of a fall scent and one last smell, the smell of a young male with exceptional pheromones that were designed specifically to create a feeling in me.

I was once again sitting in the plush velvet red couch, and next to me was him. He had the red hair, perfect complexion, and was dressed all in skater attire, looking at me with that well-known evil grin.

Devil: Welcome back, Thomas.

Me: Wow, that was fast. I just shut my eyes for a split second. Do I get any rest at all on these little trips here?

Devil: Your body does. Your mind, not so much. But with a beefed-up young brain, you should be able to take it.

I could not be sure, but recently, each time I came to this place, I would get the feeling I can sense the devil's mood more. I know he said the more I am around him, the more his personality rubbed off on me. I wonder if that works both ways. He also can read me from the inside. After time and again of being at this place, does that work for me too? It seemed I literally could feel his excitement to talk to me and a little bit of him being lonely. He did explain that it was a rare event in the history of his life to talk with humans, that very few had ever talked to him at all. An event of this magnitude is no doubt rare or has never happened to him. Maybe I am having more of an effect on him than he will admit.

> Me: I suppose you just heard that whole thought?
> Devil: What? Oh, of course. I hear everything.

He got up and walked to the bar to make himself another drink. But I got the distinct feeling he did not hear the thoughts I was just contemplating and that he was lying to me about saying he did.

> Devil: So anything to report? Smashed anyone else's head into a pulp?
> Me: If you have been watching, I guess you know the answer to that question and what exactly I have been up to.
> Devil: I am the fucking devil, you little ape. I have other things and other worlds I watch over that are far more important than you and yours.

Once again I got the distinct feeling he was lying, but I did not want to push it at this point. As I could feel his happiness to see me again, I could also sense that he was getting agitated. I decided to try not to let him get any more angry.

> Me: I'm sorry. Yeah, I never thought of that. You must have a lot going on. We are just a small part of a big puzzle, I would imagine.

He looked at me with a new expression, one I had not seen before. This one was of confusion. I saw it only for a brief glance then, as if he noticed I was observing it, changed it quickly back to the well-known evil grin.

Devil: Yes, Thomas, plenty on my plate. I do know you have used the ring. How did that work out for you?

Me: Well, it was strange the way that worked. I really did not even try to use it. It sort of decided to work on its own.

Devil: What do you mean?

Me: Like with the car. I did not want to do that, it did it itself.

Devil: Look, as I said, I have way more things going on than you. So instead of assuming I know what happened, let's just from now on have you explain everything as if I have no idea what is going on every second with you on your little insignificant planet.

Me: Hey, what's the matter? Before we talk about what happened to me, is there something going on with you? I know you put on this tough-guy, all-powerful, all-knowing thing, but I can also tell that, as immortal as you are, you get stressed too. We are partners of a sort, are we not? Somehow I can feel your stress. You said that all through creation you rarely have talked to anyone. Well, this a unique situation where you have someone here on your plane of existence, and I want to help. I need you and your support. In that giant computer of knowledge, you must be able to weigh odds and probability. The better we work together, the greater chance of success. The less stressed and clearheaded, the better equipped you are to help me. Logical or not?

He stared at me with an expression I could not read. But once again I could feel something from him, a flurry of several different emotions, always anger, but this time he was feeling something I would bet he had not felt much of before—doubt and worry. He also felt different about me. It was like a feeling of friendship, but I could also feel he wanted to resist it, that he never has needed anyone and sure as hell did not need a confused, depressed human, yet that was exactly what he felt.

> Devil: So you want a chance to psychoanalyze Satan himself. Do you think you are qualified for such a task?
>
> Me: No, not at all, but I am willing to try. I think you picked me for more reasons than you have told me and more reasons than you know yourself.
>
> Devil: In case you think I don't know, I can tell your ability to feel my thoughts is growing. It is something I cannot control. As you feel my anger and it starts to have an effect on you, something similar is happening to me. Bestowing my powers on you as well as you being in my presence are going to allow you to feel and read me as well as I have always been able to do to you. If it was up to me, I would shut that down, but once again, it's one of those little rules. I have chosen you for this, and I knew eventually this would start. But it is not healthy for you to try to stir around too much in my thoughts.
>
> Me: Agreed. But if you share with me by your own choice, you can vent some things and measure and weigh how much you put in me.
>
> Devil: How much I put in you? Is that all you think about?

Now I stared at him. I did not understand that he was making a joke. He had not done that before, so I was racing to try and figure out the meaning until he burst into a roaring laugh. It was a roaring also, to the point it shook the room. He then stopped and took his normal position on the couch next to me. Then, *plop-plop*, both DC skater sneakers smack on my lap.

Devil: If I am to open up to you, toad, you must at least attempt to laugh at my jokes, unless you did not take that as a joke.

Me: No, I get it now, Luke. You caught me off guard with a human sense of humor and a very human comment.

Devil: I will say this, you are flattered that I have picked you. In the end, you may not feel the same way. This is going to get messy and at times very stressful. My connection with you is very limited when you are conscious. So the need for you to think on your feet and do the right thing are going to be the key to success. Although you may start to more and more be able to read me, that does not mean I need your counseling. You are a smart chimp, that's why I picked you, and there may be other reasons as well, but I'm not ready to open up to you. And you, my hairless ape, are not ready for that either. I must admit I have never spent this much time with any human, and I do feel you are a clever one, in some aspects. But we need to stay focused on the issue at hand. If we fail, you and all who you love will cease to exist. It is possible that, without mankind, I may also cease to exist or, worse, lack a purpose in this galaxy. So as much as I appreciate your heart-to-heart offer, let's try to keep this on track. I have picked you, and I can't unpick you nor can I now pick someone else or want to.

Me: Don't tell me—another rule.

Devil: Yes, another rule. But I still believe although your mushy behavior is part of you being gay, it does not help us in the big picture. You are going to need to be tough, tough like you have never been before. Therefore, you can't be worried about my feelings. I can handle tough and gritty situations. So although I appreciate your new insight into me and wanting to help, stay out of my head.

When he said those last words, the room shook again and also darkened a couple shades. His eyes lit up bloodred with a glare that put a chill down my spine. I did not want to show my fear. At this point, everything could be a test, so I calmly looked down at his sneakers on my lap and untied one then the other and then removed them.

Me: Wow, even matching DC socks. I will give you this much, Luke. For a tough straight guy, you know how to shop and dress for success.

I was trying to play it as cool as possible and was looking at his DC socks and was reluctant to look up at him. But I found the courage and finally did so.

He had that "no expression" look, but I could feel the anger reduce to puzzlement. At that he reached down and took off both socks, and with the same manner as before, *slap-slap*, his bare feet came down on my lap. Then he took a gulp of his drink and returned my stare.

Devil: Okay, Thomas, touché. So maybe you are better at playing around with my mind than I give you credit for. But I still get credit because I am the one that picked you. Anyway, back to work. What happened with the ring and your car?

Me: When this whole thing broke in the news, my nephew and I went out to get supplies in case we were going to be trapped in the house for the long haul. During the venture, we came across some bad guys, and they shot up my car and put bullet holes in it. The next day, I was checking them out and rubbed my hand over them. The ring glowed, and the bullet holes were gone. I did not say any magic words or was even thinking repair, it just happened.

Devil: Yeah, first, I'm not mad, and it's good you question these things. I did not fully explain the power I put in the ring. It has its own thoughts and will do things to protect you. I assume the ring felt that bullet holes in the car could draw attention and therefore fixed them so police or others would not be questioning you about it. In fact, it may have seen some future event that the holes would cause and acted on changing that.

Me: Wait, I thought you told me the future was not written, that it can change so easily that even you cannot say for sure what will happen.

Devil: It's true. But there are odds of probability. Meaning, that of the many different possible timelines, there was a multitude of them where the bullet holes caused a situation, in fact, so many that it was reasonable to assume it was going to be a problem. Maybe it would not have been, but so many scenarios of future possibility made it a high-percentage decision, and the ring went with the numbers.

Me: Okay, I get that. But the ring is alive? I thought of it more in the symbolic sense as a magic wand for me to use. You're telling me that it's got its own mind?

Devil: Yes, in a way. It will make decisions based on statistical probability and timeline consistencies. It does not have a personality. Think of it more like a protective computer with the ability to analyze events and make things happen accordingly.

Me: That might have been something I would have like to have known ahead of time.

Devil: We don't have time for me to explain the nuances of every little detail. Some things you're going to have to just trust me on. The ring is not flawless. It makes decisions based on what mathematically seems to be the best outcome. So there is obviously room for error. But I would not waste any time worrying about it making mistakes. More likely you have a greater percentage of making things worse than the ring will.

CHAPTER 10

As we talked, I could feel him start to become more relaxed. He even seemed to get what I can only describe as lighthearted. I did not dare mention I could feel that, but it was becoming obvious I was getting more of his thoughts and feelings every second I was around him. I looked down at his feet, where he was wiggling his toes. His feet had no wear and tear to them at all, not a callous or imperfection at all. They were, of course, the feet Hollywood would use in a commercial as a foot model—smooth, well-shaped feet with toes groomed to perfection. They were not without some kind of scent though—nothing to clear a room, way less than the normal scent of the average man whose feet are smothered with socks and sneakers all day. Although the tables were now turning on who can read whom, his ability to read my mind was now very limited. I could tell he knew I was not disgusted by his feet at all. They were like the rest of him—perfect—not in any perverted sense, but to me they were works of art. The toes were like little mushrooms, and the arch and shape of his feet were beautiful, like a painter or sculptor would interpret the human physique as being a masterpiece of flawless design. So I decided to do a little experiment of my own.

As the conversation continued, I casually put my hand on his foot and just kept it there. He continued to talk and took no notice of it at all. I then gradually began to rub the bottoms and worked up to the toes. Still no notice or comment. Not until I actually started to massage them did he stop in midsentence to look down at his feet and then back at me. Expressionless once again, he gave an evil grin and resumed talking. I could sense that he was enjoying this but would never verbally state that to me.

Devil: So I want to talk to you about this doctor you will see tomorrow.

Me: Dr. Olcult? What about him? He's a dick. Tomorrow will be my last visit with him. He and I do not get along.

Devil: That might be for the best.

Me: Why? What's the deal with him? What do you know?

Devil: Nothing more than you, but just the same feeling. He's a dick. I don't like him.

Once again this newfound ability to feel the devil's true emotions came through loud and clear. He was lying to me. He did know something. If this new ability is going to continue and even get stronger, I decided I would play dumb with it. It was weird how it was working. The more I could read him, the less he can read me. In the beginning, I could not think anything without him knowing it. It now appears to be reversing.

Me: Care to elaborate on this feeling about my shrink?

Devil: No, other than you should trust my opinion on people. I have had a little more experience with them than you.

Me: Okay. I can concur with that. As I stated, I don't care for him anyway, and I was going to see him just this last time and tell him to go to your house.

The devil looked at me with puzzlement.

Devil: Are you saying I need a shrink?

Me: Joke, he can go to hell—your house. Haha.

An immediate smile came over his face. Then he looked down at his bare feet and wiggled his toes like a little kid.

Devil: Your attempt at humor.

Me: Sorry, not quite the rib-breaker joke like you tell there, Luke.

Devil: Still adjusting to this much interaction with a human. That and you're right—I am gradually losing my ability to read your thoughts, not entirely yet but, yes, less and less. In any other situation I would not be so naive when faced with a joke. My connection would allow me to know that you just told a joke. Now I have to actually rely strictly on communication and, of course, the quality of the humor itself.

Me: Well, I will try to do better. You know, I actually don't mind you being able to read me. If you wish, you can continue to.

Devil: Not a choice. It's more like…

Me: A rule!

Devil: Yes, smart-ass. Eventually I will have no read on you at all. At that point, let's both hope you are ready for the task.

My feelings were beginning to become confusing. This, after all, is the evil one himself, the prince of darkness, king of lies, the beast, yet in his young, good-looking form and in what I began to sense was his first time being in trouble and his immortality was at stake. He was like a frightened child that was vulnerable but unable to show that vulnerability. I had to be careful not to develop strong feelings for him, and it did not take six college degrees to know that would be a dangerous situation, to say the least.

Devil: So how did I do with discrediting the probe's transmission?

Me: Extremely well. As you said, there are still a couple of doubters, but overall, things are quickly returning to normal. How long until the Pelusoians reach our solar system?

Devil: I can only approximate, the future being unpredictable and all, but I would say another few weeks, give or take.

Me: You know I still have no idea what I am going to do. Does that worry you?

Devil: Not at all. You will need to react based on events as they unfold. Nothing has happened yet. I think just practicing your abilities and learning all you can is the best plan of action for now.

Me: Agreed. Can I see more of the Pelusoians? You showed me their home world, but what do they look like? Maybe even some background on them could be helpful.

Devil: Okay. They were once very similar to humans in many ways, the way they looked and how they evolved. They became quite intelligent and had a paradise-like world at one time. But they made a mistake that you humans are doing now. They started to depend on machines over their natural talent that was given to them. Let's just say the *Matrix* or *Terminator* scenario ended up happening to them.

Me: So the machines they made got smart and overthrew them?

Devil: Not quite. They were as fragile as your bodies are. The thought of death consumed them. They became medically advanced to live many more years than you do on Earth, but eventually, time always catches up. They could replace things as they wore out, but eventually, like an old car, you end up with little left of the original parts. So they saw that biological was inferior to mechanical. They devised a way to put their consciousness into long-lasting artificial creations. But the AI they had created, which helped steer them down that path, left a residual in these creations. When they transferred, they were not the beings they were as biological. Ultimately, they lost who and what they were to what they had created. Now, instead of a residual of the AI machines being left, there only exists a small portion of the people they once were. Losing the emotional aspect of offspring and the importance of living each moment, they became as they were created—pure logic with the only goal is to live on forever.

Me: Yikes. I can see us doing the same thing. I hope we don't, but we are already kind of heading down that path. Can I see what they look like?

The devil grabbed his remote and clicked it. The giant picture came on in amazing detail. What it showed was an example picture of them. Not any real film shot or snapshot. More of a textbook-looking screenshot with measurements and no background. They were beings that looked similar to us.

Me: This is them as they were before the transformation to machine?

Devil: No, this is what they currently look like. They tried their best to look like they originally did when they were biological.

They had heads, arms, and legs. Their skin was more like a transparency that showed all their insides. They were scary looking, I thought to myself, but nothing like in a horror movie, just skinny, tall, artificial-looking humanoids with see-through skin. The devil then quickly shut off the image. I once again got the distinct feeling from him—a combination of dislike and fear.

Me: So are they indestructible?

Devil: Nothing in the universe is indestructible. But they are far from fragile now. Nothing on earth short of a nuclear bomb going off right next to them would destroy them. Of course, that will not be an option. That would just destroy Earth and defeat the whole, save the humans-for-food factor.

I got a shiver from how coldly he said that. Now that I could feel his thoughts, I could see his compassion for us was only based on how it would affect him to not have us around. He was not empathetic for us but for the loneliness it would create in him. His long years of just watching us and interfering from afar and lack of actual interaction made him very self-centered.

As I was thinking of all this, he got up and went to the bar, but not before giving me that evil look; in which I realized was derived from the little bit he could still read me and my last thoughts. He did not like my conclusion, even if it was true. Yet he did not want to admit it or talk about it.

He filled his glass with a mix of a few different bottles and gave it a quick stir, sat it down, and leaned over the bar.

Devil: You are very unique in many ways. Most humans have an obsession with the afterlife, heaven, hell, and so on. You have asked me only a couple questions on that front, but you must have a whole lot more on that topic, don't you?

Me: Of course I do, but I thought time is limited, and we need to focus on the main issues? I would love to ask a bunch of stuff. How many humans get to have all the mysteries of life and the universe answered.

Devil: We do need to stay on track. But we also cannot solely concentrate on our mission. If you do not take breaks or have distractions, the constant thinking of one concept becomes distorted, and you can lose perspective. We have time for a couple questions, not too many, so make them good.

My mind raced. I can ask the questions that man has pondered all through time. There are so many. Where to start?

Me: Why does God make it seem like you are his adversary, that it will come down to a big war in the end between you two?

Devil: I would place that under the category of two concepts. One is that the Bible was translated so many times it retained approximately 25 percent of its original content. The original content was written by humans, who were writers themselves and, of course, like your movies of today, change things to make it more interesting or to put their own spin on it. I was created by God to give balance as I told you before. He made me so there can be a reality in which good and bad things happen. Otherwise there would be no reality.

Me: That makes sense. It sucks, but I can see what you mean. If every day is great, then great days become meaningless.

Devil: That is a very simplistic way to put it but actually incredibly accurate.

My next question came from deep inside of me. I looked down at the ground, and I did not maintain eye contact.

Me: What about Shawn?

At that the devil came from behind the bar and resumed his position on the couch next to me.

Devil: What about him, Thomas?

Me: Is he really gone? Does he exist in heaven or hell? Is there a heaven or hell?

Devil: This gets complex, and I may not be able to fully answer this one because it goes into such a background of things it gets really complicated. Short answer—Shawn exists still. There is a quantum number of realities from where Shawn died at birth to where he became president of the United States and almost an infinite number of scenarios in between. So is he gone? No, there are billions of him, many of which you still hang out with.

Me: Could I see one of those realities?

Devil: I don't recommend that, Thomas. That subject matter is your major weakness. It distorts you and causes you a tremendous amount of psychological pain.

Me: I can handle it. I want to see this other reality—please.

The devil took his remote and clicked the giant screen to come on. It was me talking in front of a fire, which looked like at a campground. As the camera panned back, I saw Shawn sitting on the other side of the fire. This hit my stomach hard. To hear his voice and see him laughing were something. I almost forgot what that was like.

Devil: This is a reality where he did not die that Friday after Thanksgiving. But if you remember, you guys planned a camping trip for that weekend. Well, here he did not die, and you both did go camping.

As I watched the screen, it began to hurt more and more. On the screen we were having such a good time. I did remember we had planned to go camping that weekend after Thanksgiving. I had almost forgotten about those plans. Then I saw Shawn get up and put a piece of wood on the fire and say, "Thanks for this, Tom. I am really having a good time. I needed this getaway. Makes me wonder where I would be if I had not come to Florida with you."

That stuck in me like a knife. Those words were meaningful. I had thought about that as well—that maybe, if he never met me, he would have lived a long happy life. I could not watch anymore. I put my head down in my hands and started to cry. The devil immediately clicked the screen off.

Devil: That is why I did not want to show you this. A lesson once again to listen to me when I suggest something. But no, don't listen to me. What do I know? I've just been around for hundreds of millennia. But you have six degrees that far outweigh my knowledge and experience.

He was obviously very upset and was raving and going on in a very loud and obnoxious way. But then, in midsentence, he stopped.

Devil: Okay, Thomas. I tried to show you a timeline and situation that was happy. But I could have picked something more appropriate.

Me: I asked for this, and you even warned me. So it is my fault and not yours.

Devil: Things happen that just happen. In your timeline you lost your best friend. I deal within this reality and this timeline in this galaxy.

I wiped my eyes and took a big breath.

Me: Back to the problem at hand. That holds more than enough stress and is what we should be working on anyway.

Devil: You got that right. So what do you say we do some practice again?

Me: Let's do it.

CHAPTER 11

With that we were suddenly back at Club 54. I was with the waiter, Jason, and the same two guards are grabbing me. He put me right back in the same spot and situation I had left right before my carnage happened with the security guards.

Security: I don't care who he is with. We were told to clear this place, and that is what we are doing.

The same guard was grabbing my arms, and it was all happening again. Talk about déjà vu. This time was going to be different. I will use the advice the devil gave me. Keep it simple.

Me: Mr. Security Guard, I agree it sounds like things are in an emergency situation. I think I will just leave and go home.

Jason: Kurt (*I guess Jason knew his name*), he is not resisting and wants out of here. He's taking me somewhere safe too. Please just let us go on our way.

That was very awesome of Jason to say and do. Unfortunately, I don't think they even heard him, and I was back to the point where my arm felt like it was going to break. We were at the same exact point where I splattered these guards last time. But this time, I did things differently.

Me: Kurt, go to sleep, now.

As soon as I said those words, he dropped like a sack of potatoes. My hands and arms immediately were released. The other guard, who was manhandling Jason, saw his buddy drop to the floor. He looked right at me and grabbed his baton and was about to swing it when—

Guard 2: What the hell! What did you do to him?
Me: Nothing, he passed out.
Guard 2: Guess what, time for you to pass out!

He went to swing his baton at me.

Me: Put the baton down and go help the others and forget about us and this situation.

He stood there looking at me. For a second, I thought the ring was not working. Then he very gently and calmly set the baton on the ground and headed over to the last remaining people fighting to get out the door.

Jason: How did you do that?
Me: Magic. Now let's go find Luke.

We continued to walk around, but this place was huge. Then we started to see and smell smoke. The stage where the performers had been playing was now smoking.

Me: Okay, Jason, let's get out of here.
Jason: Should we not try to find—
Me: He will be all right. Fire is not an issue for him. But we need to get out of here before we are cooked.

We weaved up and around till we hit an exit and went out the door. The outside was cold. It had been fifteen years since I had been in New York. My Florida blood was thin and not used to this type of cold anymore. Even if it was a simulation, it was that same cold I remembered from years ago.

We walked down the alley till we hit the streets. People were not just panicking in the club, it was going on outside as well—crowds running in all directions with some of them pointing up in the air.

Jason and I stood at the corner of the street. I had only been to the real New York City once, but I remember trying to get used to looking up and buildings being everywhere. If you were not used to it, it was a bit scary and disorientating. But it was not the buildings that were making the people run and freak out. We looked up to see the moon was split in half. Both halves were floating away from each other with mounds of debris all around it.

Jason: Holy shit. What the hell happened to the moon?

I could feel my heart racing and the fear in me building up. I had to remind myself that this was a simulation. Everything just seemed so real. The moon cracked, and pieces of it were circling it. It was an incredible sight.

Jason: What are we going to do?
Me: We need to go somewhere so I can think.
Jason: My apartment is just four streets down.
Me: Sounds good, let's go.

The sounds of people screaming and cars squealing reminded me of the way things were in the real world just a couple days ago. I began to wonder what the purpose of this test was. Why crack the moon in half?

We got to his apartment, which was in a very tall building. As we were about to enter, we heard shots fired. This just quickened our pace into the building and on to the elevator.

We got off on the seventeenth floor and were soon in his apartment. Jason looked visibly shaken. His apartment was pretty nice—fireplace, bar, the works. I went to his balcony to get another look at the moon. It looked even more ominous this time. Being a full moon made it show up brightly in the sky, and all the pieces would change colors as they were circling and floating around the two main chunks.

As I stood there, I felt Jason come up behind me and tap me on the back. He had a beer for me and had another for himself that was already half drank.

> Jason: Think it was an asteroid hit? Or maybe a comet?
> Me: No, not to make such a clean center cut like that.
> Jason: Then what do you think?
> Me: Not sure, but I don't think it was a natural occurrence.
> Jason: You mean aliens?
> Me: Possibly.

Just then there was a strange grinding sound, and then the whole building began to shake. It was an earthquake of a rather high magnitude. We both stepped back and got off the balcony. The sound changed from a grinding to a roaring. Then a large portion of the sky was blocked out by a ship that was miles in length. It took up the whole side of the sky from our perspective. The shaking began to lessen as I began to realize it was not an earthquake; it was the engines of this massive spaceship. It seemed to hover over the Hudson River. Then a beam of light looking like a red laser with the thickness of a car came out of it and went straight up into the sky.

The beam went directly at the remains of the moon. When the beam made contact, it hit the right half. This beam did not cut it like what appeared to have happened earlier. It completely destroyed the half section. In an explosive spray, the half of the moon filled the sky with bright explosive chunks that immediately lit up the night as if it was daytime. The chunks of the moon were now widely spread all over.

I need to do something to stop that ship. It was so big. It needed something equally as big—a nuke. I looked down at my ring and said, "Make a nuke transform in the center of that ship and detonate in ten seconds. The ring glowed brighter than I have seen and then went back to regular. Jason was standing right next to me.

Jason: Who are you talking to?
Me: I'm saving New York City, 5,4,3,2…

As we watched from outside, an eerie silence came across everything then a bright light, brighter than staring into the sun. It knocked us both down and pushed us back into the apartment.

Then there was the sound of a deep bass. But the light did not get dimmer, and the sound just got louder. I could not see a thing and began to notice I could not feel anything, like all senses were cut off. The last thing I could hear was a gut-wrenching scream of agony from Jason. Then suddenly I was back on the couch in the devil's mansion. I was sitting there, looking at the fire, and the devil had his usual position next to me on the couch with his bare feet on my lap.

I looked over to him as he took a drink from his glass and then gave me a nod.

Me: What happened? Did I destroy the alien ship?
Devil: Oh yes, a nuke in the center of the ship totally destroyed it—and New York City with all of its inhabitants.
Me: I killed everyone in New York City?
Devil: Well, in the simulation. If it was real, the radioactive fallout would have killed twice as many more. That's if the alien ship did not have some form of propulsion, like antimatter that would have combined with the nuclear explosion and would have taken out the entire planet.

I looked down at his feet with his toes wiggling.

Me: So I guess that was not the right choice.
Devil: Well, if helping the aliens wipe out the planet was the goal, then you did well.
Me: Yea, but did you see how I handled those guards? (*I tried to say it with obvious light humor and sarcasm*)
Devil: Haha. Yeah, you really handled them.

Me: So what is your suggestion?

Devil: Well, you did handle the guards better by taking my advice, which was—

Me: Keep it minimal and simple.

Devil: Did having a nuclear bomb go off in New York City seem simple or minimal? I would say very much the opposite.

Me: So what should I have done?

Devil: You still don't get it yet! I can't tell you how to handle these situations. Advice and general guidance is it. You need to be the idea man. It needs to come from your thoughts and your creativity. Otherwise I would just do this myself.

Very frustrated at this point, I folded my arms and just stared straight ahead.

Devil: Now you're going to pout?

Me: You got to admit, I don't seem to be doing very well at this.

Devil: It's only your second try. I'm not worried. You need to remember what I tell you and teach you. Keep it simple and keep it small. Think that each time before you go to the ring.

Me: So just have the ship beamed to another galaxy and tell the ring to put the moon back together?

Devil: Does that seem small or simple? Beaming, as you put it, a city-sized ship to another galaxy, does that seem small or even simple to you?

Me: No.

Devil: Does putting the moon and all its pieces back together just by willing the ring to do so?

I interrupted him out of major frustration.

Me: Once again, no!
Devil: You want the ship to leave and be destroyed. If you were on top of this situation, the moon would not have been damaged because you would have been able to do something to stop that event before it happened.
Me: How about I just turn into a superhero and do all the things that way?
Devil: You may have certain scenarios where that kind of thinking may be necessary. But that is not simple or small either. A good portion of the reason you were picked was your ability to think in the abstract and your massive creativity. Almost every situation there will be a solution just by willing the ring to do minor tasks that will create giant solutions.
Me: Luke, be honest. Are you disappointed in me? Are you having doubts? Remember, I can tell.
Devil: Then I don't need to answer.

He was right—as usual. I could feel his answer and how he thought of me and the confidence in his choice of choosing me. It was not 100 percent, but it was in the high 90s.

Devil: Well?
Me: Yeah, you have faith in me. I just wish I did. When this all happens for real, I can't make the same mistakes I am doing in the simulations. Every living thing on this planet is counting on me. You are counting on me.

With that I broke down again without knowing I had grabbed his foot and was squeezing it. They were so smooth and flawless, like those of someone who had been in suspended animation for twenty years, no wear and tear. I noticed that rubbing his feet had a relaxing effect on him, which, because of our connection, had the same effect on me. It was very therapeutic to both of us. But even with the calming effect it had on me, I could not hold back a single tear that went down my face.

> Devil: I have an idea. You need a break from all this, and we don't have much time before you will be waking up. Let's do something you will enjoy.

I could not help but to have an "adult" thought or two. I mean, he was created out of the combination of the best-looking people I had ever seen throughout my life. So he was perfect in every way to me.

> Devil: Not that, Thomas!
> Me: Thought you could not read me anymore?
> Devil: No, I still can a little bit, but I did not need to for that. I have known human nature since you guys were walking on all fours and even before that. I was thinking of something that would give you a break from the worry of all this, something you would enjoy. But if that's what you want, I suppose I could comply.

As tempting as that offer was, I can never go down that path. My gut instinct combined with raw logic made me know nothing good could come from that. I was human, and I love human contact, especially with someone who was created to be my perfect looking human.

Somehow I just knew if I did that, it would be a mistake that I could not take back and would forever distort my judgment.

> Devil: Let's put that thought on the back burner for now. Now when it comes to making decisions about using the power and stopping the Pelusoians, I cannot give you ideas, but as long as it's not to do with that, I can call all the shots. So with that in mind, do you trust

me to do something that will loosen you up and give you a break from the stress of all this?

Me: Yes, I trust you. With all due respect, can we do this on the next meeting?

Devil: You trust me, but you don't want to go. I promise this is something stress-free, and you will enjoy.

Me: Once again, I trust you, but when I wake up from these meetings, it does not feel like I have even slept. My body feels rested, but my mind feels like Jell-O.

Devil: I understand, and you are right, your mind is not getting sufficient rest. I wish we could take a night off, and if this problem gets any worse, we may have to. The thing is we need these meetings. It's important that you are ready and without criticism of the last two simulations. You need more practice.

Me: Next time we will do whatever it is you planned for me. In fact, I will look forward to it.

Devil: We still have some time. Want to try to go back to New York and start from when you and Jason get back to his apartment? Or are you too tired?

Me: I am tired, but I want to go back knowing I did something right. I still don't know how I am going to handle the situation, but I would like to have a better conclusion than that I blew up NYC and possibly the world.

Devil: Very good. I like your determination. Let's do it. But I want to add one aspect to your ring. Since you are having a hard time, I want it to give you a little bit more help.

Me: It will give me suggestions?

Devil: You know that can't happen? The ideas have to be yours. But let's give it a way to let you know if what you did was successful. When you use the ring and you have completed a task and it has been successful at more than 85 percent, it will glow green for a couple seconds. This will help you to know what you did was right, and that way you can move on. Also, you can ask it yes-and-no questions. It will flash green once for yes and two for no. These are very minor additions, I realize, but it doesn't break any rules and I think will help you. Good luck.

With that he snapped his fingers, and there I was, standing on the balcony, and Jason coming up behind me with the drinks. How do I handle this? I must stop the ship. I must get it out of here so it cannot damage anything else. But I can't just teleport it away. Keep it simple and keep it small.

The ship once again filled the sky and was preparing to destroy the remains of the moon. Keep it simple. I got it.

I looked at my ring.

Me: I want to remotely take over the ship's guidance system. I command the ship to put in coordinates to head seven hundred miles up into Earth's orbit. Then I command the guidance of the ship to plot a course directly into the sun at the ship's top speed. Engage.

This time the ring lit up extremely bright. You could visibly see the ship's propulsion initiate and quickly lift off until it was almost out of sight. At seven hundred miles above us, you could barely make it out, but being it was the size of a city, you could still see it. Then suddenly it looked like a shooting star or comet with tail and took off.

I looked over to Jason, and he had a look of pure confusion on his face.

Jason: You are like him.
Me: What? I'm like who?

Jason: It's all good, dude. I thought as much with your little trick with the guards. So if he is the devil, then are you God?

I could not help but give a small chuckle out loud.

Me: No, Jason, I'm far from that. Get me a shot, will you?
Jason: Of what?
Me: Anything, and a chaser too.

He smiled, took a look out where the ship had been and back at me, and went inside to his bar. As he was walking away, I caught a glimpse of my ring. It was glowing green for about five seconds and then stopped. I guess I was successful. I kept it simple and did not blow up NYC or the world nor did I try to transport this huge ship elsewhere. I just made it destroy itself by taking it over remotely.

Me: Ring, did the ship fly into the sun?

It glowed once green.

Me: Was it completely destroyed?

One green blink again.

Me: Did that damage anything on the way or damage the sun?

Two green blinks, meaning no.

I had done it, and the ring confirmed it. Jason came out with a shot of light brown liquid and a glass of soda.

Jason: A shot of bourbon whiskey and a cola.
Me: Thank you, Jason.

I felt a wave of confidence. The more simplistic the idea, the better it is. The outcome is always better when it's not a complex or large undertaking. The devil is correct. Keep it simple and keep it small. As I grabbed the shot and soda from Jason, I gave him a big smile, which he returned. I took the shot and chased it with the cola. As I look at Jason, it dawned on me how handsome he was. Normally that would be more evident to me, but I was not sure why it had not dawned on me more before this. Maybe with all the things going on or maybe the devil being the culmination of everyone I ever thought was good-looking made it seem like no one else was even comparable.

Jason: I have no idea how you and your boss do these things, but I am sure as hell glad I am on your guy's side.
Me: (*I laughed*) I can agree with that.
Jason: Another shot?
Me: Sounds good to me.

Knowing that in this simulation alcohol has no effect, I decided to enjoy a couple drinks. The devil did state he wanted me to take a break from stress and get some perspective. I looked up at the sky and the moon, which was still crumbling, and walked into the apartment. As I walked through the door, it went dark and then lit back up to the dim lighting I became so familiar with. I was back in the devil's mansion. He was standing by the fireplace, looking at the fire. His silhouette from behind showed the extent of his young and toned body. I walked up to him and stood on the other side of the fireplace. He did not seem to acknowledge me. This worried me. I sensed almost a sadness in him and a little anger. I had come to realize that, when assessing his feelings, anger was a percentage every time with one or more others. But anger was always one of them; it just varied on how much.

Me: So I did not blow up NYC or the world this time.

He just kept staring at the fire like I was not there or did not even hear me.

Me: I took your advice, and it was right on the mark. Keep it simple and small. I thought about that term before I committed to my decision, and it seems to always apply.

He finally looked up at me.

Devil: Yes, you did well. No casualties, no damage, and you got rid of the threat and did it all by using the minimum magic. Just taking over the ship and plotting its course to destroy its self into the sun. Bravo.

His words seemed empty and almost rehearsed. He did not speak with the flare and confidence I was used to. Now I felt another emotion in him. With the anger and sadness was a bit of the green-eyed monster us humans know best as jealousy.

Me: Like it or not, I can sense what you feel. Want to tell me what is going on, or do I just psychoanalyze you for myself?

Devil: I need to be confident. After hundreds of thousands of years, this is the first time I am forced to have so much contact with a mortal. It is taking me longer to adjust than I thought.

Me: You're right though, you do need to be confident. I need to be confident. We are faced with getting wiped out, and I get the feeling it's not just us humans. Without us humans, you're like someone deserted on a desert island with no one to talk to. Not to mention I think it goes beyond even that.

Devil: Don't get too cocky. I may need you, but maybe I have been around long enough. Maybe I want this to all end and now a situation has occurred that allows me to be released. So before you start to get that "you need me" aspect going, better think about that.

Me: Go easy. I realize teamwork is not something you are used to, but it has its advantages. Now I know the secrets behind the curtain, and you and God are not battling enemies, that he created you so there is a balance. We would not exist if it was not for you. Therefore, you are not my enemy. You are not God's enemy. It seems the only true enemy is the Pelusoians, and they are both our enemies. We both need to be at our best to win this conflict and show we are the superior ones.

He looked at me blankly and went to that evil grin that began to give me such pleasure every time I see it.

Devil: Damn good pep talk, my little chimp. I knew I picked you for a reason. I have never had such self-pity. I blame that on you and our interaction.

Me: I don't think I have ever had so much confidence that I can scold a being that can probably cause me torment at levels I could not even imagine.

Devil: Probably?

Me: Let's not go there. You and I are an unstoppable team. So let's think like winners.

Devil: You are going to be waking up soon. Have a seat, and let's make these last couple minutes worthy.

We both took our standard places on the couch—me in the middle and him at the end with his feet back on my lap.

Devil: I think you should cancel your appointment with Dr. Shrink. We have too much going on to even bother with that nonsense.

Once again I got that weird feeling when he talked about Dr. Olcult. It was hard to place exactly what the feeling was. All I was sure of was that it was not a positive one.

Me: I told you, I am going to this last appointment, and that will be the end. He is nothing but an annoying idiot who believes in… aliens?

As I said those words, I put one and one together for the first time. What a major coincidence that one of the first things this psychiatrist told me was about him being abducted by aliens as a child and we are being invaded by aliens.

I also noticed that when I said that out loud that the devil looked down and away. There is something going on with this. Suddenly this appointment felt like something much more than just cancelling with the Doctor.

Devil: Well, just don't let him take authority over you. Just listen to his psychobabble and try to get out of there as quickly as you can. Events are going to start to unfold, and we don't have time for unneeded distraction.

Me: You got it. As I said, this guy is not one of my favorite people. I was not even going to attend this last appointment, but he threatened to get the police involved if I did not show.

What was it with this appointment and this doctor? I made an effort to not just feel his thoughts but try to dig into them. When I tried to do that, he spoke abruptly.

Devil: All right, you need to head back. We will talk again soon. In the meantime, try and take afternoon naps. Your mind will start to turn to putty after a while with you spending all your sleep/dream time with me. Your mind

> needs rest time that it is not getting during your sleep.

And with that, for the first time, I felt like I was pushed out of his realm and woke up in a jolt. I got the distinct feeling he did not want me attempting to search his mind for why this appointment was bothering him so much.

CHAPTER 12

I awoke as if I had not even slept. Just as he said, my body felt rested, but my mind did not feel like I slept at all. I closed my eyes and almost dozed back off, but Toby reminded me he needed to go outside and do his business, and I needed to get up and get ready for the doctor's appointment.

I let him out the back door and noticed how things seemed so much quieter and back to normal. How quickly we adjust and go right back to a reset point in our lives. Sadly, the panic and stress have not passed for me. I knew that we were still in store for a ride and a half, and the Pelusoians were still on their way. I kept thinking back to the images the devil had showed me of them.

They looked so artificial. Of course, they are. How similar of an overall species were they to us before their transition to machine?

I got Toby back in and showered and was ready for this appointment. I was a little stressed with what was going to be said. This doctor literally threatened me if I missed this appointment.

That in itself would make this an awkward meeting. Now that the devil was acting so strange about it just seemed to add to the uneasiness.

The drive there was uneventful. There were still pockets of places that were under construction and areas still damaged from the initial news. Otherwise it was a pleasant early fall day in Florida.

As I parked at his office I kept trying to think ahead of how to respond to the doctor: with anger for threatening me or to just play it cool like it did not bother me at all. Either way, I wanted to make sure that he knows this would be our last consultation.

This may be a way to approach this: that the recent life-altering news, even if it was found out to be not true (but was), got me to reevaluate my life and has given me a new perspective on things and that this has helped me to deal with my problems better. I wanted to remember to thank him and tell him there are no hard feelings, that I just feel better now, and that's that.

As I got to the waiting room, I noticed that it was empty except for Dr. Olcult. He was sitting there as if he was a waiting patient ready for his appointment, but in fact, he was waiting for me.

Me: Hello, Doctor. I would think you would be very busy after the events of the last couple days. People all stressed and such. Instead you are out here in the waiting room and what looks to be no other patients in sight.

Olcult: Let's not waste time. Please follow me to my office.

We walked down the hallway, and he opened the door for me, and I entered. I was going to sit on the couch as I did before, but he scooted this modern-looking chair that resembled something you would see in a fancy art show over to me and had me sit there instead. That was fine for me. I did not want to get comfortable on the couch because this was not going to be a long stay.

He sat at his desk and looked at me with a very cold and unfeeling look on his face. Finally I broke the uncomfortable silence.

Me: Quite a last few days, huh? This whole probe sending back that insane message then finding out it was all just a mechanical error.

Olcult: Was it all just an error?

Me: Well, according to the news, it sure seems that way, a defect or damage caused by particles of ice in the Oort cloud. Either way, I'm glad it's over. Very stressful. Must have been for you even more so, being you were abducted by aliens when you were young.

There was a silence that was deafening. He still had no readable expression. He was blank and emotionless.

Olcult: Do you believe the news that it was all just a mechanical mistake?
Me: I do. I saw several key people from NASA and some other very well-respected and educated individuals on TV give the theory their full backing.
Olcult: Why is it I don't believe you?

He said that with such a nonchalant manner, I thought for sure I had misheard him. I sat there and looked at him with my own poker face.

Me: Excuse me?
Olcult: I think you heard me.

With that confirmation, it was time I put this doctor in his place. I was a lawyer for over a decade and have six degrees, two of which are in psychology. I decided I had played Mr. Nice Guy long enough. I stood up and looked at him with my best serious look.

Me: Okay, Doc, I gave into your request to come for this last visit, but it's time we end our association. Your level of communication—
Olcult: Please sit down now before I seat you myself.

At this point, anger and a complete stunned effect had taken me over. This guy was psychotic. I began to assess his physical abilities at this point, becoming more and more aware of his aggressive demeanor towards me. He was taller than me by a few inches, older than me by at least ten years, and did not look very muscular. My best description would be scrawny. I think if he becomes physical, I will be able to easily defend myself.

Olcult: Sit down! I will not say it again!

Me: Oh you won't need to.

At that I walked towards the door and grabbed for the knob. As I did, I heard a click. I went to turn the knob and instantly realized it had locked. It was a sturdy-looking door made of metal but did not show any locking or unlocking mechanisms on it.

I turned around quickly.

Me: Doctor, you have exceeded your boundaries as a psychiatrist and are now bordering on legal action. Is that what you wish?

He just sat there with no expression with his arms folded. I nodded my head and took out my cell phone. I went to dial 911 when I noticed it was shut off. I don't remember shutting it off, but I guess I did. So I pressed the button to turn it on, but nothing happened. I pressed again and again, each time a little harder, but no light or screen, in fact, nothing at all. I thought to myself "Great, what a perfect time for my phone to die on me."

Olcult: Your cell phone will not work in here. Now for the final time, please sit down, now!

The "now" part was literally shouted. At this point I was close to panic mode. I began to look around the room for items to use to protect myself. Just then he stood up. He made a hand gesture, and the chair I was sitting on came darting across the room and hit me behind my knees and dropped me straight down into sitting position in the chair. My butt was in the center on the seat, and my arms were on both sides of the armrests.

Olcult: It is sad you put me in this situation. I was hoping we would have more time to talk before I needed to show you my strength and control.

What the hell is going on? Locking the door is a fairly common trick, although I did not see him push any buttons or levers to make it lock. But this situation was becoming increasingly crazy. How did he get the chair to do that?

> Olcult: The cell phone was decommissioned by a localized EMP, and the office has a dampening field. The chair moving across the room is a magnetic field. You will notice that you are unable to move your arms or get up from the chair at all. It's a form of magnetism the chair creates from the iron and other metals and minerals in your body and bloodstream.

As he said that, I tried to move my arms. He was right. It was like I was tied to the chair. There was no standing or even moving my body parts. My legs were even held to the legs of the chair.

> Olcult: Now, as I was saying, this was not the way I wanted things to transpire. I wanted to ease you into this whole situation. But of course, your overexuberant behavior has put an end to that. So we will just have to jump forward a couple steps. All the better, I guess, as we both know, there is not much time before the Pelusoians arrive. If you can calm yourself and sit there and listen, we can talk, and I can answer all your questions.

My mind was flying, and I could feel my face turn red and my heart pounding in my chest. But it quickly came to me the devil's warning and how he did not want me to meet with this guy. I also know that, as impressive as his tricks in the room were, my ring could put him to sleep or allow me to take over the situation easily. With that thought in mind, I took a deep breath and started to relax, which was very difficult given the situation. Normally these circumstances would be beyond belief just a few days ago.

The fact that the more time I spent with the devil, his anger was rubbing off on me was not helping to keep me calm either.

Since I knew I could get out of this with my own tricks, I figured I would not play my hand immediately. Let's get as much information as I can from him before I make my own move.

Me: All right, Doctor, you seem to have my undivided attention at this point. You want to talk to me. I'm all ears.

Olcult: You are a special one, aren't you?

Me: I'm not the one moving objects or disabling cell phones.

Olcult: Neither am I, it's all just some very advanced technology.

Me: Let me guess, more advanced than, well, us earthlings.

Olcult: I am an earthling. I just have some very high-level toys I have been trained to build and use since I was a child. See, I was not lying to you. I was abducted when I was young. They have been in communication with me since I could read. They had no idea where I was, of course, but they could reach out to me and connect with my mind all the way from a different galaxy. They only recently learned about where I, or should I say, we are. When the *Voyager* probe entered the Oort cloud, they learned Earth's exact coordinates. What I don't understand is how the Oort cloud hid this solar system. Our human technology is nowhere near that advanced. The theory is that it's just some kind of natural occurrence the Oort cloud has. But the fact that your body temperature just went up 2.73 degrees and heart rate increased from 85 beats per second to 92, I would guess that there is another explanation, and you know what it is.

Me: Now how would you know what my vitals are?

Olcult: I have contact lenses that allow me to see many things. It also allows me to use certain eye movements to remotely control things. That's how I locked the door. This room has incredible abilities built into it. It took me years to make all these gadgets. The Pelusoians are a very advanced race and have helped me to create some fantastic stuff. Of course, there are limits because all I have to work with are the materials from here on Earth.

Me: So what does this all have to do with me?

Olcult: Good question. That's exactly what I plan to find out.

Me: Why do you think I have anything to do with this?

Olcult: The Pelusoians have been preparing me all my life for your eventual appearance. All my schooling combined with their training has had me on alert for someone who has answers to questions no one till now could ever answer.

Me: You think I am some superbeing, huh?

Olcult: My scan is showing your brain has the cellular status and activity level of a teenager. You are in your late forties. Care to answer why that is?

Me: I'm gifted. Ten years of college must have kept my brain young.

Olcult: A weak response, but not impossible. But why are there parts of your brain active that no one else on earth has? Got a good one for that?

Me: Once again, gifted, I guess.

At this point I see why the devil was so adamant about me skipping this appointment. Mental note—take Luke's advice with more weight.

Me: So just to be clear, you are human?

Olcult: Completely.

Me: And you're going to allow these aliens to eat and/or destroy you and all life on Earth?

Olcult: Not at all. I will be given my own planet to rule, a planet of clones consisting of any humans I want that will be completely under my control.

Me: Don't you care about your parents or any other humans on this world?

Olcult: No. My father used to beat me before the Pelusoians made contact with me. My Mother left when I was born. This planet is overdue for a cleansing. When it does, I will have my own paradise to live on.

Me: So what is it you want from me again?

Olcult: Playing stupid does not help or quicken this situation. My scans have showed you have been altered. Your brain was revitalized as well as upgraded. There is no compatible procedure or earthling technology that can do this, so you are in contact with outside forces. I know it's not the Pelusoians, so the question is, who are you aligned with? If they are advanced enough to do these things, they are threats to the invasion, thus you are a threat.

Me: So because I am smart and my brain is still in good shape, I am this person you have been warned about?

Olcult: On your first visit, when you were having an episode in the waiting room, I heard you say some strange things. Were you in communication with another alien race, or is it something else altogether?

Me: You're the doctor, you tell me.

Olcult: You are very calm and cocky for someone who just saw what I can do in this office. Also quite calm about finding out the aliens are still on the way, but what bothers me most

> is, when I mentioned their names, your pupil response and heart rate indicate you were not surprised. Most troubling is that you know the Pelusoians are coming to eat all the organic life on this planet. I never mentioned that. So I can only assume you know as much as I, and since your source is not the Pelusoians, well, it brings me to several conclusions. None of which you are going to like.

I did not like that statement or the tone of it, and I really did not like where this conversation was heading. My first thought was to get as much information as possible before playing my own cards, but I better not push my luck too far. It was time for action. But I must do it right. This was not a simulation this time, and I need to do this in a well-thought-out way. Keep it small. Keep it simple. I guess I will just put him to sleep and get myself released from the chair and get out of here as quickly as possible.

I looked down at my ring and thought, "Put the doctor to sleep." My ring did not light up, and in fact, it went dark. I looked up at the doctor, who had a puzzled look. Why did it not work? What if his tech is more advanced than the devil's powers? Now I started to panic!

I looked at the ring again and repeated my request. Nothing. No glow from the ring and no results. It just stayed dark. I need to stay calm. Think this through. His advantage seems to be technology. How can I use that to my advantage?

> Olcult: Well, I doubt you are going to answer my questions.
>
> Me: You said they were preparing you for me. If that's the case, you should know all about me.
>
> Olcult: No, they are very advanced, but they cannot accurately tell the future. The future has many possibilities. Their super computer, which is leagues ahead of anything we have, showed there was a 91 percent possibility that someone would rise to try and stop them.

> This person will likely be associated with the creators of humans and this planet. They have scanned and analyzed many other beings in our own galaxy and a multitude of others, but they could not find the civilization which seeded us. Of course, many in our society believe in a religious explanation of origin. But as advanced scientific beings who have charted over half of the known universe, they don't believe in such hogwash. Our culture only created religion, God, and the devil to explain the unexplainable. So the only logical possibility is you are being helped by creatures that inhabit the part of the universe they have not yet explored or analyzed.

I almost laughed to myself. Just a week ago I was the one who completely wrote off God and the devil. Apparently, as advanced as the Pelusoians are, they, like I was, don't leave room for the religious equation. Their tech is far beyond us and me. But my abilities don't rely on tech. So if I disconnect this advanced room, that may be the key.

I looked down at the ring. "Make all mechanical equipment stop functioning in this building, whether Earth based or other." This time the ring lit up. It was not just a mild glow either. It glowed bright.

As it did, there was a loud click sound. Then the lights, his computer, the fish tank—everything stopped. The room was still lit from light outside through the window. I immediately felt the release the chair had on me.

The doctor stood up and looked around. Although bright enough to see, the room was substantially darker without the lights in the room on. This made my glowing ring become obvious. The doctor glared directly at it. I looked at him and stood up.

> Me: Well, Doc, like to say it's been fun, but it wasn't. As we discussed before, this will be my last visit.

Olcult: Extraordinary ring you have there. The gem in it is made of a material unknown to my database. I may want to take a look at that. Although you may have disabled my electronic room, you also have disarmed the lock mechanism for the door as well. So I would not be so quick to be ready to leave.

I had not thought that far ahead yet. I was not sure the ring was going to be able to override his electronics. But I did not want to wait around for any of his other tricks.

I looked down at the ring, which had stopped glowing, and thought to myself, "Super strength." But I thought back to the simulation with the blood and brains of the security guard all over the wall. I thought again, "Ring, unlock the door." The ring glowed very little, nothing like the glow to shut the building down. Then I heard the lock mechanism disengage. The doctor was taking in all these actions, the ring glowing again and the door unlocking, but just stood there.

I walked over to the door and turned back and was going to say a very sarcastic final farewell, but he was gone. No trace of him at all. This put a chill down my spine, and I now decided that any further conversation or delay may be a big mistake. I turned the knob on the door and quickly exited. I walked very fast down the hallway. The corridors were creepy with an eerie darkness from having no hall lights on. I kept expecting something else to happen. I totally underestimated this guy and was ready for anything. I walked to the elevator and realized they were not working and went to the stairs. As I got to the bottom floor, I noticed that there were no other people around. I got to the exit door and opened it, and I was outside. Standing there was the doctor with his arms folded.

Olcult: Thank you for reassuring us that you are the threat I was warned of. Also, thank you for using your gizmo ring. It will take some time to analyze how it works and what its origin of power is, but since you used it directly in front of me, my friends, the Pelusoians, saw what I saw and are already figuring that out.

Me: Well, good luck with that. Good-bye, Doctor.

Olcult: Oh it's far from good-bye, Thomas. In fact, I can guarantee we will be seeing much more of each other from this point on. That is till my friends arrive. Then we will see if your little ring can do more than barely get you out of a locked room.

I was tempted to say something sharp or smart-ass back but just held my tongue and walked calmly to my car. As I sat in my car and started it up, I looked over to where he was standing, and he was gone. I started up the car and drove home. This was not the experience I had thought it would be. I needed to go home and run through all these events again. Things just got a lot more complicated.

CHAPTER 13

I got home, and my Toby greeted me as always. Even though he could no longer see, he always could find me at the door and know it was me. His eyes were so white and glazed over with the cataracts. But nevertheless, his tail was wagging, and he would bark and spin around as if he was still a puppy.

I sat on the couch, and Toby jumped up on me and, after a minute or so, began to lick my face. I was shaking and a nervous wreck.

Toby always could sense when I was like that and would do his best to comfort me.

I tried to review the events of this doctor's appointment. I wanted to talk with the devil but knew that was not going to happen until I slept that night. So I best review all that happened and what I wanted to ask. The big thing is who is this guy? But biggest of all, why did the ring not work when I tried to put him to sleep? It made me begin to contemplate if the devil's powers were far from limitless. It seemed it was two different forms of power. The devil had his powers from God. His powers were based on real magic and miracle where the Pelusoians' abilities were based on advanced technology and science.

I had a hard time with that concept. To me there was no magic. Magic was just technology we had not yet figured out. But maybe there is a difference. These were things that definitely needed to be discussed.

My assessment of how I handled the doctor was pretty good. I kept it simple and kept it small. But I still felt I was unprepared. I decided to lie down in my bedroom. Maybe a nap would get a brief visit. I was very impatient and wanted answers. But as I lay there, my mind was speeding through everything. No hope of getting myself to calm down and sleep. I even considered taking a couple sleeping pills but did not want to go down that path again.

Then I had a thought. Maybe I can get some answers before I confer with the devil. I had remembered the new ability he gave the ring to answer yes-and-no questions. Maybe I can get some things answered. Being limited to yes and no would keep it general but better than nothing. What to ask? Let's start simple.

> Me: Is the doctor really human?

The ring blinked once.

> Me: Has he really been in communication with the Pelusoians since he was kid?

The ring blinked once.

> Me: Why could I not put the doctor to sleep?

Nothing.

I knew it was not a yes-or-no question but thought it was worth a try. It was difficult to try and get what I wanted by only asking yes or no.

> Me: Does the doctor have powers like me?

Ring blinked twice.

> Me: But he does have powers?

Ring blinked twice.

> Me: I know he has powers. He moved objects. But maybe it's not him, it's just advanced technology.

I really was just thinking out loud and was not really asking, but the ring blinked once. He is just a human, a human with scientific gadgets way beyond anything we have here on Earth.

As I lay there, I found it harder to think of yes-and-no questions. My brain was exhausted with a combination of the semisleep I get at night and the events of the day. Maybe I should just take a break, think of something else for a little while. With that I turned on the TV. The news was still on a loop about the probe and the alleged false information it had sent back. There were still some riots, and insurance companies were taking a pounding after the stealing and robbery that went on.

Then the TV picture froze. It was not that uncommon with satellite in Florida. Any storm or heavy clouds and this was the result. The screen was stuck on a picture of a store with the shelves empty.

Then the sound made a scrambling noise. The picture got bright and then dimmed to show Dr. Olcult sitting in a chair. It looked like he was back in his office. This gave me a jolt as I was not prepared to see him or his office, at least not that same day or on my TV.

> Olcult: Hello, Thomas. How are you doing? Not sure how, but you seemed to seize up every system in my building quite effectively. It took a full restart to get everything going again. I'm not sure exactly how you were able to do that or what technology that nice little class ring of yours uses, but be assured we are working on that puzzle and will know soon enough.

As I stared at the screen, I used my remote to change the channels. The channels did change, but the picture remained the same.

> Olcult: If you think that was the end of our chats or you have permanently escaped us, you would be wrong, as you will soon find out.

This guy was clinically insane from the way he talked to what he said. His confidence was abundant as well. I shook my head at this new nerve-racking event and talked out loud to myself.

Me: I am so sorry I went to see this nutcase.

Olcult: You have not yet begun to be sorry, and there is no reason for name-calling. Yes, I can hear you as well as you can me. I am a wiz with electronics. I am contacting you to see if we can come to some kind of civil agreement. Let's meet and see if we can talk this out. Maybe we can come up with a way I don't have to come to your house and slaughter your nephew and dog.

That statement hit hard. After losing Shawn, death and threats were not something I was good at tolerating. Combined with my time with the devil, which made my anger level increase, that caused me to get very upset very quickly.

Me: Is that a threat, Olcult? If you are going to make statements like that or threats about my loved ones, then maybe I will have to put an end to you.

Olcult: See, just as I said. We need to meet and work through our obvious problems.

Me: No, I see no reason to meet with you. Remember, we had a deal. That was our last appointment. If I were you, I would just stay as far away from me and my house as you can. Otherwise I may give you a taste of what I am really capable of.

Olcult: But see, Thomas, I want that. We want to see just how far these abilities go and who is behind enhancing your brain and what that ring can do so we can analyze its origin.

Me: So you had to reboot everything to get your advanced mechanical building working again, you say?

Olcult: That is correct. It was very surprising to us that we could not locate the origin of how you got it all to completely stop working but…

As he was rambling, I looked down at the ring and said to myself, "Shut down his building again and burn out some key electronic materials so it will take more than a reboot." The ring glowed dim for a couple seconds and then bright for just a quick flash. Then the TV went to a crashing static and gradually faded back to the regular news program I was watching.

I lay there looking at the ring. Olcult had drawn a line in the sand and had threatened me and the ones I loved. The devil is right that I need to start to thicken my skin and be ready. Olcult is just one human. Granted, he obviously has some powerful and advanced toys, but I have a whole invasion of advanced cybernetic beings on their way to put an end to mankind, so I better be able to deal with this guy. I also need to think in terms of having some of my own abilities ready to use. I may not always have time to access the ring's power and request a solution.

The first thing is I need to keep my house safe. How do I do that without drawing attention? When making spells (we will call them that) with the ring, you have to word things very precisely. The slightest little misinterpretation could create a disaster. I know one thing: I don't want Olcult here with his gizmos. I looked down at the ring.

> Me: May there be an invisible barrier that will keep Olcult and anyone working with Olcult as well as any of his advanced devices off the premises of this house and property.

I was pretty happy with the way I worded that. After I said it, the ring glowed and stopped. No worry of him sneaking in and doing harm to me or anyone else in my house.

Now, as far as instant help, abilities that I don't need to access—that was one to think about. Have powers of a superhero? As cool as that would seem, I can see danger in that. I also think the devil warned me about the superhero thing as only a last resort. As much as I tried, I could not think of anything. I decided to leave that as something to ask the devil and get his opinion on.

Just then I got a knock on my door. It had a very authoritarian sound to it. As I went to the door and opened it, I could see two police officers standing there.

Police: Hello, we are looking for Mr. Williams.
Me: I am him. How can I help you?

There stood two officers who both seemed very similar looking. They had the same height, weight, size, and even looked alike. The only difference was one was a blond, and the other had black hair. The black-haired policeman seemed to be the ranking officer, as it was he that did all the talking.

Police: We need to talk to you about charges of assault being pressed against you.
Me: Assault? Are you kidding? Who did I allegedly assault?
Police: One Dr. Olcult. I believe he is your psychiatrist.
Me: Ex-psychiatrist due to his unorthodox behavior and forms of treatment.
Police: Well, you may not agree with his treatment methods, Mr. Williams, but that is no reason to physically injure him or anyone.
Me: Dr. Olcult, and I use the term *doctor* very loosely, is making this whole thing up, I'm afraid. He is upset because I terminated my sessions with him after he tried to hold me in his office against my will. In fact, he locked me in his office. If you go see him, you will find he has no injuries and is just making this up out of spite.
Police: We have seen Dr. Olcult. In fact, he is in our police car. Would you like to see him for yourself?
Me: I certainly would.

The police stood there as one waved his hand for me to follow him to the car while the other stayed behind me—Some kind of backup police training, no doubt.

As we walked to their car, which was parked on the curb in front of my house, I could see that there was someone in the backseat. As we approached, the back door opened, and Dr. Olcult came out.

His face was bruised, and both eyes were blackened.

Olcult: Oh, Mr. Williams, I am so sorry it has come down to this, but you would not allow me to talk to you and rudely cut me off. I was going to let my injuries slide if we could just have talked civilly, but you would not have that. So now we are down to this.

Me: Pretty impressive marks, Doctor. But you know, self-mutilation is a very serious mental disorder.

Police: Okay, Mr. Williams, you are obviously not sorry for doing this, and we are going to need to bring you in for questioning.

Me: Officers, I did not do this. This is all a big mistake. With all the looting and dismay after the misinformation of an alien invasion, you tell me this is a priority?

As I said that out loud, it dawned on me that I was exactly right. Police and civil defense are still trying to recover from a couple days ago. These officers are either fully taken in by his story or not officers of the law at all. I did not have time for this and needed to take immediate action. As I looked at Dr. Olcult, I gave my best imitation of the devil's grin.

Me: Nice chess move, Doc, but I will not allow you to do this. I must once again override your plans and—

As I was saying that, I looked down at my ring and was ready to overtake the situation when I heard Olcult say he was going for a weapon. Then I felt a shocking pain in my side, which made me unable to move, and a second sharp pain in my neck, and I recall everything going dark.

I woke up in front of my nice warm fireplace with a big fire roaring. I was back in the devil's mansion, except this time I was lying down on the couch. That was unusual since normally I appear sitting on the couch. I turned my head and looked at the devil sitting in his chair with a drink in his hand. I sat up and felt a little dizzy. That too was new and unusual.

Devil: Just had to go meet with Dr. Jackass.

Me: Hey, if you would have told me he was more than just an annoying human shrink, I would not have gone to the appointment.

Devil: And I have told you that I cannot dictate what you do. I can suggest and push you in the right direction, but ultimately, it is your choices and decisions that are final. I believe I have said that to you already. It's a pity if I have to repeat myself. I guess rejuvenating your brain did not have the results I'd had hoped for.

Me: Come on! Okay, you're right, and I will take your advice with more importance from now on. Do you think this is really the time to argue?

Devil: On that you are correct. We don't have the usual amount of time. You were Tasered and then given a shot. This was an artificial way of putting you to sleep, thus why you're feeling grogginess and disorientation.

Me: That son of a bitch of a doctor. I am going to deal with him properly when I wake up.

Devil: Let me catch you up to speed, my simpleton hairless chimp. They have brought you to the police station and put you in a cell. They are about to wake you with smelling salts, so you are about to be pulled back there any minute. You let Olcult see you use the ring. He has had them remove it from your finger.

Me: Holy shit, with that ring he can do almost anything, and he can almost do that now with Pelusoian advanced tech.

Devil: No, idiot stick, only you can use the ring, but the question is, how are you going to get out of the cell now?

Me: I guess you are going to have to help.

Devil: Once again, do you recall any of our conversations? I am very limited on what I can do in the real world. By letting you into my realm, helping you, and giving you enchanted items, I won't be able to get you out. Well, you are about to wake up. I cannot help you. Get out of that cell, or Olcult will kill you the first chance he gets to be alone with you.

Me: How am I supposed to do that without the ring?

Devil: Good question, but mine, yours, and the entire human race is riding on this. Better put that rejuvenated brain to work. Remember you still…

In the middle of the devil talking to me, I awoke. My head was swimming, and there was a foul smell. Above me was an officer waving something that looked like chalk back and forth in front of my nose. I jumped up from a lying position, which they had me in, on a cot in a jail cell.

I was immediately grabbed by two sets of arms that belonged to the two officers in the cell with me with Olcult standing in the background.

Police: I would calm yourself unless you like being Tasered again.

I tried to relax and lay back down. I looked at my hand and saw the devil was right. They had taken my ring.

Police: Now if you stay calm, we will not need to put any restraints on you so you can be free to walk around the cell. But if you are ornery at all, Straitjacket City, *comprende*?

I shook my head in the affirmative. Both cops released their hands from me and backed away. I could see Olcult's face in the back, all bruised and two black eyes and an ear-to-ear smile.

They all walked out and shut the cell door behind them.

Me: Officer, where is my class ring? I have had that for over thirty years and is very valuable to me.

Police: Standard procedure is we take all jewelry while you are being held. It's safe right now.

I noticed as he said that he patted his right shirt pocket. As he did, I zoomed in with my best enhanced vision to see the outline of the ring in his breast pocket.

Me: I don't see how my ring can harm anyone. Could I please just have it back while I wait in my cell?

Police: Well, let's see, I guess we could make a special consideration for you and break our standing rules. So no, I don't think so!

At that point all three of them walked away from my cell and stood around a desk that was in sight from my cell bars. I was worried, to say it mildly. I was in trouble. The devil said Olcult would kill me. What am I going to do? First thing is not to panic. As they all stood around the desk, I closed my eyes and tried not to move and concentrated on listening. Like my eyes, my hearing was very improved, thanks to my brain overhaul. I could hear Olcult telling them how dangerous I was and that I was delusional. Then he remarked that he would like to examine the ring. The officer started out against it and was explaining that it is not proper procedure and it needs to be put in an evidence locker as it may have skin or blood on it that can prove I assaulted him.

The officer explained he needed to catalog it and that there was no way he could give it to the doctor as it was important evidence.

Olcult asked when it would be returned to me and was told not until I was released several days or weeks from now.

Olcult: But maybe I can do the forensics on it for you gents. I'm sure you are all very busy with all the commotion over the past few days.
Police: Thank you, Doctor, but we have specialists who do that for us, and being you are the victim, it would not be ethical to have you do the forensic tests.
Olcult: Yes, of course. I need to use the restroom.
Police: They are around the corner on your right.
Olcult: Maybe when I come back you will feel different about it.
Police: Ha-ha, I don't think so, Doctor, but feel free to use the men's room, and we will get the paperwork going on this case. We have a couple forms we will need you to sign.

With that he scurried down the hallway. I did not like the comment that they may change their mind. Why does he not just take the ring with all the toys he has. Then it dawned on me that he may be very limited on what he can pull off at this point with the wrench I put into his advanced building and my last ring request to shut down his stuff. Either way, I am still stuck in this cell for what they claim could be weeks, and Olcult will certainly figure out a way by then to get the ring or have me killed. As I lay there, I thought to myself, "Come on, brain, you have been revamped, turboed, and made young again. Figure out a way to get me out of this."

As I watched the two officers talk and hand paperwork back and forth to each other, my mind was racing. I blamed myself for not listening to the devil's obvious warning about this guy. He has picked me because he feels I was the right choice with the best chance of success. But my current situation had me doubting his choice and myself once again.

CHAPTER 14

One of the officers was called out of the room, and just one stayed and was diligently working on paperwork. He was mumbling and put his head up and looked at me.

Police 2: What is your date of birth?

I lay there and acted like I did not hear him.

Police 2: Hey, I am talking to you. What is your date of birth?
Me: I am not answering any questions till I get my phone call and get my lawyer here.
Police 2: Dr. Olcult says you are a lawyer, a NY one. Don't you trust your own abilities?

"My own abilities. My own abilities. My own abilities," the officer's request echoed three times like we were in a canyon. It did not seem like the officer heard it like I did because he made no bother of it. But it was not a natural thing. My first thought was I was having a reaction to being shocked by the Taser. But it was too clear and too precise. The more I thought about it, the more I began to believe it only echoed in my head. Someone was trying to give me a hint.

The police officer was still looking at me for a response. I had an idea, and it was my only hope.

Me: I'm going sue this police department so bad you will end up being overqualified for the position of greeter at Walmart. If you want my date of birth, come here and say please and kiss my ass, and maybe I will consider it.

The officer's face turned immediately red as he stood. He grabbed a clipboard and headed to my cell.

Police: I need your signature that you will not cooperate. Please do me the favor and not sign it so we can take this to the next step in your lack of cooperation.

As he approached my cell, I stood up and met him at the bars of my cell. He was scribbling some final parts of the form as he approached the bars and reached out and put the clipboard in my hands.

Me: I may need a pen to do that.

As he took a pen out of his shirt pocket, I could see in the opposite pocket on his chest was the outline of my ring. He grabbed the pen and held it out, making a point to look me right in the eye to show his authority. When he did that, I matched his glare. I remembered the events several days ago with the guy in the store and years ago with classmates in school.

Police: You trying to eyeball me, boy. 'Cause I was in the army for five years.

His voice faded off. I felt the hair on the back of my neck begin to rise. I felt the connection of our minds. It was like I was back at the store, but actually, it was much more intense. I was getting flashbacks of his army days and a bunch of images flashing quickly through my mind. I had to try and block the onslaught of his history and things he was thinking of. I said in my thoughts, "Stop and clear your mind." The images stopped, and his expression went blank.

Me: I need you to take my ring out of your pocket and hand it to me. (*I said into his mind.*)

In his mind he tried to explain why he should not, but I spoke loudly in his mind this time. "You need to give me back my ring as if it is the most important thing in the world to you." He went into his pocket and got out the ring. It was in a clear protective Baggie.

He looked at it for a brief second and then handed it to me. I took it from his trembling hand. I removed it from the Baggie and put it directly on my finger. I signed the paper and handed it back to him. Then I said in his mind, "Go back to your desk and finish this paperwork. As you sit down at your desk, proceed with doing your job and do not remember giving me back my ring as though it never happened at all."

In a blank and almost zombie-type way, he took the clipboard and returned to his desk. The moment he sat down and started writing, I released our minds' connection, and he immediately went back to his normal expression and attitude.

Police: Thank you for signing that without the need to get your lawyer in here to hold your hand.

Me: No problem, Officer. I am here to cooperate.

The officer looked at me with a frown of disbelief. I returned to the cot and sat down. My ability to control people in a limited way still works. But no time to pat myself on the back right now. Olcult was still there, and I needed to get out of this cell. I don't just want to break out though, then I am going to be fighting the cops, Olcult, and the oncoming alien invasion. Maybe I should have kept the cop under mind control, but I fear my ability to use that is very limited and is no guarantee. The ring is the key. Okay, keep it simple and keep it small.

I looked down at the ring and thought, "Completely heal Olcult's bruises to his eyes and any injuries to his face." The ring did a very quick and dim light up. I began to think that the brightness and duration of the glow seemed to directly relate to how much divine intervention is used. If so, apparently this did not take a lot.

While still sitting there, I decided to pad my help. I looked at the ring and said in my mind, "Let there be a file showing that in the past Olcult was known for false insurance claims where he would use cosmetics to make himself look more injured than he really was and create a situation where this will be discovered by the other officers right now. Make it a historical event in the computers that is completely authentic and impossible to denounce. Once again, the ring glowed a dim glow and a short blink.

I then lay down and told myself I was only going to give this plan a couple minutes to work. Then if necessary, I may have to resort to something less "small and simple" if it did not work quickly. But as I was thinking that, in came the second police officer with what looked like a printout in his hand.

Police 2: Something just came across the wire, Jim (*apparently the first officer's name*).

He handed it to the first officer. He looked at it and read it. He looked back at the second officer and then looked at me. He put his hand on the other cop's shoulder and maneuvered him so they both faced away from me and whispered to him. Normally it would not be audible to me, but my improved hearing allowed me to listen to it all loud and clear.

Officer 1: Look, this does give credibility to Mr. Williams's story about Olcult making it all up, but remember, he is a lawyer. So we were only following up on what the doctor told us. We will just hold on to this information for now and—

As he was about to finish his remark, out came Dr. Olcult from the restroom with a paper towel, drying off his hands. His once severely blackened eyes and bruised face completely healed as if it had never happened at all.

Olcult: Well, gentlemen, I am sure you will keep me informed about the charges I will need to file and whatever paperwork I will need to sign.

The two officers looked at him for a good thirty seconds without saying anything then looked at each other then looked over to me. I was standing up at this point, giving my best Academy Award expression of surprise combined with a hint of "I told you so" look.

Me: Wow, Doctor, are you related to Wolverine?
Olcult: I would suggest you keep your mouth shut. You are the one in the cell.

He apparently did not know yet that his face had been completely healed, and he was still walking and talking with his full level of confidence that he had me right where he wanted me.

Me: Officers, I think it's time for my phone call. I think my lawyers are going to want to come down and get this taken care of ASAP and maybe some local news crews as well.
Officer 1: Doctor, do you mind explaining to me why you no longer have a mark on you?
Olcult: What are you talking about? My face looks like I was hit by a train.
Officer 2: Does it?

The second officer grabbed Olcult and roughly pushed him in front of a wall mirror that was hung in the police station. Olcult's face dropped to a look of misery.

Olcult: You gave him back the ring, didn't you, you fuckin' morons. You said he was not going to get it back, and when I leave the room, you return it to him.
Police 2: What the hell does that have to do with your injuries vanishing? We also just got this report that last year you made a claim in a car crash, and it was later discovered you used

makeup to create the illusion of bruises and cuts. Then later you were found guilty of insurance fraud because of it.

Olcult: What are you talking about? Nothing like that has ever happened to me…unless…

Olcult then looked over to me and gave a look of pure hatred.

Me: Officers, I want to once again elaborate that I need to call my lawyer—unless it seems you have realized I have been telling the truth all along and the good doctor here has been playing you guys like a fiddle. If I am released from my cell and replaced with Dr. Olcult, I am sure there will be no need for further legal issues or actions. I have no anger toward you officers, at this point. You just seemed to have been conned by a con artist. I am willing to even sign your RWC-201 form that states I won't hold this department responsible for their mistake and chalk this all up to a complete misunderstanding.

Both officers were silent as they looked at each other then at me then at Olcult. At that point Olcult turned around and looked as if he was going to leave. Both officers grabbed him roughly as one took out his handcuffs and tightly put them on the doctor. They then sat him down in a chair, and one of the officers walked over to my cell and unlocked the door. I remained in the cell until the officer made a gesture for me to exit.

I walked over to their desk and stood there. I could feel Olcult's eyes glaring at me, but I did not look at him.

Officer 1: Of course, we are very sorry for this obvious mix-up. You were present and saw what we saw. We also got this report just moments ago that Olcult has tried to fool an insurance company into believing he had

> injuries that he created himself with makeup. So you can see how we only were going on what we had at the time. But now we have new evidence that seems to corroborate your story. Now you mentioned you would sign a RWC-201 release form. Is that something you would still be willing to do, sir?

Wow, from name-calling to "sir" in minutes. If this cop was not careful, he was going to strip his mental transmission. I tried to keep a straight face with a hint of aggravation as I folded my arms and looked at the officer.

> Me: Well, Jim, I think I said I would be willing to do that on two conditions. One was that I be released, and second was that Dr. Olcult takes my place in the cell.

As soon as I said that, the first officer gave a look to the second one, who immediately grabbed Olcult and got him to his feet and quickly scurried him to the same cell I was occupying just moments ago. At the door of the cell, the second officer gave Olcult a little push and then slammed the cell door shut. He then looked at me in such a way that seemed as if he was searching for my approval.

Olcult did not resist or say anything. Upon being put in the cell, he went over to the bed and sat there looking directly at me. The second officer, who seemed to really be showing signs of worry, walked over to me.

> Second Officer: I want to fully apologize for this misunderstanding, sir. We make mistakes like everyone else. Hell, we are only human.

I had to hold back from letting out a giggle. What ironic phrasing that was, I thought to myself. "Only human" with what's going on and "hell" speaks for itself. But I kept my composure.

Me: If you have that paperwork, I would be glad to sign it now and be able to return to my home.

First Officer: Of course, Mr. Williams. Let me have the secretary get that right now.

He then got on the phone and was telling someone to have all the paperwork ready and do it pronto. The second officer once again smiled at me and shook my hand.

Me: What will happen to Olcult?

Officer 2: We have several charges in mind for him, but no matter what, he will be our guest here for quite some time.

The other officer got off the phone and told his partner to go downstairs and get the paperwork from Carol. He immediately left the room to go retrieve it.

Officer 1: You would not believe the last few days we have had, Mr. Williams. All my nine years, I have never seen anything like this. I mean, how they could get something as important as an alien invasion so wrong? Even when it was discovered all to be a mistake, the aftershock of damage done has overwhelmed us here.

Me: Yes, that's why I was so surprised when you were at my door for an assault with the national guard still trying to get the general public back in order.

Officer 2: To be honest with you, Olcult has friends in pretty high-up places, and we were kind of put in a position where we had to follow through with his complaint. Obviously they did not know about his criminal background.

Me: Oh you would be surprised.

As I said that, I looked over to Olcult, who still has said nothing but just sat there staring at me. When the officer mentioned him, then he stood up.

> Olcult: You are right about that at least, Officer Jim. I do have friends in high places, and they are not going to be very happy about this, I can assure you. But all in good time.

Just then the second officer came back out of breath as if he just ran a three-mile sprint. He handed the first officer the papers and sat down to catch his breathe.

> Officer 2: Okay, Mr. Williams, since you knew this release by name, I am sure you understand it and what it means by you signing it.
> Me: Yes, I do.

The out-of-breath cop handed me a pen before I had a chance to ask for one, and I signed it in all three spots and the one spot where it needed an initial without being shown.

> Officer 2: Haha, I see you still know your law, Mr. Williams.

I then handed him the clipboard and the signed release. The second cop rose from his seat and shook my hand and reassured me again how sorry he was for this mishap. Then the first cop did the same. I went to walk out the door and realized I had no idea how I got there. I assume I was brought in the back of a cop car.

> Me: Gentlemen, how am I getting home?
> Officer 1: Oh I am sure my partner can give you a ride.
> Me: With all due respect, I would rather have a taxi. Problem is I did not bring any money with me.

Officer 1: Not a problem, sir. We will gladly pay for a taxi. He gave a hand gesture to the other cop, who got on the phone and made the call to have a cab pick me up.

Me: Thank you once again, gentlemen.

Officer 1: The taxi will not charge you, he will know it's a free fare.

I nodded my head and started walking to the door when I heard Olcult say something.

Olcult: See you soon, Thomas. You play this game pretty well, but you are playing checkers while I am playing chess. You will soon figure that out.

I turned to give one last look at Olcult when I heard the other officer jump to his feet and start to yell at Olcult about keeping his mouth shut and that he was already in enough trouble at this point.

As I walked out the door, I caught him giving me a look of pure hatred and revenge, which I returned with a smile and a look of pure joy even though deep down I knew he was far from done or that this would be the last time I would see him.

As I got to the first floor and exited the police station, there was a cab waiting for me. In no time I was back home. The taxi was of no charge, as the officers said. I walked into the door to be greeted by my Toby, as always, tail wagging and doing his little happy doggy dance. This time though I was also greeted by my nephew. Justin had a glare in his eyes that told me he was upset and he knew something.

CHAPTER 15

Justin: What happened with your psychiatrist? The police left a message on the answering machine that you beat him up!
Me: No, I did not beat him up, and yes, I have talked to the police.
Justin: The neighbor said they saw what happened out in front of the house and that they Tasered you in the front yard and took you away.
Me: All true, but it ended up all just being a misunderstanding. I was released, and they discovered my shrink is a nutcase himself and put makeup on to look as if I had beaten him up. But the cops found a file of him doing this before, arrested him, and let me go with their full apology.
Justin: Holy shit, you're kidding me!
Me: Nope, I'm not, and I have had a long day in a cell and still jittery from getting Tased. So I'm going to lie down.

At this point it was night. I had lost track of time from when I was knocked out, and the police station had limited windows, so it was hard to tell even the time of day or night. I can only imagine how long I was unconscious.

I lay down on my bed, and Toby immediately hopped up with me.

I went to turn the TV on and then stopped. I was reluctant to do it even though I knew Olcult was taken care of for a while. I did not want to chance it. I could not take too much more in one day.

I slept so much from being knocked out that I knew sleeping was going to be a problem, but I also knew there was a lot I'm sure the devil wanted to cover with me. From what I understand, he must have seen what transpired at the jail. He can observe whatever he wants but is very limited on intervening with events. That short time I talked to him when I was knocked out, he was genuinely worried. He has been around for at least thousands of years, yet through all the turmoil of the ages of man, apparently being invaded or the extinction of man has not occurred. It's such a strange concept. He has been portrayed all through time as the evil one, the one who torments us and tries to destroy us. But that is not the case. Although he is far from benevolent and I could hear and feel that in him, he is doing all he can to save us—even if it is for selfish reasons. Without us, it's just an empty galaxy for him.

If I remember my college astronomy, there are billions of stars in our galaxy, and there are billions of galaxies. So to us the Milky Way galaxy is so vast we will likely never be able to explore all of it. So if God created the whole universe, are there devils in other galaxies since our Luke only has domain in this one? Or maybe the other galaxies don't have the negative influence the devil brings to the table. Or maybe there is very limited life out there at all. Maybe we and the Pelusoians are the only ones. But according to Olcult, it sounded like they have explored half of the known universe, and they did not think any others were giving me these abilities. Meaning, it sounded like there are others.

Wow, I had to shake my head and reboot. That was getting into some deep philosophy but a question maybe I can get answered by Mr. Devil, but not right away, for sure. There are way more important things needed to be covered before I get educated in universal philosophy. I barely escaped this little situation. If it was not for my own innate ability, all could have been lost. Even though that ability does seem to be consistent in its ability to work, I don't like to rely on it. Who is to say at some point I am so nervous or injured I cannot perform that little trick? The ring is the key, and even that was easily removed from my finger and taken away from me. That cannot happen again.

I must come up with a way to not let that event happen again. I also have to have "ready to use" tricks that I do not need to stop and request from the ring. I thought about just waiting to go to sleep and covering this stuff with the devil, but I realized I now had a paranoia about the ring being taken so easily. So let's deal with that one on my own before I go to sleep. I looked down at the ring and thought to myself, "Ring, let no one else, human or otherwise, be able to remove the ring from my finger. Only I can remove the ring." The ring gave a very bright glow that lasted several seconds.

As I have started to determine, the brightness and length of the glow after a demand upon the ring seems to indicate how much "magic," let's say, is needed to fulfill that request. I would think of all the ones I have made so far. That one was a very minimal, but the ring sure did not seem to think so. That seemed strange, so I decided to make a mental note about that but did not linger on it. There were a lot more pressing things developing and a lot more important aspects to consider.

As I tossed and turned and as bad as I wanted to sleep so I could get back to that realm and figure out our next moves and ask all the questions I had, I realized there just seemed no way. My adrenaline from the day's events was just too strong. I considered the sleeping pills again, but with Olcult now angrier than ever, I couldn't drug myself. I needed to attempt to sleep the natural way. So I used some meditation I remembered—peaceful thoughts and calm waters. I also worked on my breathing—slow, deep, cleansing inhales and exhales. All muscles relaxed more and more with each breath.

Wow, I thought to myself, I never really tried any of these meditation techniques. I always thought they were kind of hippie-type stuff with no real basis in logic or reality. But I could feel myself relaxing. It took at least fifteen minutes of doing this, and I felt so relaxed but still not sleepy.

I decided to open my eyes and checked the time, but when I did, I was lying on the grass in a field. The sun was shining, and I could smell all kinds of wild flowers. As I stood up, I heard a voice behind me.

"Thought that was funny back at the jail, huh?"

I knew at once who that was. As I turned to look, it was a gruesome sight.

A human-sized spiderlike insect was looking back at me.

"Like my new look?" it said to me in Olcult's voice.

> Me: Where am I?
> Olcult Bug: You are just where I want you to be—
> at my mercy.

With that he lifted one of his tentacle-like legs and swiped it at me at a speed that was barely visible. When he did this, it took my left arm completely off at the elbow. I looked down and screamed in pain. Then it swiped at me again, this time across my throat. The speed at which it could do these things was beyond anything I could do to stop or defend myself. As my hands went to hold my throat from where the slice happened, I felt weak, and suddenly the field began to spin, and I fell to the ground in a circular motion.

The right side of my face was in the dirt. I tried to look up but could not move, but what I saw made my mind go cold. I saw on the ground my headless body twitching and fingers opening and closing. He had decapitated me, and where my head used to be above my shoulders was just torrents of blood spurting out. I went to scream, and nothing came out.

The sight of my headless body was way too much for me to handle. If this was it, then I would shut my eyes and let nature take its course. But then the smell changed. No longer was it the wild flowers of the field but the smoky smell of a fireplace. Then there was a voice, not of Olcult but the one I thought I was going to be hearing from the beginning.

> Devil: Pretty scary, huh? You did not do so well in
> that scenario.

I opened my eyes and was on the couch of my well-known place.

The devil sat in his chair with a drink in his hand, as always. I was lying down on the plush couch back in the mansion. First thing I did by instinct was grab for my arm and the other parts of my body. This, of course, made the devil laugh. I sat up and tried to keep my composure and tried not to show I was unhappy about the start of this meeting but was too shook up to attempt any brave smirk or clever comment.

Me: What was that all about? Don't think I have been through enough today?

Devil: It was a wake-up call, excuse the pun. This human, Olcult, is dangerous. What I just let you experience could very easily happen in real life. Although human, he has been trained and taught with Pelusoian intellect and knowledge. He is very dangerous. You have not even seen his whole bag of tricks at this point. It's not just the advanced toys either. This guy rivals my own sense of evil. He has been brought up to kill anyone who opposes him or could impede the plans for invasion.

Me: Why did you not tell me all that instead of just a warning telling me not to go to the appointment?

Devil: At some point you are going to be faced with a situation that will make today's look like a game. The simulations are fine, but you know they are only artificial events with artificial consequences.

Still shaking, I put my head in my hands. I felt defeated and over my head again. He's right that I need to be ready, but when the time comes, will I do the right thing? Will I be able to be as ruthless as Olcult?

The devil got up and sat next to me. He put his arm around my shoulder.

Devil: Look, you did really well, I mean, with no help from me or the ring, and you turned that whole situation around. You got the cops to release you and drop all charges and arrest Olcult. You did all that without making a huge scene or blowing out a wall or injuring cops, which would have created its own share of new problems. You kept it simple and small. Implanting information about Olcult being an insurance fraudster and then fixing his injuries, that was pure genius.

Me: Then why?

Devil: You've got to be ready. You have to realize how dangerous this is and that he is ruthless and won't think twice about taking you apart. Now the spell that no one can remove the ring—very good. I was hoping you would think that one through. This event was a learning lesson, and we will use it to be ready for the next bout.

I was still very shook up but did not want to show it. That was a very real simulation and very hard for me to shake. So I pulled myself together and tried to talk slowly and calmly.

Me: Okay, I got some questions.

Devil: Fire away.

Me: When I was in Olcult's office, I tried to put him to sleep with the ring, and it did not work. Why?

Devil: That's because the Pelusoians are from another galaxy. Their origins are from a place far away, and they are made of materials that don't exist here. You are not going to be able to take over their minds or put them to sleep or anything even similar to that with the ring.

Me: But Olcult is not a Pelusoian. He told me he was human.

Devil: That is true, but his DNA has been altered at birth to be similar to them. I guess this was necessary because they needed him to be able to understand and use Pelusoian technology, so although he is human, he has parts of his neural pathways that are not, thus the powers I have put into the ring will not allow you to use mind control on him or any of the Pelusoians.

Me: Why do your powers not work on them? I mean, you are the devil himself.

Devil: They are from another galaxy. This galaxy you mortals have called the Milky Way galaxy is my domain and so are all the creatures and materials in it.

Me: So another rule.

Devil: Think of it more as a law of physics than a rule.

I stood up quickly, which abruptly pushed his legs off from me. I did not mean to do it. I just needed to stand up. The devil gave me a glare that once again put a chill down my spine.

Me: Sorry, I did not do that on purpose. My mind is overwhelmed. I think you know that.

His expression went from surprised anger to what I can only describe as understanding.

Devil: It's all good, Thomas. I know you would not harm me even in the smallest way. But I am concerned. I have been around for eons, and I am a bit, let's say, edgy. This is a lot for a human to bear, and me as well.

Me: It sure is. I thought I was going to die in that cell.

Devil: I did too. But you did fantastic. Your idea and final solution was, well, I'm not sure I would have come up with a final solution that good. But things are not going to get easier as time goes by. In fact, it will be just the opposite. My advice to keep it simple and small may have to be thrown to the side when the actual Pelusoian ships arrive. You may need to forget small and clever ways and think big and destructive.

Me: Does Olcult have mind control?

Devil: I hate this answer, but I'm not sure. My best guess is no.

Me: I've got to ask, since you are talking "think big and destructive," why don't I just use the ring to destroy all Pelusoians before they even get here?

The devil took a big sigh and patted the couch for me to sit back down. When he did that, I could feel a couple of his emotions: frustration and what I can only describe as anger and fear. I sat back down, and he took off his sneakers and put his feet back on my lap.

Devil: I may not be able to explain all things to you, not because I don't want to but because you simply will not understand or to get you to understand would take lifetimes. I don't mean this as an insult. I picked you because you are one of the more clever humans, but even your best and brightest would have a hard time with some concepts.

Me: I get it, and no offense taken.

Devil: You cannot wave your magic ring and make all Pelusoians disappear because they are in another galaxy. Keep the concept of my, let's say, jurisdiction always in mind. But even when they do arrive in this galaxy, if we just wipe them out, they will send more. If we wipe them out, then more will come. These beings have expanded to such a degree that they don't just inhabit one planet, instead they occupy entire systems of planets. These beings have infested a multitude of systems and have almost filled their own galaxy. This is why they are starving for resources.

Me: Now wait, what is the end plan then? If there are that many and to just keep destroying them will not work—

Devil: Exactly why this little probe leaving the protection of the Oort cloud has created a chain of events that will be hard to stop. Your little brains have evolved you into exploring space. Instead of being safe in this solar system, cloaked and protected, you have opened yourselves up to this.

As he was saying this, his voice became loud, and I could sense an anger building. To feel his anger was frightening. It was so dark and so explosive.

Me: Hey, I'm on your side, remember? To question and explore is in our nature. We need to know, even if it puts us at risk.

Devil: Well, you did, and it has.

Me: Anyway, if destruction is not going to work, what exactly am I supposed to do?

Devil: I'm not saying destruction won't work. Enough of them are eliminated and they may eventually stop. But there are so many of them it would take a lot of killing. I was hoping for you to come up with something clever that will deter them from this, seek another galaxy to rampage. Normally just wiping their minds and memories of Earth would be enough, but that won't work on these creatures. I don't even have an idea to try and hint to you.

Me: So normal combat is out.

Devil: No, not at all. At first that's all we can do to keep them from getting to Earth is to give them a bloody nose, but in the long run, you need to come up with something that will make them give up on Earth and not come back.

Me: Oh that's all. That should not be a problem.

The devil chugged the remainder of his drink and stood up and went to the bar and made another one. As he walked to the bar, I could swear he was unbalanced and walking funny, almost as if he was drunk. I remember him saying I could not feel alcohol while I was here with him, but I know he does.

Devil: You know, being a smart-ass may not be a wise move for you right now.

Me: Sorry, but this is the first I have heard of this. An enemy that outnumbers us, is a hundred times more advanced, and we are limited on our ability to manipulate them—a lot more grim than was currently imagined.

Devil: Yet you have a ring that is virtually limitless with power that gets its abilities from me, and my abilities come from the creator of this entire reality. I would think we would still have the upper hand.

As he said that, he was no longer sipping mixed drinks; instead he was doing shots. When he was talking, he was slurring on a couple words. This is great. I am no rock when it comes to security or confidence. Now I got the devil drowning his worries in alcohol. What happens if he gets too drunk? I remember he stated the more I am around him, his anger and personality traits rub off on me. So it looks like the more he is in proximity to me, the more human he becomes. I could feel his sense of worry. After millennia or more of being the devil and a confident entity over us puny humans, he—for the first time—was unsure. We were faced with an enemy that he cannot fully control, that could wipe out the human race and maybe him too or leave him alone and empty in a deserted galaxy of lifeless systems.

As he did his sixth shot back-to-back, he slammed the bottle down on the bar, and it shattered. Pieces of glass went everywhere. Then he looked up at me with a nasty look.

Devil: Bet you love that you can feel my anger and doubt. I bet that makes you feel like I am the great loser the Bible portrays me as, the one destined to loose.

I kept eye contact with him but felt my stomach go in a knot. He was drunk and coming apart. I have always been proud of my education and the way I have used that to legally help people and psychologically aid others. But I was way out of my league with this. How do I counsel the devil, a being that has been around for ages. I was not sure how, but I had to attempt to talk him down from this, at least till the alcohol wears off, if and when it does on an immortal being.

My best idea was to get him talking about something other than the Pelusoians and the invasion, allow him to show and tell me about his vast knowledge and maybe, along the way, get him to relax and refocus.

Me: Why is this all up to you? If we and the universe are God's creation, why does he not help? Where is he? He must also care about us.

His glare mellowed a bit.

Devil: Good questions, but I don't fuckin' know.
Me: When did you see him last?
Devil: Before humans, when the universe was first created.
Me: What makes you so sure he won't show up?
Devil: I don't. But unlike me, he controls many galaxies and many universes and many alternate dimensions, so this little blue speck may have been forgotten about as far as I know.

When he said that, I felt his jealousy. Although he had virtually limitless powers, he was limited to just this galaxy. I say "just" this galaxy while there are billions of planets in this galaxy alone.

To us humans, the size of this galaxy is beyond what most of us can comprehend.

Me: Alternate dimensions? So how many more of me are there?
Devil: Countless. Every conceivable you exists. Every time a decision is made, a split occurs, and two possible timelines are created.
Me: So how many are there of you?

With that he stopped in the middle of his wild glares around the room and looked straight at me. He came from around the bar and sat next to me, not close like usual, but intentionally on the far side of the couch.

Devil: There is only one of me.
Me: So the other dimensions don't have a devil in them. I thought that was a necessity so there is balance.
Devil: The other ones have me too.
Me: Huh? How does that work? I mean, you're good, but that's quite a trick.

I said that with specific intentions of a compliment and to get him to explain and give a chance to show me his great knowledge. I was really just trying to get him to talk and say things that kept him explaining but in a way that was not irritating yet allowed him to give his opinion and even vent a little.

Devil: Not sure you will understand. But let's say some I have already done. Some I have yet to do. But they are all me. Unlike you, who has several versions, it's just me.
Me: So if you lose us, then you go to another one so you would not be alone.
Devil: I would not go to the next one if I fail. I will be left in this one. It's too hard to explain to a mere human. But this dimension or reality has

a special significance. That's the best explanation I can give you.

Me: That's good enough. I sort of get it, and that's plenty, Luke.

He then seemed to loosen up and calm down a little, but instead of diving back into the main topic, I figured I would keep him in this answer-question conversation. It seemed to be good for him, and I certainly had plenty of other questions.

Me: I know there are other solar systems and other galaxies, but there are several universes? Is that where the other me's exist?

Devil: No, the other "yous" are in other dimensions. They take up the same space but vibrate at a different speed. The other universes are all side by side in an infinite number called universe clusters. To which there are clusters of universe clusters. Has your mind exploded yet? Hahaha!

Me: Just about. It does not become overwhelming to you at all?

Devil: It could if I let it. But I rule over my domain. The entire Milky Way galaxy is mine.

Me: To us humans, it would take us years at light speed to get to the next star. It is almost incomprehensible to even think in terms of the far side of our galaxy, let alone to think of a multitude of galaxies. For me to think in terms of several galaxies making up the universe to now find out we are only one of many universes, and there are a bunch of "universe clusters," I mean, we are nothing in the "big picture."

Devil: Trust me, this galaxy was God's favorite. Above all of them, he gave this one all the extras and everything needed to allow you humans to advance into your own godlike state.

Me: I have to ask, you call your power Magic. Is not magic just science not yet figured out?

Devil: Yes and no.

Me: That's a good specific answer. (*I tried to say it with a lighthearted laugh of my own.*)

Devil: My power is more like magic than Olcult's scientific little tricks. The Pelusoians are advanced. They have had centuries to build up their knowledge and technology. Cavemen would think a gun or flashlight was magic when it is just technology just as modern earthlings would see a matter transporter or creating a controlled wormhole to skip through galaxies to be godlike, although you humans are getting there rapidly. But the abilities I use and summon, which your rings uses, are from the maker or creator of all you see and understand as well as what you don't. He made everything, so it's by his rules that everything works. Advanced tech uses the rules of science to do things. My power does not use the rules. Its origin is from those rules.

I did not want to say it, but that was pretty deep and was going beyond my limited ability to comprehend abstract concepts. But I certainly did not want to let on to that or show it. Even if I did not understand the how, the fact is that the what is clear. What he does is real magic, and what Olcult does, as impressive as it is, is science. That was a good concept to know.

Devil: Quite the little shrink you have turned out to be. I don't have to still be able to read your mind to know that you are talking me down from my temper.

Me: No, I was just asking.

Devil: It was a compliment! And I am not wrong, so just take it as such.

I did not want him to return to his angry, miserable, and drunk state of mind, so without hesitation, I just went to another question.

Me: Olcult is a dangerous man. He wants to kill me.

Devil: Of course he does, you're the only thing that stands in his way of having his own utopia that was promised to him. He had it rough as a kid too. Smart but twisted—the perfect mix for this assignment in my opinion.

I looked at him with that statement.

Me: Is that why I was picked too?

Devil: You're a little like that too, in a sense. But I would bet on you over him, and I guess I already have.

He definitely had lightened up. Whether he knew I was trying to do that to him or not, it worked.

Me: So I should have the upper hand? Magic, as you put it, trumps science.

Devil: Of course. I mean, you have easily put a hurting on his abilities to do things against you with his technology. You shut down his building then put an extra whammy on his other tech with just a thought and the ring. He will eventually fix what you have decommissioned, and he also has other places he keeps his advanced gadgets, but you can stop all his machinery with a thought. But that's not what worries me about Olcult. He plays dirty. He will find your weakness and use it against you. He, like you, uses psychology to his benefit.

Me: You just said magic trumps science. How can he find the weakness in something stronger?

Devil: Not talking about the powers. It's you. Your human weaknesses he will use. He just found out you are the one he has been trained to stop. Now he will research your past and find the weak links to hurt you with.

Me: Weak links. My fear of spiders? That I can't swim? I guess those are things that could be used against me.

Devil: And worse.

Me: What are you getting at? Let's not play games, I can tell there is something more specific you are talking about.

Devil: Shawn or your dog, but the spell on your house will keep Toby safe enough. But with Shawn…

Silence came across the room. That topic had been lightly treaded on, a topic that, now that I've thought about it, was my Achilles's heel.

Me: You mean like when you showed me him being incinerated at the crematorium or that he was calling for me before he died?

Just saying that out loud temporarily decreased my physical attraction toward the devil. It also made me realize we had come a long way since that day. How mean he was back then and sometimes still is, but he has changed to be more personable toward me. I would even go as far enough to say he likes me. When I was in jail, he was worried like a father or brother or maybe something more. Then again, it could just be worry because if I fail, he fails.

Devil: I just showed you an event from the past, and it hurt you more than any physical pain could create. He may take it a step further. You will need to be ready for that too.

Me: What does that mean? (*I said that in a "what now" type of way.*)

Devil: He could do more than speak of Shawn or show you past events.

Me: Shawn is dead. No new events are going to occur.

Devil: Shawn is dead, but think about what you are dealing with. He might be able to do things.

Me: Like what, bring him back to life?

Devil: Shawn is dead, but Olcult could clone him. He would be as much Shawn to you as you remember—memories, scars, and everything.

Me: That would not be good—not at all. Won't be able to…

Devil: What you have to remember is that won't be Shawn. It's a facsimile, a copy. The Shawn you knew and remember is beyond Olcult's ability to harm. You must remember that. The real Shawn is under the best protection there is—God's.

Me: So he is in heaven?

Devil: Let's not go there. He is protected by God. Am I lying to you?

He looked at me with that look as if to say, "Go ahead and check," and I did. I could not sense any deception. In fact, it was a strong feeling of truth.

Devil: You just have to remember that. No matter what Olcult does, you remember that fact and that I am telling the truth, and he loses that advantage on you.

With all the events over the last few days, I have not thought about Shawn that much until now. I say "that much" because I am always thinking about him. Commercials on TV, songs, candy bars—there are a million things that remind me of him.

Me: Maybe if Shawn was here, I could be stronger. He always did that for me—gave me strength in hard times. He would be a big help against this invasion too.

Devil: Don't go there. And what you have not found out yet is if you try to use the ring for something that is not directly related to the mission, it will not work. So don't try to bring Shawn back or return your dog's eye sight because it won't work.

Me: Naturally I risk my life and/or being physically or mentally tortured but can't do anything to benefit me.

Devil: Oh cry me a river. Think it would be better if you all end up as dinner for these alien assholes?

Me: No, no, I would not. Sorry, Luke. I'm still not sure I was the right choice for all this.

Devil: Well, I had my doubts too. You did not do well with the simulations, and your depression is an easy thing to feed off from for Olcult, but the way you handled Olcult with that jail situation made me realize you are the one without any doubt at all.

Me: Because I got this mutant-like ability to get people to do things. You don't have to butter it all up. That's probably the one and only reason I was picked.

Devil: Guess again. Your little Jedi mind trick is impressive, but I was referring to what you did after: no big explosions, no big "headline news" events that would have created more problems and curiosity for the cops and the public, a very subtle solution that worked perfect and tied up all loose ends. Maybe a reward system is in order. What would you want?

Me: You said me and Olcult are similar. Maybe I want a planet of all good-looking human beings who do whatever I want?
Devil: Sex? Really? I thought you were more than that.
Me: Well, I am human after all. Besides, I'm not talking sex—well, not completely. But I have lived my life with very little human contact. I would not mind some semilustful events.
Devil: Well, let me think on that one. The thing about that is, who would you want?
Me: Never mind, that's not what I want.

The thing that bothers me is the devil was created to look like my ideal guy, the culmination of everyone that my mind has ever found noteworthy all combined into what I see when I look at him. But I can feel in my belly and Spidey senses, to fall for or even fool around with the devil would be a bad thing that would never work out in the end.

Devil: Well, now that you have used your vast psychological ability to calm me down and sober me up a little. Maybe we should finish talking strategy before you awake.

As he said that, he kicked off his sneakers and socks and plopped his feet on my lap. Then he gave me the smile and wiggled his toes. My affection for feet was not really sexual. A little of it is, but since I was a kid, it was the admiration for feet. We put all our weight on them all day. They get us around to where we need to go, yet they are the pit of jokes because we smother them in socks and heavy footwear, and because they sweat, we label them a smelly and gross part of our anatomy. To me, they are like art. Each toe is like a little mushroom. They are often smooth, unflawed by pimples or blemishes. This was, of course, very true with the devil's feet. Just like him, they were the combination of every cute dude's foot I have ever seen. Once again, I am only human.

Devil: Go ahead. You want to massage them, and to be honest, I like it too, and of course, you know I'm telling the truth

I could tell he was.

So what the hell. It's not sex, and it's actually very innocent, so I began to massage them. I found it also therapeutic. It made me relax and concentrate in a more positive way. I deserve a little enjoyment. I have the weight of the world on me, not in a figurative way, in the real way. As I rubbed them, I could feel the devil's enjoyment of it. Since I was tuned into him, I got a super strong impression of his enjoyment towards this. When my enjoyment combined with his, it was a strong level of pleasure.

As I was doing this, I got sleepy. This was weird because it was the first time this had happened while I was in the devil's realm.

Normally I was always fully awake and alert. Besides, I was asleep. But nevertheless, the enjoyment of rubbing his feet from heel to sole back and forth was so relaxing I yawned, and my eyelids got heavy.

Devil: You have not had any real sleep in several days. Whenever you fall asleep, you end up here talking to me or doing the simulator or whatever, but your mind is getting no breaks. That's not good, and as much as I wanted to cover some more ground, if your mind turns to jelly, we both could be in trouble. So I have an idea. I will let you sleep here for just a short time. It will give your mind some down-time—I hope.

Me: I hope? What does that mean?

Devil: Not sure how this works. Some of this stuff is a first for me too. But you should get some rest for your mind.

It was hard to dispute how tired I was. The devil moved his feet to the side, and I lay down next to them. The couch was huge, so I was able to sprawl out easily. It did not take long and I was asleep in my sleep.

"Wake up, wake up, this is the most sleep you can do."

I opened my eyes, and I was still on the couch, and the devil was standing above me.

Devil: Feel better?

I did feel rested. It was just a strange sleep. It was hard to describe. But allowing my mind to shut down for who knows how long was definitely needed. I could feel how badly my mind needed some downtime until it was given it. I sat up and looked around.

Me: How long was I asleep?
Devil: That's hard to tell since technically you are still asleep. Time runs different here and in your realm, but the point is you feel better.
Me: Yeah, I do. Almost feels like I'm on speed or something. My batteries feel totally recharged.
Devil: Well, since you took your nap within a nap, we don't have much time. I wanted to tell you to come up with some kind of addition.
Me: What do you mean addition?
Devil: Something built in to you which will allow you to have some form of a weapon for protection without having to access the ring—something that you can use as offense.
Me: Like what?
Devil: You tell me, genius.

I thought for a second. Although my mind seemed recharged, I was still just waking up and not ready for this immediate task.

Me: I don't know. That Taser really messed with me. I think I still got the shakes from that. How about that, a Taser? Make the ring a Taser.

Devil: Electricity is a good idea. Can be used in small doses to knock out people or larger doses as lightning bolts to do damage in bigger situations. But not with the ring. Let's make it a built-in ability. Just like the brain tune-up, your hands will control it. No need to take the time to summon the ring's power. One finger will be a little zap to lightly deter, and each additional finger will add more. All five fingers will produce enough current to take out a building. It will work with both hands, separate or together. Excellent idea.

As I looked at him, I thought to myself how far he is stretching this "he can't come up with ideas, has to be all me" type thing. Seems like as long as I come up with any small portion of the idea, he can take it and go from there. But if it's within the rule book and helps me get out of the more sticky situations, I am not going to complain.

Me: Sounds like a good app to me.
Devil: App?
Me: Application, like a cell phone gizmo. Never mind.
Devil: Well, use this app carefully. All five fingers are going to carry quite a punch, and this is not a simulation. Also, try to keep it on the down low, drawing the least attention to yourself as possible, even though Olcult might make that impossible soon. Keep the advice of keeping it simple and small until that no longer fits the situation. When they arrive, we won't care about keeping this all secret anymore.
Me: Sounds like you know I am in for some shit until we talk again.
Devil: I told you about seeing the future. But I can see some possible scenarios that may get rugged. Besides, Olcult is already out of jail.

So be on alert for him at all times. Take him out if you want—if you can.

Me: If I can?

As I said that, the room got shaky and then dark. Next thing I knew I was back in my room, lying on my bed. I was covered in sweat. This was a first. Never had that happened. Must have something to do with my sleep within my sleep. Either way I was awake and fully charged. But as positive as I was when I woke up, I knew it would not last long. For some reason, I had a feeling it was going to be one stressful day.

CHAPTER 16

I got up and took a shower, brushed my teeth, and got dressed. Toby wanted to go out, so I brought him out the back door. It still amazed me that a dog that blind could still be so self-sufficient. It was a warm day, as they all are in Florida.

As I stood there, I remembered my new ability to defend myself. Like a kid with a new toy, I wanted to try it out. But I rationalized to myself that it was more that I should test it out so I was proficient at using it when and if the time came, not some cool new ability that I could not wait to try out.

In the backyard was a huge oak tree. I looked down at my hand and pointed one finger out and touched the tree. Nothing happened.

So I did two fingers. Nothing. Was this some mistake? Is the devil messing with me, or had Olcult found a way to override the devil's magic? So I gave it one last try and folded my thumb under and pointed all four other fingers at the tree. A very bright blue and white jagged surge of energy came out. It was thin like approximately four inches wide. The surge went into the tree, came out the other side, and down into the ground with a rather large snapping sound. When it hit the grass, it made a small explosion, like a couple of M-80 firecrackers would leave if you lit and buried them. It left a foot-and-a-half-wide hole that went down only a couple inches. The tree had a surgical small hole that went cleanly through it.

The sound, of course, frightened Toby, and he ran into the house. I was amazed at how powerful this new gift actually was. That was only four of five fingers, and it cut through an oak tree like butter.

Once again I got the feeling of being irresponsible. I should have just tried three fingers instead of just nonchalantly jumping the gun and going for much more. What would have happened if I did use all five fingers and it took the tree right out and it fell on the house or, worse, Toby? I got the overwhelming feeling of insecurity about myself and that I'm what the inhabitants of Earth have to count on as their hero.

I kicked some of the dirt back in the hole and returned into the house. I sat down in my chair and tried to regroup. I was so full of energy. That sleep within a sleep really worked. It was needed too. Several days of dreamland with the devil had been taking its toll on me more than I realized until now. Having finally had some brain-off time was needed, and it may be necessary to try and do that again, even for a short time, each visit with the devil.

I looked at the TV with questionable doubt. I was full of energy, but I also recently have had bad experiences with it. But I do need to keep apprised of current events. So I turned it on and went to the news. The news was still full of controversy over the probe.

Before all this, the conspiracy nuts were always coming up with things to broadcast, but this just lit them all up, and reporters were all over anyone who thought they had some shred of proof, information, or any connection to it at all.

This one guy (who had been on the Internet) stated there was an alien base on the moon. While being interviewed, he said these recent events showed we are being monitored from space and that it was all a government cover-up. Not as far from the truth as he thinks, I thought to myself.

My cell phone text alert went off. I took it out and checked it. The text was from an unknown user and said, "Thomas, I think we started off on the wrong foot. May I please call you so we can talk? If not, I will find other ways that we can communicate that you may not like."

As soon as I read that, my heart rate sped up considerably. This guy scared me. As the devil said, he is similar to me in many ways, and I need to never underestimate him. If I do not let him call me, he will just come up with something diabolical to get me to talk with him. I have to show that I am not fearful of him. It has to be like he is not even a concern or worry to me. So I text back, "Okay, Olcult, but I am a busy man and don't have time for your little tricks, but I will await your call."

I was happy with the way I phrased that. It was the impression I wanted him to get from me. Within a minute, the phone rang.

Olcult: Mr. Williams, how are we today?
Me: Let's cut the pleasantries and just get to it. I'm a very busy man.
Olcult: First I want to congratulate you for your cleverness at the police station. Still trying to figure out how you did that. The jail cams showed you did not have your ring, yet somehow you got the officer to hand it to you. No EMF disturbances, but somehow you got him to reach into his pocket and just give the ring back after he was clearly against it when I left the room.
Me: Well, that's me, Mr. Convincing. I guess I just have a way with people.
Olcult: Yes, not too far from the truth, I suspect. Some ability to control the human mind. According to records, even your third-grade teacher made a note saying you used to have a strange way of controlling the other kids. I guess you apparently still have it.

Although shocked he was able to get access to that information, I kept my calm and acted like that barely even registered to me.

Me: Yeah, I'm a real Mr. Wizard.
Olcult: But the ring is something altogether different. We believe its powers originate from a galaxy we just started to survey, a very advanced race that even makes claims they created us humans and the conditions which make up Earth.

This did not bother me. What was he talking about? The devil is not from a distant galaxy. He is the creation of the creator. But I did not show my concern outwardly.

Me: Wrong again, Olcult. Must be getting used to that by now. Of course, with your creditability ruined from all those insurance frauds you did, it must be hard to get anyone to believe you.

Olcult: Haha, yes, that was a slick move, but you should not try and outdo me with computers or technology. In that area, I am way beyond you. I have fixed the false data you put into the system, but don't worry, I am not going to try the police thing again. I'm sure you will just put it all back, and I would have to fix it all again, back and forth and we will get nowhere. I have much more permanent plans for you.

Me: Oh my, should I be worried?

Olcult: Most definitely. Once we find out more about these beings and the galaxy they are from, we will be able to neutralize their technology and that ring.

Me: Well, good luck with that. It's not technology, and you are never going to be able to neutralize the ring.

Olcult: Don't tell me you're that stupid. I took you for someone equal to my own intellect. What did they tell you, that they are God and are helping you from heaven? The Pelusoians have come across many beings that make that same claim. I hope you are not falling for that line. A person so well educated in areas such as psychology, law, and science knows that there is no such thing as magic or gods, just different advanced beings with other kinds of tech. Magic is just science not yet understood. I will be truly discouraged if you have fallen for that old gag.

As he talked, my mind flooded with what he was saying. What if this person I have come to believe as the devil is not who he says he is and is just from another race of control freaks with another mind-bending story, using our own human folklore against us. I can't go down that road. Olcult has been against me from the start, and the devil has been nothing but helpful toward me. He has given me powers as well. Although I will retain this information, I will not let it persuade me to go against the devil and believe this moron who has tried to kill me.

Me: I know exactly who I am and what I am doing. Who says anyone is helping me? You see, I can control the will of the human mind. Maybe I am the threat alone, Olcult, me and me alone with abilities inherent that you will never be able to understand.

Olcult: No, the ring gives off a special EMF and vibrates at a different speed than this dimension. I still believe the Pelusoians are on to something in this other galaxy. Maybe it is not in our universe at all. Maybe it's from one of the other multiverses. Either way, we will figure it out by the time they arrive, and your little human pet tricks' ability will do you no good at all. Because of all the trouble you have caused, I'm sure the Pelusoians will want to take special care of you and anyone or anything you love. Say hi to your cute little dog. What's its name? Ah yes, Toby. Say hi to him for me.

Me: Nice try to go there. Just as he said you would.

That was a slipup that I did not mean to say, but the threat on Toby took me off my game temporarily. But I kept talking without acknowledging I had made that admission.

Me: I already have erected a shield around my property which will prevent you or any of your cohorts from doing any harm to him. I will do whatever it takes. I am not someone who would backstab their own human race for the promise of a land of beautiful people to rule. You are the one being told a story, tricked to behave the way they want, but I am also not a cold-blooded killer and have an appreciation for all living things, but if you come near me, I will eliminate you, Olcult. Killing you is as easy as a thought, so keep that in mind while you make your plans to hurt me or my dog.

Olcult: Who is he, Thomas?

Me: Maybe the he is my other personality that does not have the same mild-mannered temper as I do. So you should hope I don't let him out for a walk.

Olcult: I don't think so, but it's all good. We will know all we need to know about you and your friends.

Me: How do you know you're not being played? What makes you so sure they are going to make good on their promises to you?

Olcult: Logic. Why train me as child for this to just lie about it all? They are getting almost seven billion humans and countless animals to satisfy their carnivorous needs.

Me: Why not help me, Doctor. You went through all those years of school. Remember the Hippocratic oath? You are smart, maybe the smartest human on earth. Together we can stop this. I'm sure saving the earth will have its perks too—maybe not your own world of gorgeous slaves, but a lot of very thankful people.

Olcult: People…humans…I have been abused as far back as I can remember and not just by my parents but bullies and others. I hate the human race. They destroy each other, and their hatred runs rampant. Look at WWI and WW2. Look at 9/11. This planet needs to be cleansed of the cancer best known as humans.

Me: And the innocent animals?

Olcult: We already kill them by the droves. Chickens and cows are allowed to be created just so we can slaughter them. What I am doing is the most humane thing possible as well as the only solution.

Wow, this guy has his negative points, and they are not all inaccurate. It's tough to argue the merits of the human race with someone super intelligent because we are barbaric in many of the most fundamental ways. Just a week ago, I would have agreed with some of his philosophies on this matter.

Me: Well, you might be right about some of that.

Olcult: Might be right? I am on-the-nose correct about all of it, and you find it hard to defend them.

Me: Well, let's use that brain and your advanced knowledge to make it better. Fix these problems. Change these flaws that exist in us.

Olcult: I plan to, Thomas. The Pelusoians are preparing for their voyage here, and it won't take long once they are ready. When they get here, all the issues I have mentioned will be taken care of and so will you.

Me: I see there is no talking to you about any of this. You have been programmed, just like one of your high-tech computers, and lost your way. But let's be clear. I have not even began to show you a fraction of what I can do. If you think you're going to easily take me out of this equation, you may want to think again. We may be flawed and in many ways still developing, but we are worth being given the chance to go on and become a universal powerhouse ourselves. Keep your distance from me and the ones I love.

Olcult: I don't doubt what you say at all, Thomas. In fact, I know you do wheel some pretty high-level abilities. But everyone and everything has its weakness. When I fully know and understand the origin of your powers, they will be analyzed and turned off just like a light switch. Till we meet again, Thomas.

I was going to come back with one of my own remarks, but I heard the phone disconnect. He certainly gave me a lot to think about.

The worst thorn in my side was my doubts he planted about the devil being no more than just another alien from a race of super beings with their own agenda. It will be hard to prove that either way. For now, all I can stick with is Olcult trying to kill me and wipe out all life on the planet, the devil helping me and saving the creatures of Earth. When you melt it down to that as the very basics, it seems pretty cut and dry.

But I need a plan. Just waiting for this impending invasion is not the way. Maybe the world should have been left knowing what was going to happen. They would at least be preparing our armies and military and begin to create some kind of defense. What am I saying? We are going against beings that can travel through interstellar space, not just cross galaxies but jump galaxies. Any beings with that kind of means, our defenses will be a joke to.

So back to needing a plan. I need someone to confer with here on Earth, someone like a Stephen Hawking, someone who knows physics, astronomy, genetics, and the whole deal. But who can I trust? With Olcult out there, I don't know. Should I just kill Olcult? All I have to do is look at the ring and think it and he's gone. But how would I be any different than him if I do that. I may still have to if the situation calls for it, but I am not just going to kill him in cold blood. Maybe I can still get him to change.

My mind was on overload. In all of history, there has been people put in incredible situations with many lives on the line, but I can say with all surety, no one has ever faced this before—at least not on this planet. But there are many Earths. The devil told me there is a multiverse of other realities, a place where every eventuality, every scenario has played out. So maybe that would be a good place to find the help I needed. Use the ring to drop in and talk with a genius or super genius. But who? If every possibility exists, then everyone I ever knew has a reality where they are a mastermind. So if that's the case, then I just have to figure out who I want to work with, someone I would like and feel comfortable with, someone I would know even if they lived a completely different life and turned out to be a super genius; they would still, at least in a small part, be the person I knew.

CHAPTER 17

The Shawn I knew dropped out of high school but was by no means dumb. He was a mechanic and could fix anything that had an engine. But I would visit a dimension where Shawn was the Einstein of his time. The devil warned me not to bring back Shawn and also warned me about doing things that benefited myself. It had to be only things that pertained to stopping this invasion. But this was. I need a genius, and it needs to be someone I can relate to. This does not violate the rules and will certainly benefit me with planning, strategy, and knowledge.

I'm going to do it. I had made up my mind. I went to my room and lay in my bed. While looking at the ring, I thought to myself, "I want my consciousness to go to a dimension where Shawn turned out to be one of the smartest humans alive. I want to visit Shawn on a dream plane like the devil does with me. My body will stay here, and I will go to the timeline where Shawn is a genius. I will visit and talk to him while he is asleep. Let the room be just like the mansion the devil brings me to. Let's start by bringing me to that room."

As I said that, the room transitioned around me into the exact same room I go to for my talks with the devil. I was sitting in the king's-type chair the devil always sat in.

> Me: Now bring me the Shawn I just spoke of, but he will be here as he sleeps in his world, and this will be a dream to him. But I want him to have his full mental capacity and be in every way the same as when he is awake.

With that Shawn appeared on the couch. He did not have his goatee and was dressed in a suit, which I think I only saw Shawn in once at a wedding. He also seemed to have less acne, and his hair was more blond. But in every other way it was Shawn. The sight of my best friend took the air out of my lungs. The last time I saw him I was pounding on his chest, trying to revive him. But of course, that was a different Shawn.

Me: Hello, Shawn.

He looked at me in a surprisingly calm way. He took a deep breath and looked around the room. It took all I had to hold myself together. From that dark day I found him in his room not breathing, I dreamed of a day where I could see and talk to him again. But I had to use all my self-control to play it cool. I needed to remember that this was not my Shawn. This one lived a different life in a different universe. Although in one sense it was him, in the most basic sense, it was not.

Shawn: Hello. I don't recall ever seeing this place. Dreams are usually the culmination of your memories reorganized to fit the script your subconscious has written. But I have no recollection of this place at all.

Me: That's because you have never been here before. Do you recognize me at all?

He took a few seconds to look at me.

Shawn: Sorry, I do not. Should I? I have been told I have a photographic memory. But I just do not recall you at all.

That was not surprising to me. This Shawn had lived a very different life. In his timeline we never met that night in Upstate New York while he was homeless. His path was very different from the one I knew and the Shawn I was familiar with.

Shawn: Should I?

Me: No, not necessarily. I need to explain, this is not your average dream.

Shawn: I can agree with that. Although my dreams are quite detailed and vivid, this one is exceptionally colorful and realistic—right down to the smell of the fireplace.

Me: Yeah, that was the first thing I noticed too.

Shawn: Really?

Me: It's that way because I have brought you here. You are in a dream, but one where I have created and controlled the environment. I need your help.

Shawn: Love a good adventure dream. How can I help?

Me: Shawn, there are many different realities. I am not from the one you know. In mine we were best friends.

Shawn: You talking about quantum realities and the multiverse?

Me: Yes, precisely. In my universe, we are in trouble. The earth is about to be invaded by an alien race known as the Pelusoians. They are from not just another planet but another galaxy.

Shawn: How did you bring me here?

Me: I was given powers by an angel.

I did not want to explain the devil aspect. There was already too much to explain. Plus the devil was an angel who was kicked out of heaven, at least according to the Bible. Not even too sure that's accurate. I will have make a note and ask him about the validity of that next time.

Shawn: An angel. I'm disappointed. My subconscious usually does better than that. I don't believe in God or religion.

That was not strange to me. The Shawn I knew was an atheist too. Plus most super geniuses are atheists. The level of science and education make the concept of a supreme being and the Bible seem farfetched. Just a week ago I was the same way.

> Me: I'm not going to try and talk you out of this not being just a normal dream. If that's what you want to believe, that's fine. I just need you for your super intelligence. So could you help me out?
>
> Shawn: Sure, I will go along with this. But I want my questions answered first.
>
> Me: Seems fair to me. Shoot.
>
> Shawn: You say we were friends in your timeline, past tense.
>
> Me: Yes. (*I said this slowly and with great reluctance.*)
>
> Shawn: Why past tense?
>
> Me: Because you died in my reality.
>
> Shawn: How?
>
> Me: You choked in your sleep the day after Thanksgiving. I tried to resuscitate you with CPR, but I was unsuccessful.

I was having a hard time and choked on the words as I was relaying them to him. My eyes began to water. My attempt at being strong and at holding it back were failing. Shawn could see this.

> Shawn: I can see this bothers you. Were we that close?
>
> Me: You were like a brother to me. You knew me better than I knew myself and the same in reverse.

He stood up and looked around the room. The ring did an outstanding job recreating the room the devil and I converse in. He walked over to the bar and grabbed a shot glass and poured himself a shot of rum and drank it down in a quick gulp. He looked at me and said okay.

He then walked over to a wall that had several books on it. He grabbed one and opened it. He continued to look at it as he returned to the couch and sat down.

Shawn: In dreams you are not able to read. Yet I am reading this. That shot was warm and burning all the way down. I am not totally persuaded this is not a dream, but there are some intriguing aspects that make me wonder. Not that I am convinced but I give some credence to this situation. If you say you know me better than I know myself, then you should be able to tell me who was the name of my favorite professor at college.

Me: I would not know.

Shawn: As I thought. That's where the bridge breaks down.

Me: I don't know because the Shawn I knew never went to college. He never even graduated from high school. But he was born with a bad right knee. He had it checked, and it was not an injury but a congenital problem he was born with.

Shawn immediately grabbed his knee as he looked down at it. He then raised his head slowly and looked right at me with the most serious look he could manage. If this was my Shawn, I would say I hit the bull's-eye.

Shawn: Most impressive. But if it's a dream, then my subconscious would know that too. My sense is that there is something unique about this dream. Not sure if it's an out-of-body experience with someone from another dimension or just the salmon I ate for dinner. Either way I'm going to go along with it. What is your name?

Me: Thomas. And the Shawn I knew did not like salmon. He used to say it tastes too fishy.

This got me a long quiet stare. He was blank and expressionless.

Shawn: I don't like salmon either—for the same reason. If what you say is true, you did sincerely care for me or the other me a great deal.

Me: Yes, a great deal. Your death, or his, I should say, just about ruined my life.

Shawn: I am a man of science. There is so much out there we do not understand. If what you are telling me is true, it's far from the most incredible things out there.

Me: On that we can both agree.

Shawn: Enough about me then. Tell me your situation. Have these aliens attacked?

Me: No, not yet. The probe we sent out back in the seventies, *Voyager*, finally made its way out of our solar system. As it entered the Oort cloud, it was detected by the Pelusoians. That's how they discovered us.

Shawn: Why only in the Oort cloud?

Me: The Oort cloud was apparently hiding our system from outside beings.

Shawn: Well, that's a flaw in the story. The Oort cloud is just ice garbage left over from the creation of our galaxy and, more specifically, of our solar system. There is no way that would block anything.

Me: You're right. That's the same conclusion our scientists came up with. But when *Voyager* entered the Oort cloud, we turned it around to look back at us and our planets, and they were not there. The Oort cloud is some form of cloaking field that completely blocks us from the rest of the universe.

Shawn: Outstanding. In my universe, we don't have anywhere near the technology to do that.
Me: They don't in mine either.
Shawn: So what's the explanation?
Me: I'm not sure. Maybe God did it to protect us.

Shawn laughed out loud. As different as this Shawn was, his laugh was exactly the same. Many things were similar. Many were not. Mannerisms were similar. Accent was not. My Shawn was far from dumb but was not book smart. I remember his ability to read and understand were way above average. I used to tell him on many occasions that he could easily be able to complete college.

But he always told me that he was not that type and it was not his thing. But seeing this Shawn reminded me of the path not taken. The seeds of intelligence were there; it's just this Shawn pursued them.

Shawn: Getting back to logic and science, how do you know the Pelusoians saw *Voyager* and are on their way?
Me: Somehow they took over the probe and had it send us a very ominous message back. Basically it said they were on their way and we should prepare ourselves.
Shawn: Where are these Pelusoians supposedly from?
Me: Another galaxy.
Shawn: Not even from our own Milky Way galaxy? And they were able to detect our small probe from that distance?
Me: Apparently. There's more. Even though they have never been able to locate us, they knew we existed. They have been training a human from here on Earth to pave the way for their arrival. They have been in communication with him since he was a child and have been teaching him. So in other words, he is smart

and has used earthly materials to create some very advanced machines and electronics.

Shawn: How do you know all this?

Me: Because he was my shrink. Come to find out he is way more than that, and we have been after each other ever since.

Shawn: Shrink, huh? Why were you seeking psychiatric help?

Me: Mostly 'cause a friend of mine died in my arms and messed up my psyche, causing bipolar level depression. Want to guess who that was?

Shawn: Not me. But I get what you're saying. So if he has advanced knowledge and technology, what do you have? What gave you the ability to bring me here to talk to you?

I raised my hand and pointed to my class ring. He focused on it for a few seconds.

Shawn: Beekmantown Eagles school ring. That's where my father went to school. Were you friends with my father? Or your Shawn's father, I should say?

Me: No, I met him a few times but did not really know him.

Shawn: And my mother?

Me: No, she divorced your dad and left after you were born.

Shawn: You live in a bizarre world from mine. My parents are both alive and well and have been the reason I made it through college and had so much success.

Me: Maybe my Shawn would have had that same success if he would have had the same support.

Shawn: Hard to say.

Me: Anyway (*I was trying to not let the last couple statements bother me as they did*), you seem to be familiar with the *Voyager* probe. Does that mean you also had one in your universe?

Shawn: Yes, we had two actually. One did not make it past the asteroid belt, and the other was pulled in by Jupiter's gravity and dissolved in its atmosphere.

Me: Lucky for your world.

Shawn: Possibly luck or maybe not. Maybe my world was spared.

Me: Could be.

Shawn: So back to the original point. How does that ring have such abilities?

Me: That's a long story, much of this all is. To summarize, I was chosen to try and save Earth from this invasion. A being with powers different but equal to or greater that believes in the human race and their future endowed it with—let's call it—magic. This being has put me in charge of its use and ways to help save my world.

Shawn: Are you implying that God is the one helping you and empowering the ring?

Me: No, I am not. In fact, some intel appears to show that the ones helping me are from an even more distant galaxy, possibly even the ones that seeded us on Earth.

Okay, that part I took some liberty with from what I know and moved it around. I just want to keep him from incorporating his nonreligious beliefs into this.

Shawn: How does the ring work?

Me: I told you, it's powered by advanced—

Shawn: No, I mean how do you get it to do the things you want?

Me: Oh, yes, sorry. Well, I look at it, and what I want to happen, I say in my mind. The ring glows, and it happens.

As I continued to talk, I felt my energy start to leave me. The recharge that the dream within the dream had given me was wearing off. It was all happening very suddenly. As this tiredness came upon me, I started to even feel dizzy. Something did not seem right, so I decided to end this conference for now. I had laid the groundwork and the basics. I will send him back so he remembers this (his) dream and he can mull over the situation and maybe come up with some thoughts.

Me: Well, Shawn, it takes a lot of energy to make this connection with you. Please consider all I have told you. We will talk again.

Shawn looked surprised at the abruptness of this conclusion to our talk. But as he has with everything so far, he took it in stride.

Shawn: Very well, Mr. Williams. I will try and remember all you have told me and do my best to think in terms that may help you.

Me: Thank you, Shawn. By the way, my first name is Thomas. You can call me Tom.

Shawn: Very good, Tom. Can I plan to see you every night I fall asleep?

Me: No, other things may come up, and it's also not good for you. These meetings take place while you are asleep, and therefore your mind does not get a lot of rest. But I assure you, we will talk again, and it will be soon.

As I said that, I looked down at my ring and thought, "Return us both back where we were. Let him retain all of our conversation." Shawn smiled and then just faded away. But I was still there. I went to look down at the ring to return myself, and I heard a voice from behind me.

CHAPTER 18

Devil: Have a good talk?

I turned around to see the devil at the bar making a drink, looking sharp as ever, toned and athletic in a very sharp skater-looking outfit.

Me: Drinking again, I see.

Devil: Yeah, why not? An interesting choice you have made—the intellectual super genius version of Shawn.

Me: Do you disapprove?

Devil: Yes and no.

Me: Definitive as ever.

Devil: I am in agreement that you should chose someone smart to bounce ideas off from. It's not like I can help as much as I would like with all my restrictions. But to use Shawn, not so sure about that. Don't you think that could cloud your judgment? Would it not be better to get someone impartial?

Me: I think someone who I can relate to and feel comfortable around making life and death decisions outweigh the impartial factor.

Devil: Well stated, Councilor. We don't have much time to talk.

Me: You made me tired and feel exhausted. I can sense that from you. I don't feel like that anymore. Why did you do that?

Devil: Something has happened. We needed to talk, and I did not want to barge into your conversation, especially since you went so far out of your way to not include me in the explanation.

Me: So what's the important news?

Devil: Olcult has moved up the timetable. He has let the Pelusoians know about you and the problems you have caused him. Instead of months or weeks, it now will be days before they arrive.

Me: I guess I should have just killed him.

Devil: No, that would not have helped. Losing contact with him would have created the same outcome or worse. I think he may play a bigger part in all this yet. He has a weakness we might be able to use—something from his past.

Me: So what does that mean? I am not to harm him?

Devil: Oh no, not at all. He is out to kill you. Do whatever is needed to defend yourself. If you have to take him out in a conflict, then do it. I am just saying no using the ring to just make him melt or anything.

Me: Melt, huh? Maybe I will have a drink too.

I got up and sat at the bar. The devil was behind the bar and seemed to be delighted I was going to drink with him. He grabbed a bottle of bourbon whiskey and filled a shot and then gave me a soda loaded with ice.

Me: You want me to do the mixing?

Devil: It's a shot and a chaser. Is that not how you used to drink them?

Me: I thought you could not read my mind anymore?
Devil: Always so black and white with you. I know this from your past, not reading your mind. Since you now know you can come here anytime you want, there is no need to wait for sleep.
Me: Why did you not just tell me I could? Because you can't help or give direct advice? That rule is being put to the test.
Devil: Test it all you want, just don't break it.

He seemed pretty upbeat for giving me such dire news that the Pelusoians are arriving way ahead of schedule. I took the shot and gulped it down and chased it with my root beer chaser.

Devil: I thought we would have more time for simulations and practice, but we will not. In three to five days, a wormhole will appear somewhere in our solar system. Their war ships will exit and head to Earth. They will not wish to talk to the leaders. They will not give terms for the human race to surrender. They will come and send ground forces to wipe out and package all life.
Me: No laser beam to take out the planet?
Devil: No, they want you guys for food. Seven billion meals—that's just the humans alone. Ground troops with advanced weapons to get things under control, I am guessing.
Me: And just me to stop them? Me against an entire army of advanced half-cybernetic aliens—seems pretty fair to me. I think I will have another shot.

The devil, with no anxiety in his voice or actions, smiled and filled my shot glass again.

Me: Why are you so calm? Has something changed I should know about? Because I am more than a little apprehensive about this, and you act like you're getting ready for a party.

Devil: Either you win or you don't. I hope you win. But if you don't, I will have to deal with the outcome and make the best of it. As far as your apprehension, you have all the power you need in that little ring on your finger. Unless they catch you by surprise or you fuck up, you should have the upper hand.

Me: Wow, that's quite a pep talk. Olcult said something interesting to me. He said that they have been analyzing the power of my ring when I use it, that it's similar to a race of beings in another galaxy, not ours or the Pelusoians but much farther away. He thinks you are not the devil but just another life form with advanced knowledge, that it's all part of a con.

The devil made his well-known poker face, an absolute emotionless expression.

Devil: Well, what do you think, Mr. Smart-Ass. Am I lying to you?

Me: Just wanted to get your opinion on that.

Devil: I think he is a top-level liar and manipulator, and that opinion comes from the best there is. His high-tech gadgets are quite challenging. But his greatest asset is his ability to make you doubt me, you, and the whole situation, make you wonder who is telling the truth and if you are on the right side. I am who I say I am.

He knew I would be able to tell or sense if he was lying. Although I clearly felt he was not lying, there was something in there that was not a full 100 percent rating. What he was saying was mostly and almost fully the truth, but there was something.

> Me: All right, don't get all defensive on me. I believe you. Just wanted to tell you what he said to me. I think you should be as informed about every move and conversation as I am. How else can we work together to defeat them?
>
> Devil: Very true, Counselor.

I began to notice that every time he referred to me as counselor, it was a way of sarcastically saying that I was using my communication skills to dance around topics—just as he does.

> Devil: Anything else you want to tell me?
>
> Me: No, that's about it. Olcult is a smart man, but he is self-consumed with this paradise they have promised him. Do you think they will really give him what they say?
>
> Devil: Maybe, who knows and who really cares. Not relevant. With the timetable moved up, any ideas of how you plan to handle this attack?
>
> Me: Not really. But I work best spontaneously. When the time comes, I will do whatever is necessary to stop them and defend my planet.

That was my best poker face and remark. I have no plan and have no idea how I will react when the pressure is on, but I sure was not going to let him in on that doubt. As far as I can tell, he is a neurotic mess. I need him. If giving him false confidence helps, then it helps me.

> Devil: Until the waves start to come and the one after that. We need to get them to give up on Earth altogether, forget about this planet, and never attempt to come back. The first few waves I'm sure you will do fine giving them

sufficient damage. Eventually though, a plan will be needed that does not rely on sheer force.

Me: On that I will take some advice.

Devil: You know I can't. But maybe Smart Shawn can help you come up with something.

Me: Are you being sarcastic or for real? Getting harder for me to tell.

Devil: I mean it, you want input from a genius, and you have chosen one, so use him to see if he helps.

Me: That's my plan, Luke. It's strange. In his reality, the *Voyager* probe's never left the solar system.

Devil: I'm sure many things are different. It is, after all, a different dimension and an entirely different timeline?

Me: What did you do in that timeline? You said you exist in all of them, just not at the same time. How are you in that timeline?

That deep, theoretical question and comment got me the classic evil grin.

Devil: Not how it works. Why do you waste time on things like that when you have so much on your plate? You can't figure out how to save Earth in this dimension, but you want to know how my feelings are in another?

Me: The more information I have the—

Devil: Don't use that card this time. That knowledge gives you no advantage in this situation.

At that he swung around from behind the bar and slammed himself down in his king chair in front of the fire.

As good as a performance as he could put on, I always could feel the doubt, fear, and anger in him. He was being honest about the "if it works, it works, if it don't, it don't" mentality. I guess it was his coping mechanism. Maybe his life was not on the line like us mortals, but a life without us was worse than existing in exile. His complete reason for being was about us. Even if it sometimes was about tormenting us, we were still his whole world.

I did another shot and walked over to my usual position on the couch. It felt like once again he needed to talk. As many degrees as I have, being a psychiatric counselor to the devil himself was just becoming too difficult. But what the hell, saving the human race from an alien invasion was well beyond my area of expertise too. So the game is, wing it.

Me: Look, you picked me because you thought I had the best chance for success. You have been around for ages, known every living being that has ever existed. You have experienced all scenarios. We have the power of the creator of space and time itself. Your power and knowledge of this galaxy is only matched by God himself. I'm scared too. But we are going to—not going to say *win* because it would be easy to win. We are going to put things back to where we are not on the radar of these beings or deter them so much that searching the universe for another choice will be, by pure balance of logic, a much more appealing decision.

Devil: You are good at shoveling it. I will give you that.

Me: If you could read me you would know I have doubt, of course, but what I am saying I do believe.

Devil: I think you do, Thomas. I also hope, when things get tough, you remember this confidence because you are going to need every bit of it.

Me: Do you have any idea why Olcult thinks you are one of these beings from this distant other galaxy? He even says they analyzed the ring's power when I used it and had a similar, if not the same, signature as them?

Devil: Maybe. But I think he is bullshitting you more than anything. I don't think, as advanced as they are, he has any clue. They think the aspect of religion is just a human-made belief created by early man to cope with life and death. I don't think the ring gives off any detectable scientific signature at all. As I explained, it's not science. Its powers are derived from the creator of all things.

Me: So he is using pure speculation? Feeding me information.

Devil: I would guess he's bluffing to see if he can get anything they can piece together.

Me: Since we are both on the same team working toward the same goal, it would be absurd of you to not be completely honest with me.

Devil: Yes, it would be, and since I can't lie to you, I would think it becomes obvious.

Once again, I can feel the truth with that 1 percent of something that I would not describe as a lie but something withheld. He stared at me and then at the fire.

Me: Do you think it's possible at all, that if things looked very grim, that God himself may make an appearance?

Devil: Anything is possible, but I would not hold my breath on that. He likes to create, put things in motion, and see how it all works out without him directly intervening.

Me: Sounds more like the rules of an experiment rather than the logic of a supreme being.

This got one of those roaring laughs out of him, which I took as a good sign. Someone who is letting doubt of the future and worry get the best of him can always use a good belly laugh. It tends to put things back in perspective, even if it's just for a little while.

Me: Is it breaking the rules if you let me know when they do arrive?

Devil: No, it would not. I am also willing to bet that it will be immediately observed by the masses. The wormhole they use to travel is quite large as well as bright when it opens on this side.

Me: Good, that helps.

Devil: Although the wormhole is large, they will only be able to have one ship at a time go through it. But the ships are the size of a city.

Me: So where are you while all this will be happening? In the Bible you were always messing with mankind on Earth. Will you be in the crowd, watching, or in this simulated alternate realm, watching on a big-screen HD television?

Devil: What did I say about the Bible? Do you even listen when I tell you things? Much of it was written by the best fiction writers of the time. But to answer some of your questions, I have walked among you on occasion. Not very often, but I have. When the time comes, I will be with you, not in the physical sense but in a way that's actually closer.

Me: I doubt you will be one of those they will be feasting on if it all goes bad.

Devil: No, I won't.

To that I got an overwhelming anxiety attack. Trying my best to disguise it, I put my head down in my hands and closed my eyes. The next thing I felt was the devil getting up from the chair and lying down on the couch where I was sitting. Off went what looked like $300 sneakers. And then the distinctive skater socks right after that. Then, *plop-plop*, both feet were on my lap.

Me: Does this make you feel better?

Devil: Makes us both feel better. It's your obsession with my feet.

Me: Let's get this clear. I don't have an obsession with feet. I would not even call it a fetish like many people like to label it. Some people hold hands. Some people hold much more intimate things. Feet are just feet. To me they are not smelly and ugly things, they're just feet.

Devil: Hey, I get it. It's not weird either. God likes when you humans appreciate any part of the human anatomy, feet included. He sees the whole human body as his best work of art. So you find that he did a great job on the creation of feet. I see nothing wrong with that, and God himself would see nothing wrong with that either. Lighten up.

Sometimes it is so hard to tell if he is making fun of me or making a point. Yeah, I could read his mind to a degree. Actually, it was more like reading his feelings. So when it came to him saying something like that, it was indistinguishable whether he was making a point or being a dick.

Me: Why did Shawn die?

Devil: Lack of oxygen to the brain due to shallow—

Me: No, not the forensic description. Why him? Why at only twenty-eight?

Devil: That's human free will. Events culminated creating that outcome. You know I did not do it. Ancient man used to love to blame me for every bad event. I don't intervene like that. You should know that by now.

Me: Not directly, but you do that whisper thing.

Devil: Overall, I cannot make any mortal being do anything they don't want to. The final choice is theirs and theirs alone. I realize that makes for very little help on the explanation front. It is what it is. Where did that come from?

Me: He's always with me. Seeing his alternate version has brought back a lot of memories. I know you don't bring back the dead, but if I pull this off, could we take an alternate Shawn, maybe one that is the mirror image of my Shawn, and let him exist in this timeline?

Devil: So how would you feel if, instead of dying, Shawn disappeared one day, no explanation, no idea whatever happened to him, just disappeared? How would that make you feel, never knowing if he ran away or was kidnapped and tortured, no clue at all?

Me: Obviously I would not want that. What does that have to do with my question?

Devil: Because that's what would happen to the people in the universe where we would steal him from.

There was a silence as I pondered that. It was a good point, and I really had no answer. I looked down and started to massage his foot. Not a bruise or callous—a podiatrist's dream. The devil was so attractive, and I did not have a lot of dating. Growing up gay is a nightmare for a kid. It was no different for me. I had desires. I certainly did not have the model-type dudes talking to me. It was difficult to not enjoy the contact with him. Although I could not be sure, but reading his feelings, I would guess it was a sensation he never experienced in his immortal state either.

Me: I can't do this.

Devil: You have been given the biggest responsibility of all time. I think you can give yourself some leeway.

Me: You must realize this doesn't help my situation. It only makes it more complicated. I feel you are doing this for your own enjoyment, not mine.

Devil: So what if I am. You are also enjoying it. Where's the harm?

I stood up but not before gently putting each of his feet to the side.

Devil: Getting you that wound up, huh?
Me: Look, let's not go there. Let's keep this on a professional level.
Devil: I will give you this much, you have excellent restraint. But it's up to you. Let's keep it business only.
Me: Thank you.

Suddenly he got a weird expression, one I had not seen at this point. I also immediately felt worry and caution, maybe best described as anxiety.

Me: What? What is it?
Devil: You need to head back. Something is happening at your house.
Me: My house? I put protection on my house.
Devil: And it's working, but you better go back now. Remember, you don't need to fall asleep anymore to come see me. Before you go, you can't kill Olcult—at least not yet. If they lose contact with him, they will start sending ships immediately. We need these extra few days. The ring will not let you kill him. Not every idea you have will work. I can't explain now, but if you try to use the ring and it goes black, that means it is something you should not do and will not work. That's all I can say for now. Just use the ring wisely, but for now go, now!

CHAPTER 19

The urgency in his voice was alarming. My heart rate doubled, and I could feel myself sweating. I looked down at the ring and thought, "Bring me back home." With that I was back in my bedroom. I stood up fast and yelled for Toby. But in my panic I did not see him lying right next to me until I took a deep breath and looked around. Toby, as he always could, sensed my panic and stood up. I grabbed him and kissed him on his long sheltie nose. I told him to stay and got up and left my room and shut the door.

I went room to room, but the house seemed fine and empty. Again I wondered, Is this some kind of joke the devil was playing on me? But after a second thought, I remembered how strongly he felt about there being a problem. Just then my cell phone rang. I looked down, and the caller ID showed it to be the brewery where my nephew worked. I was so conditioned to expect the worst that I answered it so quickly I almost dropped the phone. I answered it.

Me: Hello. Who is this?
Justin's Work: Are we speaking with Thomas Williams?
Me: Yes, who is this?
Justin's Work: My name is Curtis. I am the owner of the brewery your nephew Justin works at.
Me: Yes, Curtis, what can I do for you?
Curtis: I am afraid I have some bad news. Your nephew has been in an accident. One of our forklifts went haywire on us. It turned on without anyone even on it and drove across

the plant and struck your nephew. He was brought to the emergency room. I am so sorry for this. Would you like—

Me: I will head there now.

Curtis: I have not even told you where.

Me: You don't need too.

I hung up the phone. I felt a wave of nausea come over me as my stomach tightened up. I protected the house but did not even think about Justin going to work. There was no way this was a mishap, a forklift starting up and driving itself. Olcult! As I went back to my room, I grabbed my keys and looked down at Toby. He was shaking. His connection with me went beyond science or magic.

He was empathic with every feeling I have. I picked him up and hugged him. I rubbed his center forehead and told him to relax, that everything was going to be all right. Was I telling Toby or trying to convince myself? This all happened while I was massaging the devil's feet and enjoying my own warped pleasures while Justin was being targeted.

The overwhelming feeling of doubt and guilt came over me. How could I be so dumb? How could I have overlooked such an obvious problem? I can't even keep my immediate family safe, and I'm expected to save the world. I am not the right person for this. Just then my cell rang again. It was from an unknown number. My first thought was it was the hospital calling to tell me some new bit of bad news. I quickly answered it.

Olcult: Hello, Tommy Boy. Having a bad day? Not nearly as bad as your nephew's, I would be willing to bet. I actually wanted to get to your dog, but that's quite a force field you have around your house. It's like nothing we have ever seen or analyzed before, some very impressive technology, if that's even what it is.

Me: What have you done, Olcult? You have just made the biggest mistake of your life, what little you have left of it.

Olcult: Well, if you would like to discuss this in more detail, I am right outside your house.

With that I kissed Toby. I looked down at my ring and thought, "Make sure the house protection spell is working and flawless. The ring blinked positive. Make sure my automatic protection is at maximum and fully functioning on me wherever I am and on anything used against me. Once again the ring blinked in confirmation. I put Toby on my bed and kissed him on the nose again.

Me: You are safe here. Don't be afraid. I will not let anything happen to you.

With that I shut my bedroom door and walked to the window by the front of the house. There was Olcult leaning against what looked like a Porsche. I walked to the door and grabbed the doorknob. I took a big cleansing breath, put on my best confident poker face and opened the door.

Olcult saw me right away and got off the sports car and tried to take a step toward me by putting a foot on the lawn, and I could see a blue glow encompass his foot and leg and repulse him backwards a couple steps. It appears my house force field was working well.

I walked across the yard and went to the edge of the grass. I was now standing less than a couple feet from him.

Me: Can't go after me, so like a coward, you go after my family.

Olcult: There are no rules in the game of war. I warned you to stay out of this. If you had listened to me, your nephew would be fine right now.

Me: Yeah, until the Pelusoians arrive and everybody becomes a human Happy Meal.

Olcult: Haha, human Happy Meal, that's clever. Love your sense of humor. But to go see your nephew, you will need to leave the protective area of your house.

Me: That's true.

As I said that I looked him right in the eye and stepped off the grass. Olcult, not expecting this, looked shocked. I grabbed him by the throat with my left hand and punched him with all my normal strength across the chin, knocking him to the ground. I then watched him look up at me and grin and say out loud, "Now!"

Just then I heard multiple loud bangs. As I did, I saw bullet fragments stop and dissolve about a foot from my face, at least two by my head and four to five around my torso. When the bullets stopped and crumbled into super small pieces, an egg-shaped field of see-through protection seemed to envelop me. When the bullets dissipated into nothing but smoke, the field seemed to disappear.

I realized there were shooters all around me. I guess Olcult was trying to get me to come get him in hopes of shooting me full of holes. I could not see any of the shooters, but it was obvious they were there. Olcult looked surprised and tried to make it to his feet and get in his car. I looked down at my ring and thought, "All shooters or anyone with Olcult who will endanger me will fall asleep instantly for twenty-four hours. The ring blinked its acknowledgement. The only thing I saw was a person in the distance in camouflage falling from a tree.

Olcult rushed to get into his car. He opened the car door and started the Porsche. As he slammed it into gear, I took my hand, and with my thumb tucked under, I pointed all four fingers at the trunk of his car. As with the tree, a lightning bolt of energy was released and sliced into the back of the car, basically removing the entire trunk section of the vehicle. The trunk flew up in the air and landed on the street. Although the car sustained major damage, it was not enough to make the car undrivable. As it raced down the road, I pointed my hand again, this time planning to use all five fingers, when I realized there were several people all standing in their yards, staring at me. As I looked back at them, I got the same feeling I do when with the devil. I could sense many of their feelings. Fear and disbelief were most prevalent. My advanced hearing started to pick up a couple of them talking.

> Neighbors: Did you see that? He shot lightning bolts from his hands. Maybe he is one of the aliens that were coming for us.

Many of them were thinking similar things. I guess the devil's rule of keeping it small and simple was not used this time, and I have let the whole world in on the situation. But reality came back to me quickly. Justin—I have to get to him. I went back in the house and into the garage and got in my car. I looked down to the ring and said, "Let me know which hospital," and I immediately did. I squealed out of my garage and on to the road. There were still many people standing around and many of them pointing at me as I drove off. I had created a whole new situation, but right at that moment, I did not care. My priority was to get to Justin and help him. This situation with my neighbors will no doubt be a problem but one I would have to deal with at a later time.

It was a strange sensation that I knew right where to go. I made each turn on each street with no idea which hospital it was. I just knew where to go. Luckily I was not pulled over on the way there because I drove with a very heavy foot. I parked and was in the hospital. The front desk was packed with people and commotion. I did not have time for this. I looked down at the ring and said, "Get me to his room." I thought that, like with finding the hospital, I would just know where the room would be. Instead, I was transported from the entrance to the room. Not being ready for that event, I was a bit jolted. Luckily there was no one in Justin's hospital room as I materialized next to his bed. He was in bad shape. He was hooked up to multiple machines, and his face was mostly bandaged. As I stood there, a doctor walked in.

Doctor: I'm sorry, sir, this is ICU. There are no visitors allowed.
Me: Doctor, how is he?
Doctor: Are you related to him?
Me: Yes, he is my nephew. He lives with me.

The doctor's expression changed from mad to sympathetic. He put his hand on my shoulders.

Doctor: What is your name, son?
Me: My name is Thomas.

Doctor: Thomas, I'm sorry, but it's not looking good. He has broken seventeen bones and fractured his spine. He also has suffered a major concussion. He is in a coma. We don't expect him to come out of it. If he did, he would likely be paralyzed from the neck down. I am sorry. We will do everything we can to keep him comfortable, but I don't expect him to make it.

Those words hit hard. Justin was all I had. He, Shawn, and I had done so much together. I can't let this happen.

Doctor: I'm going to have to ask you to leave. This area is restricted. I know that seems cold. But it is necessary.

I then did just what the doctor did to me, and I put my hands on his shoulders. As I did, he looked on both sides of himself and then directly at me. Our eyes met, and without much effort, I felt the hair rise on the back of my neck. I made the connection with the doctor. As has happened with everyone I have ever done this with, I started to get a rush of his memories from his past, and with them came a bright whiteness with the memories, a warm feeling of calm and security. This had never happened when I did this to anyone else, but I just chalked it up to him being a doctor of high intelligence and him caring for humans and his patience, although there seemed to be more to it.

I quickly stopped that train of thought and said in my mind, "It is okay for me to come in here. You will let everyone know that. You will do everything in your ability to save Justin. In your mind, his life is linked to the world's life. If he dies, so does the world. You will show him every concern and do whatever it takes to keep him alive and recover. Is this clear to you?"

Doctor: Yes, of course. To save Justin is to save the earth. All efforts must be made to save him and thus saving my family and all families.

Me: Very good. Now give me a few minutes with him.

Doctor: Of course, take your time.

The doctor replied not in some robot or controlled zombie voice but sounded very normal and authentic. He turned and left the room. I had to try and see if I could help him. I looked down at the ring and said, "Ring, repair Justin and make him just as he was before this injury happened." Nothing happened. The ring did not blink, and Justin did not change. I repeated my request. Still nothing. I did it a third time, and something very strange happened. The blue stone of my class ring turned black. I mean a black so dark I had never seen anything like it before. This was the first time that the ring did not fulfill my request.

Even though I had a feeling it would not work from what the devil told me, it was still very devastating. I started to cry and felt incredible anger, anger that was like the heat of a thousand suns combined. But I brought myself back from it. I am sure I can work something with the devil to bend this rule. He bends them all the time. It's time I get one. In the meantime, I had to do something to keep him protected so Olcult could do no more damage. I looked down at the ring and said, "Ring, protect Justin from any further injury. Create a shield, like at the house, that will guard him from anything that would cause or attempt to cause him harm so I can concentrate on the Pelusoians and not be worried further." The ring went from its dark black back to the blue and glowed brightly and then went back to its normal blue stone. Apparently the ring allowed some leeway for my well-worded loophole on this one occasion.

I took Justin's hand and spoke to him.

Me: You will be okay, Justin. You are safe now. I will make sure you are as good as new. Until then, just rest and have good dreams.

I put his hand back and felt the rush of sadness and anger come over me again. Olcult will need to be punished severely for this; I will make sure of that. I took one last look at him and turned and left the room, knowing at least he was safe from any further danger.

As I left the room, I was bum-rushed by two nurses who were very aggressive, grabbing me and yelling that I was not allowed on this floor or to visit patients in this wing. As I was in no mood for this, I was about to use my loudest voice toward them when the doctor that was in Justin's room came out of nowhere.

Doctor: Nurses, this gentleman has top clearance from the government. You will release him and know from this point forward he is free to come and go on this ward as he wishes. Are we absolutely clear on this matter?

Both nurses took a step back and cringed as if they were children being scolded by a parent. They both looked at me, and one of them spoke.

Nurse 1: I am very sorry, Doctor, we did not know this.
Nurse 2: We will certainly make a note of this on the chart and tell all the rest of the staff so he will not have any further problems.
Doctor: Very good. Please go back to your assigned duties.

The doctor then looked at me and winked and walked away. I don't recall my ability to control another's mind to have ever worked so well and have the person respond so specifically to it.

As I walked back to my car, my mind was full of thoughts. I was, of course, worried about Justin, but part of me felt sure the devil would bend the rules for me to allow a full recovery. Olcult is still out there and is using snipers to try to kill me—not a very high-tech way, but since I have jammed up much of his equipment and have showed that I can easily override all his advanced toys, I can see why he is resorting to such barbaric methods to do me in.

The devil said I cannot kill him because it would move up the Pelusoians' timetable on attacking Earth. But when that limitation is lifted, he is done. At this point I am willing to bet he is already knee-deep with a new plan for my demise. Although my autodefenses seem to be quite effective, as they showed with blocking and pulverizing the bullets to dust, I still need to be on full alert.

As I was walking up to my car, my cell phone rang. Before I answered it, I knew who it was.

Olcult: Hello, Thomas. How is your nephew doing?

Me: A lot better than you are going to be. Want to test me?

Olcult: That lightning bolt out of your hand trick is very fascinating. Each time you do a display of power, we get one step closer to figuring out its origin and a way to stop you from accessing it. So please keep up the show. Eventually we will discover its origin, and then they can put a bed next to your nephew and you both can stay in a coma until it's time.

Although his remarks were stabbing me like knives, I kept myself calm and acted like none of it bothered me and I have it all under control.

Me: So would you like to meet again, Doctor? I would be glad to.

Olcult: Not quite yet, but very soon I will take you up on that offer. Until then, I'm sending you a video through your cell you may enjoy. Are you ready?

Me: Actually, I am not interested in your videos.

Olcult: Oh I think you will find this one quite interesting.

As he said that, my phone beeped, indicating I had a message.

When I checked it, it showed a video message. As reluctant as I felt to watch it, I knew I had to. I have to play his game till the time comes when I can stop him once and for all.

As I pressed play, I saw Olcult's face. Then he said, "Hello, Thomas, I am here with a friend of yours. It was a little difficult to get through the protective shielding around your house, but after your last magical display, we came up with a way to take it down."

Those words hit me hard. Only Justin, Toby, and I lived at the house. It was obviously not me; Justin was in the hospital.

> Olcult: What a furry and friendly little guy he is. I love the name too, Toby. It's so cute. Such a shame he has lost his eyesight.

As he said that, the video showed him picking up Toby and petting him on the head. I had to take a deep breath for I felt myself become lightheaded. It certainly looked like my Toby. As he petted him, the petting became harder and more aggressive until the petting was more like hitting, and Toby began to whine with each hit. Then he grabbed him by the throat, pointed him at the camera, and said, "Say good-bye." He then took his head and twisted it all the way around in a quick snap. Toby gave a yelp and then just went limp. The camera panned up to Olcult's face.

> Olcult: I hated to do this, Thomas. I have no negativity about dogs. It's humans I dislike. I even had a dog myself that I loved a great deal. Now that I have demonstrated my point, I think you get the idea of what you can look forward to.

Then the video ended. With my hand shaking, I put the cell back to my ear.

> Olcult: You bring the worst out of me, Thomas. Why don't you just give up this battle between us, and no one else has to be hurt.

In my calmest voice I could muster, I said to him, "Please hold." I muted the phone and looked down at the ring. I said in my mind, "Ring, was that my Toby from back at my house?" The ring blinked in the negative. "Is my Toby still safe at home?" The ring blinked in the positive. I then unmuted the phone.

Me: Very nice special effect, Olcult.
Olcult: It was no special effect. I can assure you.
Me: Well, I happen to now that my Toby is safely at home. But what you have done is assure that I will take no pity on you when the time comes. You hear me, you piece of shit? You're going to pay for everything you have—

Just as I was about to finish my well-worded threat to Olcult, a pickup truck came from nowhere and headed right at me. I had no time to run or block or even point my hand. The truck was going at least eighty miles per hour, and as it got about five feet from running me down, it stopped dead as if it hit a cement wall. The front of the vehicle crushed in almost all the way to the driver's compartment. The driver was catapulted out of the driver seat and hit the same invisible cement wall and exploded into what could only be best described as a chunky and slushy human blender mix. Blood and bone spattered on to the invisible wall, displaying to me all the gore of the human body, looking like it went through a chopper blade and thrown at a plate glass window at me. A second later, the truck itself exploded in a loud and bright spray of fire and truck parts.

I instinctively ducked even though there was no reason to. The smell of smoke, fuel, and a couple other unrecognizable smells became immediately obvious. I couldn't hardly see anything except the sun shining through a red tint of blood and smoke. I could hear voices everywhere and could barely see two security guards making their way toward me. There was no way I was going to be able to explain this. It would take too much time to clear all this up. In the back of my mind, I also wanted to get back to the house and confirm that Toby was really all right.

So once again I decided to not drive but teleport home. I looked at the ring and said in my mind, "Bring me home in my room."

Instantly the carnage and smoke were gone, and I was safely back in my room at my house.

I looked down and saw my Toby looking confused, no doubt from me just appearing instead of walking in as he was used to. Even though he was blind, his other senses always made up for the difference. I went to pet him and noticed that the cell was still in my hand and was still active. I put the phone to my ear.

> Me: Nice try, Olcult. I am keeping track of all the people you have killed and all the things you have done to piss me off.
>
> Olcult: That was most impressive. Your shielding is incredible, a technology never seen before by us.
>
> Me: Whatever, I am at home, and my Toby is fine, so I have no idea what you are trying to pull.
>
> Olcult: You're home, huh. So you have teleport ability too. Well, I need to let you go. I have a lot of data to analyze after this last display of your magic. Your neighbors saw you shoot lightning from your hands, so I am sure you will have your hands full at your house. I will see you soon, Thomas.

He then hung up. I looked down and sat on my bed and picked up Toby to hold him. I kissed and hugged him for several minutes and burst into tears. This is all becoming too much. Olcult is a single human being, and he has me all twisted and stressed out. Justin is in a severe medical condition. My neighbors probably have told the cops and the *National Inquirer* about what happened outside my house by this point. I hate to admit it, but Olcult is right. I have my hands full, and I am very unsure of what my next move is going to be, let alone a plan for a battle with the soon-arriving armada of alien ships.

What happened at the hospital I'm sure was captured by the parking lot cams; no doubt Olcult tapped into them with his higher-than-average tech skills. And with my neighbors seeing me blast off the back of a car with lightning coming out of my fingers, it's safe to say my secret is out of the bag. I could waste a lot of time and energy fixing this, which I am not even sure I can do at this point. Or since the timetable for the invasion has been moved up, and the whole world will once again be alerted to what is going on, and this time there will be no going back, so why try? I will soon have to display great feats of power to have any chance of stopping this attack.

I cannot be wasting time doing a cover-up. But this means everyone will know. In a few days, all hell will break loose, and I can't be fighting the government and the rest of the world, who will likely be fearing me and preparing a defense.

I need some advice. I need help. Since the devil is limited by rules on helping me, it's time to fall back on the person who can give me the most intelligent advice—Shawn from the dimension where he is the leading genius.

CHAPTER 20

I knew I did not have long before I was going to have knocks on the door and crowds of reporters wanting to know what happened. So I decided to contact Shawn again. I looked down at my ring and said in my mind, "I need to talk to the same Shawn I talked to before with the same conditions." I figured that would cover our meeting place and him dreaming. Just like that, the ring glowed, and we were back.

Once again I was sitting in the main king chair and Shawn on the couch. He looked at me and smiled. That alone gave me strength and confidence. Shawn's presence always had that effect. Even though this was not my Shawn, it still seemed to work the same way.

> Shawn: So here we are again.
> Me: Yes, we are, and things are not getting any better.

I explained everything that has happened with Olcult and the situation with the car and lightning bolt as well as the hospital event and the fact that everyone knows now. Unlike the first time, he seemed to accept this as more real this time or at least seemed to go along with the situation more seriously.

> Shawn: Well, it was inevitable you were not going to be able to keep this situation and all your abilities secret much longer. I am surprised you managed it this long. Not to mention if Olcult is as clever as you say, he will also want your secret to be out in order to put additional

pressure on you and add to your mounting situation.

Me: That's very true. Olcult is damaged in the mind, but that does not mean he is not super smart, not just with advanced technology but psychology and warfare.

Shawn: Well, if he has been training all his life for this event and is eons more advanced than us, it would seem logical.

Me: Well, if the cat's out of the bag now, what do you suggest?

Shawn: He is trying to make all this as public as possible to derail you and add as much pressure as he can. It's time to let those bricks out of your backpack.

Me: What do you mean?

Shawn: I mean you need to let the governments of the world know what is happening with you and the pending disaster. It will eliminate the aspect of you trying to do everything in the dark and will give them time to prepare, and Olcult will lose his advantage. I realize your timeline is almost identical to mine. So that means there is little our missiles, ships, or planes are going to be able to do, but at least they can begin some kind of contingency plan to help protect the people when you start this war with the Pelusoians.

Me: That's also true. Maybe I should have not hidden this information the first time.

Shawn: No, you did the right thing. That was not the way for the world to find out. The government has considered this possibility for a long time. They will have some ideas on how to handle it. Let the government take the reins with the human population, Tom. With all the abilities you have, I think you have enough responsibility on your back.

Me: Any ideas on how I should do this?

Shawn: Normally I would say go to the UN, but that may cause too much commotion and too many opinions. The United States is the strongest country in the world. Go to the president and explain it to him. Let her figure a way to distribute this information to the rest of the world.

Me: She? Did you say "she"?

Shawn: Yes, President Hillary Clinton. But not in your timeline, I take it.

Me: No, in mine it's Barack Obama who is president.

Shawn: Interesting, how liberal your dimension must be to have a black president.

Me: That's funny, I was thinking the same thing. A female president seems "liberal" too.

Shawn: Well, either way, the president has a book with a contingency plan for first contact. It mostly refers to a peaceful joining of beings, but it was also created if the worst scenario were to happen too.

Me: Thank you, Shawn. I just wanted you to know.

Right at that moment, I lost it. Everything just caught up with me at once: seeing Justin in a coma, seeing the images created by Olcult of Toby having his neck broken, the guy in the truck turning into mush right in front of me, and talking to Shawn. Even though he was a very different Shawn, he looked so much like him. The pressure and, literally, weight of the world on my shoulders, all of this hit me at once, and I broke down into tears.

Shawn: Hey, Thomas, I know this has to be overwhelming. No human, no matter how well balanced, could easily deal with this without doubting themselves. I can tell you are a smart guy, maybe not as smart as me, but right up there.

He said that last part in jest and patted me on the head—something my Shawn used to do. That same gesture of a couple taps on the top of my head to signify that I was letting too much build up in my mind and also the joking at a very serious moment were just what my Shawn always did to lighten the mood.

Shawn: I don't know who chose you as the one to take on this burden, but I can tell you that I see why. You are a good person, but moreover, you have the perfect balance of craftiness and compassion. With the situation you have been thrust into, you will need both and just the right amount of each. I am not going to tell you what I think the percentages are of you saving mankind, but I will say, I would have picked you too.

I wiped the tears from my eyes and pulled myself back together.

Me: Thank you, Shawn. That was just what I needed. Even though I think much of it was a pep talk over the truth, I still appreciate you saying all that.

Shawn: You're welcome, my friend. I can see why the me of your timeline was best friends with you. Now enough of this mushy shit.

Me: Agreed. Time I stop this emotional merry-go-round and get down to action. I guess it's time the president and I have a conversation.

Shawn: The Secret Service may not just let you in the front door.

Me: Well, actually your Secret Service might be better than ours. Lately people have been walking right into the White House here.

Shawn: Really?

Me: No, but it's just a recent event that occurred with someone getting all the way into the White House, and the Secret Service has been taking the brunt of everyone's jokes lately.

Shawn: How close did they get?

Me: The news said he was still a couple rooms away.

Shawn: Is there any way that ring of yours can tell you if the president is the president or if he was under any kind of mind control?

Me: I'm sure it can. Why?

Shawn: It may be something you want to test before you tell the whole story to him. He may be fine, but I would confirm that before you let him know the whole situation.

Me: You think the president has been compromised?

Shawn: I don't know, but it's a precaution that would not hurt.

Me: Never thought of that. You are absolutely correct. I will do that first thing. Thank you again.

Shawn: That's why I am here instead of dreaming of playing golf with Albert Einstein. (*He smiled.*)

Me: Same sense of humor.

Shawn: What?

Me: Nothing, just my Shawn was the same way, always with a joke.

Shawn: Well, you need to lighten up a bit. Not like you are the savior of all life on Earth!

Me: Ha-ha. On that topic, do you have any ideas for me when the Pelusoians start coming through the wormhole?

Shawn: I have a couple, but let's wait on that. You need to get to the president before your house ends up being the center of all news.

Me: You're right. Thank you again. You have helped me in more ways than you can even conceive. And I am willing to bet you and your help are going to play a huge part in saving this world.

Shawn: I hope so, Thomas.

Me: Just call me Tom. That's what my Shawn called me.

Shawn: Very well, Tom. I am sure I will be seeing you again soon so we can talk strategies.

Me: That is a definite, my friend.

Shawn: Till then, stay strong and keep your confidence up. Someone obviously believed in you, or you would not have been chosen, and I am also convinced you are the right pick. So lose the self-doubt.

Me: You got it.

With that I looked down at the ring, and it blinked without me having to say anything. When I looked up, Shawn was gone, and I had returned to my house. I was hoping the same thing as last time would happen, and I would remain in the mansion, and the devil would show up to talk. I wanted to see if I can help Justin and talk him into allowing me to use the ring to bend the rules. But it did not happen that way. I was back in my room and back at my house.

I walked out to the living room and pulled the curtain back a little. Outside were several clusters of neighbors, all talking and occasionally pointing and looking at my house. I was sure it would not take long before there were officials and authorities out there as well. It was time to start thinking about how I wanted to handle this with the president. I considered coming to him in his dreams like I do with Shawn, but somehow I felt that would lack credibility.

No, I was going to have to meet him face-to-face in real time. There was no other way.

The president is always surrounded by people. I need the ring to notify me when he would be alone and in a room by himself. It seemed the ring and I were beginning to melt together. Just as I no longer needed to say things in my mind to send Shawn back, it also blinked when I was just thinking about having it notify me of when the president would be alone. I also felt it understood me.

This was an improvement for sure. Not only was it a time-saver, but it was more accurate. The need to worry if I worded something wrong was no longer a problem. It was instantaneous and on the nose with what I wanted.

Knowing the ring was going to alert me when the right time would come to talk to the president alone, I decided to watch television and see if what happened on my street or at the hospital had gone viral yet. As I turned it on, I scanned the channels and saw nothing immediately about my two events, but on the big news network, they were talking about something to do with the probe again. This, of course, was of great interest to me, so I locked in on that and began to watch. It was a reporter talking to a NASA astronomer.

Reporter: So when did you first notice the probe doing this?

NASA guy: We, of course, have had Hubble and several of our other best telescopes fixed on the probe since it transmitted what we once thought was a message. For days we were continuing to track it through the Oort cloud when suddenly it stopped. It lost all velocity and just halted at a very specific coordinate and stayed there.

Reporter: Do you think it ran out of fuel, or is it having another malfunction?

NASA: I don't think you understand. *Voyager* was the fastest-moving man-made device ever created, then it just stopped dead. There is no scientific explanation. An object at that speed does not just hit the brakes, and if it could, it would not stay stationary. It would drift. It would have some kind of movement or continued momentum.

Reporter: Well, what is your explanation?

NASA: We don't have one.

Reporter: Are you still in communication with it?

NASA: We were until this sudden stop in space. At which time we have lost all guidance and communication. We were lucky to get a fix on it by its last known position.

As the reporter was about to ask him another question, several gentlemen in military suits came from behind him and whispered something in his ear and then grabbed him by both arms and started to walk him away. The NASA guy did not resist but seemed very surprised about being manhandled this way. The reporter tried to ask the military guys what was going on, but she was stopped too, and then the cameraman seemed to be grabbed, and the signal and picture from in front of the NASA building was stopped completely, and it went back to the studio. The lead broadcaster tried to make light of it and said there were some technical difficulties, but it was obvious what had happened.

I switched it to other channels, but it did not take long for that one interview to be on every news station. It would not be long before things were right back to a panic mode around the world.

I began to wonder why the probe would just stop like that. What would be the benefit? Whatever it was, it was not a benefit for us as earthlings and was only the first of many bad news updates we were about to get.

Each channel had its own take on the probe's sudden stop in space—some with logical explanations, others with conspiracies, and some just suspecting that the original message and situation were the truth and the government was just covering it all up so the world would not fall into chaos.

With these new events, it was more obvious than ever I needed to talk to the president. I could not wait any longer to be notified by the ring that the president was alone. With the current events, he probably has nonstop meetings and is surrounded by advisors constantly. The ring needs to make him create a situation where he is alone. "A headache which he needs to lie down to and not be disturbed for an hour, yeah, that's a good idea," I thought to myself, but I also realized it was like I was being told that and not thinking of it myself. The ring is bonding more and more with me. When the headache idea came to me, I looked down at the ring, and it glowed brightly for a brief moment. I somehow knew that it was telling me it was all clear and it was time.

I looked down at the ring and thought, "It's time, Ring, bring me to the president. Make sure when I appear I will not be seen and we will not be disturbed by anyone." Then everything went black and then transformed into a dimly lit room. I was no longer in my house but in a very large plush bedroom. There was a huge bed bigger than any I had ever seen. I was standing at the side of it. I took a quick look around. I was in the White House at what appeared to be the president's bedroom. As I looked down, I could see it was him, and he was very sound asleep and snoring at a very high decibel.

I was very nervous, and I was not sure how I was going to do this. So I kept it simple. First thing, I looked down at the ring and thought, "Is this the real president? And is he himself and not taken over by other influences?" The ring gave the positive response. "Okay, Shawn." Even though he was not under any influence, it was still a worthy question and a reasonable precaution.

Me: Mr. President, Mr. President.
President: I told you, Scott, I need at least an hour to let the aspirin kick in. This headache came out of nowhere, and I need just a little time.
Me: Mr. President, this is not Scott. My name is Thomas, and it is imperative that we talk.

With that the president quickly pulled down the covers on his bed and sat up and looked directly at me.

President: Who are you, and how did you get in here? Damn Secret Service can't do anything right these days.

I could see he was trying to push a button that was under one of the side tables by his bed in an inconspicuous way.

Me: I told you I was Thomas, and none of your warning measures are going to work. I need to have a few minutes of private time with you so we can talk about the probe and the pending disaster our world is facing.

President: For your information, I have pushed a security alarm, and there will be a dozen armed men in here any moment. There are also cameras on me 24-7, so you are being seen as we speak.

Me: Well, I have made sure we won't be disturbed.

This was taking too long, and it was time we did not have. I looked down at the ring and thought, "Bring us to the mansion." With that the room changed and so did our positions. The president was on the plush couch where I usually sit, and I was sitting in the big red king chair where the devil usually is. Once again I began to become more aware of how quickly and efficiently the ring and I were communicating.

The president jumped in a startled fashion and then stood up. He looked around the room and then back at me.

President: This is some kind of dream?

Me: You know it's not. You were just sleeping in your bed at the White House. I need you to think clear for a second. You know this is not a dream.

President: Yes. Are you one of the aliens? When my people discover I am missing, they will search for me and not stop.

Me: They can search all they want, Mr. President, but I have frozen time where we are. We are in a separate dimension from the one you and I know. I brought you here to get your assistance and explain how I am trying to help.

President: I noticed you did not answer my question. Are you an alien?

Me: No, I am human, but I am aware of the impending invasion and am here to help. I was given abilities by allies of the human race to help defend the world from these attackers to our planet.

President: Are you God?

Me: No, I am not.

President: Are you an angel? Did God give you these abilities to help us?

Me: Not exactly.

I did not want to explain that I and the devil are working together to save the world and that he had given me powers, which I am using to do these things. I just had a feeling the truth was not the right thing to do at this point. So I decided to go another way.

Me: I was given these powers and abilities by a race that helped seed Earth many millennia ago. They are enemies of the Pelusoians.

President: Pelusoians?

Me: Yes, that is the name of the race that is going to attack Earth. Our probe, *Voyager*, after several decades, left our solar system. When it did, it entered the Oort cloud and was detected by these hostile aliens, who are so abundant that their race takes up almost an entire galaxy.

President: Why have we seen no data on this?

Me: The Pelusoians are far away. They are not even from the Milky Way galaxy. The Oort cloud protected us from being detected by other life forms in order to keep us safe. But unfortunately, our curiosity got us in trouble this time.

President: So you are on our side and are going to help us fight this enemy race?

Me: That is correct, Mr. President.

President: So if these Pelusoians are able to get here from another galaxy, they must have scientific technology that is way beyond anything we have.

Me: That is correct.

President: What about the beings that gave you these abilities? Are they equally advanced?

Me: Yes, sir, maybe even more so. But they are not coming to our rescue. They endowed me with powers to defend Earth, and it is basically all up to me.

President: So it's you against an entire army of Pelusoians?

Me: Yes, sir. Something else you should know. There is a man. He is a psychiatrist by the name of Dr. Olcult. He has been in communication with the Pelusoians since he was a child. He has much of their technical knowledge and has been brought up to facilitate their arrival and stop anyone who may endanger that mission. He has been after me for the last couple days and has displayed some very advanced toys and tech. I have been able to keep him under control so far, but he has attempted to kill me several times already.

President: Let me guess, you are from the state of Florida.

Me: Yes, sir. How did you know that, Mr. President?

President: I was given a report about multiple eyewitnesses seeing a man arguing with another man, and when he drove off, theses witnesses claimed this individual was able to shoot electricity out of his hands at the car he was driving away in. Then I watched some video footage of a person standing in a hospital parking lot, and a truck going very fast tried to run him over. The truck was crushed in the front, and the driver was mutilated by what appeared to be an invisible shield. Do you know anything about these events?

Me: Yes, I do, Mr. President, both occasions. Dr. Olcult was in front of my house and tried to kill me with hidden snipers. He tried to escape when it did not work, and I used one of my abilities granted to me by our allies to try and stop him. I was also the one who they tried to mow down in the hospital parking lot, but I have a protective shield that is created around me during events where I may be in danger. But this is the work of Dr. Olcult. He is a very dangerous man and should be considered an enemy to any living being on this planet.

The president took a deep breath and sat back down on the plush couch. I was trying to read him, but there were so many emotions at once it was hard to put my finger on any one. I did get the distinct impression he believed me and it was not a dream, but he was skeptical on whether to put his trust in me.

Me: I know this is a lot to take in. Trust me, the last few days have been unreal for me as well. But with the recent events by NASA and the probe just stopping dead in space, people are going to start to become unruly again, and this time I will not be able to hide the truth.

President: What do you mean by that, "again"?

Me: When the probe first transmitted that ominous message---that really happened. I made it so it seemed like it was a glitch.

President: Why would you try and deceive me and the people of the United States in that way?

Me: I thought it was for the best. It just seemed to be more advantageous to wait until I had collected more information. As I am sure you are aware, when that announcement came out, the planet was in a state of anarchy, national guard and all.

President: Now all of a sudden you have changed your mind about all this.

Me: The Pelusoians have moved up their invasion plans because Olcult has informed them of me and my ability to stop him and his invasion force. It's also too difficult to try and hide this constant battle between us, just like the intel you got about what happened in front of my house and at the hospital. I can't be worrying about continuously covering things up. I need to be able to concentrate on how I am going to stop them when they arrive.

President: That makes sense. You realize you are going to have to go in front of congress and quite likely the UN and tell them everything you just told me.

Me: I don't have time for that. You are the president, and soon enough the world is going to witness everything I have said for themselves. I need you to stop Olcult's plan to expose me. I have my hands full already, Mr. President. You need to keep them off my back and allow me to concentrate on saving our planet.

President: Sounds like a reasonable request to me. But I may need to have you eventually do something for me. Not sure exactly what that will be at this moment. Like you, I find this a lot to take in at one shot. How do I get a hold of you?

Me: Just ask for me and say my name out loud, and I will do my best to get to you as quickly as I can. Given I am being put in some incredible situations at every turn these days, it may sometimes take me a bit, but I will always show eventually. And as far as Dr. Olcult, can I count on your help with him and that situation?

President: I am going to contact your local authorities and have my best "PR" guys put a positive "spin" on what your neighbors claim they saw, and do the same for the incident in the hospital parking lot.

Me: Thank you, Mr. President. I am sure, working together, we will come out of this far stronger.

I was surprised how quickly the president accepted all this. But with him knowing about the probe, seeing the videos of what happened to me, and the information his people gave him about the lightning bolts from my hands, I guess the pure weight of everything combined was enough to allow him to be open-minded and therefore accept this incredible chain of events as true.

President: Thomas, what are the real chances of us surviving or winning this battle? For years our best scientists have told me any creatures who can traverse interstellar space are as far ahead of us technologically as we are to a colony of ants. If you wish me to be honest with you, I expect the same courtesy back. What are our chances?

Me: I can't give you numbers, Mr. President, or percentages. It does seem sort of like a David-and-Goliath-type scenario. But the powers I possess to defend Earth and mankind are beyond their best technology. In fact, it would not be lying to say, it's not even in the same ballpark.

He stood up and put out his hand. I did the same and firmly grabbed his hand while he gave me a strongly gripped handshake.

President: I have been put in situations over the last six years which made me toss and turn at night, worrying about thousands of our troops. Stress so bad you can see I have gone mostly grey. Even when the situation looked grim and my best and smartest people were telling me we will be fine, I could see in their faces they were saying that for my benefit and not for the reason of telling the truth. So when

I look into your face, I see a man who is being optimistic and yet has enough self-doubt to fill an ocean. I guess what I am trying to say is, I can imagine the pressures you must be under, but I can't even begin to relate to something of this magnitude. For your decisions to be right, you have to believe in them, which means you have to believe in yourself. I believe in God, Thomas. I also believe in destiny. You were not picked for this as a random name from a hat. Someone put this in your lap. They must have known you are our best chance. I have only talked to you for a couple minutes, but I believe, as they must have, you are the right choice.

Wow, that was a pretty good pep talk. I guess all those years of giving them made him pretty good at it. It did give me a sense of confidence and self-assuredness. I was not giving him all the facts and was distorting some of the truths, but still he was given the gist of our situation and still felt as though I would be able to do my best.

Me: Well, Mr. President, I think it's time we get you back to your bed. I hope that headache is gone at this point.

President: Oh yes, Thomas, that headache is long gone. The one I have now is a whole new breed of headaches. (*He said that with an obvious chuckle.*)

Me: I am going to put you right back where I first woke you up. Please immediately try to take care of the situation at my house. I think the reporters were about to start setting up tents in my front yard.

President: It will be the first thing I do. There was already a man we had in Florida on his way because of the video we watched. What about Olcult? Do you want my men to take him out?

Me: No, sir, I will take care of him. He may play a part in this I have not yet figured out. And if not, I want to be the one that makes him pay for his decisions. If nothing else, keep an eye on him and have some people follow where he goes at all times. That certainly could not hurt.

President: Consider it done. What about you? Who should I tell about you?

Me: You can tell your closest and most trusted staff. But I would limit it. As I said, it won't be long before everyone will know what is going on. Till then, just tell only who you feel you have to.

President: Very good.

With that we each gave the other a half-smile of false confidence, and as I looked down at the ring to think the thoughts to return him, it was done. I was back in my living room, and I'm sure he was safely back in his bed at the White House.

CHAPTER 21

I decided to check the outdoor situation again. It had gotten much worse. There were multiple news vans with satellites on their roofs and dozens of people now. I could see from my living room window there were notes on my door. I wanted to see what that was all about, so I went to the door and tried to open it a crack and grabbed the several pieces of paper stuck and tacked to my door. I did it somehow without any of them seeing. All the notes were from different news services asking if they could interview me.

As I sat down to read them, I could hear some people walking up to my door. My finely tuned hearing picked up one saying, "Oh look, the notes are gone, he must be in side." They then walked to the door and started to knock and ring the bell at the same time. They were doing it relentlessly with no break or pause in between.

There was no way I was going to answer, so I grabbed Toby and went to the back of the house where the family room was.

I sat there with Toby for a couple minutes, petting him. As always, Toby could sense my distress and started to shake himself. It really bothered me when he did this. It made me feel guilty that I did not have enough self-control to keep calm. I could hear more and more people coming to the door and the nonstop ring of the doorbell. I found where the bell for the doorbell was inside the house and unplugged it. That helped, but it did not stop the continuous knocking on the door.

To try and distract me from this, I turned the TV on. Of course the TV was overwhelmed with the same footage being shown over and over of the NASA guy being pulled away by two military guys.

Some stations just kept showing that same thirty seconds in a loop while muting the event and talking over it with their own speculation and constant update about the *Voyager* probe frozen in space. I kept clicking through the channels until I came to one station that was interviewing a professor from Syracuse University in New York. He seemed to be a very intelligent man who had some interesting things to say. I was kind of lost on why the probe stopped dead in space myself and wanted to hear some theories.

The man's name was Professor Kettermen. He had a theory why it stopped and what it means. I stopped on that channel and turned it up to try and drown out the banging on the door.

> Ketterman: It is my belief that the original message may have been authentic at this point. I am not sure how it was so easily dismissed, but if it is all true, then who or what took it over is still coming. Making it stop dead in space would give them better coordinates to find us. If it continued at the speed it was going, they could still pinpoint its original location, but now that it's stopped, they can more easily and accurately follow its route back. I fear if these beings can hold the probe in place like this from an incredible distance, they have abilities we will not even begin to understand. If my theory is true, then the original message is one not of peace but of war. If that is the case, our only hope is to try and communicate with them and let them know we are a peaceful race and we would only like to welcome them and share our knowledge with these galactic friends.

It was hard to criticize this man. His theories were logical, and his intentions were pure. But the Pelusoians do not want to come in peace, and it was certainly not going to be a civilized welcome and first contact. They were here to feed their race, and we are the dinner. No communication was going to help or change their minds.

While watching I noticed I could barely keep my eyes open. I was exhausted, and in the middle of watching another interview, I fell asleep. It was hard to tell how long I was out for, and I was not sure why I was allowed to just sleep and not be whisked to the mansion, but I was abruptly awoken by bangs on the door that became louder and more aggressive.

Not only were they pounding on the door but they started to pound on the window next to the door. Toby became fully alert to all this. Even from the back of the house, it could all be heard loudly. I could feel him begin to shake, and then he barked. It was obvious I could not just sit there and wait until they busted in the door or broke the window. I got up and put Toby in my room and went to the front door. I grabbed the doorknob and took a deep breath. I then opened the door to get a rush of cameras and microphones pushed into my face. I tried to speak and told them that they need to leave my yard at once. There were at least fifteen to twenty altogether, and with them all asking me questions at once, I could not understand what any of them were saying nor could they hear a word I was trying to tell them. I guess the shielding only protected me from actual danger and not annoying reporters.

Then came the push from all of them that backed me right into the house and allowed several to enter. My patience was running thin at this point. They already had a clue as what I was capable of, so what was the difference? I looked down at the ring, but before I thought anything, I heard police sirens—many of them. This made most of them that were pushing their way in retreat outside. Over them I could see multiple police cars pulling into my driveway at rapid speeds and stopping in front of my house.

What appeared to be sheriff, state, city police cars and some unmarked vehicles with government plates, proceeded to stop all around my yard. To my surprise, I also saw my Mazda pull up with a man in a very expensive-looking suit driving it.

The police all ran up to the door and started grabbing the reporters in a slightly physical way and started pushing them back away from my door. After a few were manhandled rather roughly, the others decided to retreat to their news vans on their own. The officers never spoke to me as they just seemed interested in getting every reporter and cameraman off my yard. The only one who paid any attention to me was the one in the nice suit who was driving my car. He walked right up to me. He asked if I was Mr. Williams and shook my hand and introduced himself as Special Agent Brock.

Brock: Mr. Williams, I am very sorry it took us so long to get here. I had no idea things were getting so out of hand at your residence. I wanted to bring your car back to you. Quite the vehicle. It truly is the Batmobile, isn't it?
Me: Yes, I love my car. Thank you for bringing it back to me. I went to visit my nephew who has been in a serious injury at work, and I ended up deciding to walk—

As I was saying that, he raised his hand to silence me.

Brock: May I please come in, Mr. Williams?
Me: Yes, of course, please come in.

He turned around to one of the plainclothes officers.

Brock: Detective, do you have this under control?

The officer gave a nod and returned to herding all the reporters back to their vehicles and left the property. Then Brock walked in, and I closed the door.

Brock: Mr. Williams, I am here from direct orders of the president of the United States. You do not have to lie to me or tell me anything if that is what you wish. My orders are to see you are safe, left undisturbed, and do anything I can to help you if needed. I was given very little information other than that, but I can assure you, I will do all those things with utmost efficiency and effectiveness.

There was no doubt by the way this guy talked and held himself that he was all professional and took his job very seriously. He did not look any older than thirty, but you could tell he was used to being in a position of authority for quite some time.

Brock: Do you have any questions, or is there anything you would like me to do?
Me: Right now the angry mob of journalists was my main concern. I thought they were about to kick my door in. (*I said this with a partial laugh and also a note of seriousness.*)
Brock: I can assure you they will not be bothering you anymore. I am posting fourteen officers twenty-four hours a day around your house, in which they have direct access to fifty more at any time if they feel they need them. You will not be disturbed again. If you need to go somewhere, you can take your car and be escorted or ask any of the officers to take you. They are under strict orders to help you in any way they can.

I have never been a big fan of the police, but it was hard not to like this guy. He certainly gave you the feeling of trust and that what he tells you is the way it is going to be, no ands, ifs, or buts about it.

Me: Thank you again, Agent Brock. I feel better already. I would like to have my car in the garage. Is it safe for me to go out there?
Brock: If you will open the garage door, I will see that one of the officers will drive it in and give you the keys.
Me: Thank you. I appreciate that. And yes, I will open it right now.

I went and pushed the button to the electric garage doors and opened them and saw an officer drive it in and park it. He got out of the car and handed me the keys. He nodded at Brock and walked back outside.

Brock: Anything else, Mr. Williams?
Me: I would appreciate it if you could see that my nephew also has some guards around him just in case. With all these reporters knowing who I am—
Brock: I will see to that immediately. I will have a dozen officers at the hospital at all times. I would also recommend that if you need to shop, as in need food or any other supplies, you just ask one of the officers outside and let them do any errands you may need done.
Me: Yes, I will do that. All I can say is thank you again. Your help is greatly appreciated.
Brock: I have two sons and a daughter, Mr. Williams, and love them more than anything on earth. Please do not worry about thanking me. Do whatever you need to do to keep this country and this world safe, and you will have my eternal loyalty.
Me: I have many people I love too, Agent. I will do my best to do just that.
Brock went into his breast pocket and pulled out a cell phone. It was not like any I had ever seen before. It was small and had an antenna, which was rare to see these days. It only had two buttons on it where there would normally be the screen.
Brock: This is a very special cell phone. It will never lose its signal and will work anywhere on earth. The button that has a B will connect you directly to me. That one you can use 24-7. The other has a P, which will connect you to the president. I would imagine, given the situation, that one can also be used 24-7. I myself will never be far from your house,

never more than five minutes, usually less. I am at your service for anything at any time. Is that clear to you, sir?

Seemed strange to have him call me sir, but I could hear in his voice and feel in his mind that, although his exterior showed a calm and professional man, on the inside he was worried and slightly nervous.

Me: Yes, Agent, I do have a request.
Brock: Of course.
Me: Don't call me sir. Makes me feel uncomfortable. Let's go back to Mr. Williams. Better yet, call me Thomas.
Brock: If that's what you wish, Thomas, sir.

I could not tell if that was an attempt at a joke or a person so well mentally trained he just could not help himself. I shook his hand this time. When I did, he gave me the full-on serious look.

Brock: 24-7, Thomas, I mean it. We need to keep you safe, and that's my job, and I have never failed an assignment yet.
Me: Understood, Agent Brock, and trust me, I won't be bashful. If I need you, I will call.

He then turned and opened the door and left to go back to the front yard. As he did, I could see there was no longer a reporter or news van in sight. The only thing outside my house was police cars and officers lined up on both sides of the street. I watched as he walked over to the other officer who drove my car into the garage and started to give all kinds of commands. He was pointing all around the neighborhood. I could see a couple of my neighbors still looking out their windows, staring at the police and my house. I shut the door and locked it. I will have to say this about the president—there was no doubt in my mind he believed me and was taking everything I told him 100 percent to heart. He also wasted no time getting these guys here. As much as the pressure was incredible on me, this did give me a little piece of mind and a small but needed feeling of reassurance.

What to do now? Knowing the ring's power will keep Olcult and anyone related to his evil doings away from the house combined with a multitude of law enforcement led by Agent Brock, it would allow me to concentrate on the big picture.

CHAPTER 22

Time was going by fast, and now with the invasion moved up, I really needed to start thinking about strategy. I know they are coming with large ships through a controlled wormhole in which only one ship at a time can go through. Being they have frozen the *Voyager* probe, they have a symbolic space arrow pointing to our solar system in the Milky Way galaxy. With that, chances are they will form the wormhole inside our solar system. They also will probably not create the wormhole too far from Earth. With all that in mind, what would be a good defense?

As I was pondering my strategy, my cell phone rang. I could see by the caller ID it was the hospital that Justin was at. My stomach instantly went into a knot. As much as I did not want to answer, of course, I needed to.

Me: Hello.

Dr. Ashton: Is this Thomas Williams?

Me: Yes.

Dr. Ashton: This Dr. Ashton. I am your nephew's doctor. We spoke at the hospital. I'm afraid I have some bad news. Your nephew has come out of the coma.

Me: Well, that is good news.

Dr. Ashton: Well, normally yes. But in your nephew's situation, it is not. His injuries are substantial. By him being awake, he now feels them at a conscious level, and the pain is no doubt excruciating. Now I have given him painkillers to help, but a very small dosage. He is in such bad shape that it would be unsafe to give him what normally a person in that medical condition would get to cope with the pain. The only other option is to induce a coma state, but once again, because of his condition, that is very dangerous as well. We need to do something. He cannot be left as he is, and some kind of action needs to be taken, but the options are very limited.

Me: What do you suggest, Doctor?

Dr. Ashton: To put him back in a coma would allow him to not suffer the pain of his injuries. It also makes it so we don't have to keep pumping him with morphine, which is not medically a good option to do in his state. But to put him back in coma has its own risks. It's up to you, Mr. Williams.

Me: Let me call you back.

Dr. Ashton: There is not a lot of time to make a decision. I cannot emphasize the importance of that.

Me: It will not be long, Doctor. I will call you back within the hour.

Dr. Ashton: Very good, Mr. Williams. You may call me back on this number. I have the hospital routing your calls directly to me.

Me: Thank you and thank you for all you're doing. I will call you shortly.

I then hung up. This situation never stops. Am I being tested of some kind? Is dealing with a pending invasion not enough? I looked down at the ring. I have to try. I looked at the ring and said in my mind, "Ring, I need you to fix my nephew. I need him to be repaired and be back as he was before this accident." The ring turned black. I knew what that meant.

The ring could not or was not allowed to do what I asked. I felt like I had been punched in the gut. I collapsed in my chair in the living room and started to cry. And it was not just a whimper but a full-blown cry where the tears are streaming down your face and you have a hard time breathing—the full deal. What am I supposed to do? The ring won't work, and that means it's beyond what the devil can do. The rules cannot be broken.

In the midst of this complete breakdown, my cell rang again. Thinking it was the hospital once more, I tried to clear my throat and disguise my complete emotional breakdown.

Me: Hello.

Olcult: Hello, Thomas.

Me: I don't feel like talking to you. I do have a gift for you, and it's coming very soon. Forget about that paradise world being promised to you. Your chances of being around when the smoke clears have just dropped to zero.

Olcult: Listen, Thomas, I'm not calling as your opponent. I am calling to see if we can talk and work this out.

Me: Oh I see. Getting sick of having snipers try to take me out or trucks run me down. Now you want to talk and be friendly?

Olcult: No, but what I would like to do is tell you the truth, what is really at stake.

Me: I know what's at stake.

Olcult: You think you know. But you're being tricked by one of the best ever. You're being lied to and led to believe you're the savior when it's exactly the opposite.

Me: I don't have time for these games. You are the enemy. You have betrayed your own human race. You are a sick and twisted piece of garbage.

Olcult: But, Thomas, I'm not the one who is working with the devil.

There was a silence for a few moments. How did he know that? Last I talked to him, he was still analyzing the source of my powers.

He thought I was working with another form of advanced beings in a far off separate galaxy from ours.

> Olcult: I see by the silence I have gotten your attention.

I certainly liked it better when he was wrong about the origins of my power. It gave me the feeling of having the upper hand. I was not about to let that advantage go so easily.

> Me: Wow, Olcult, I knew you had issues, but the devil? Really? Are we living back in the seventeenth century? Are you sure it's not Zeus or the tooth fairy?
>
> Olcult: Yes, I agree, I had a hard time with it at first as well, just as you must have in the beginning. But we both know it's true. Analysis shows when you transport or do your many other wonderful magic, it's just that, not advanced technology but some form of power that leaves a molecular residue of the origins of creation itself, but not that of the creator but more like one of the creator's first creations.
>
> Me: I really don't have time for this. I am going to hang up. Whatever drugs you have prescribed yourself, you better go easy on them.
>
> Olcult: If you give me ten minutes to hear me out, I will see to it that your nephew makes a remarkable recovery, just for ten minutes of you hearing me out.

I did not trust Olcult. He could just as easily have me hear him all out and do nothing to help Justin. But what do I have to lose to give him the ten minutes?

> Me: I don't believe you. It's hard to believe anyone who has tried to kill you more than three

times in just a few days. But what the hell. Let's hear your little mythical story.

Olcult: Hell indeed. Ever read the Bible, Thomas?

Me: Some of it.

Olcult: Well, I am more interested in the part about Revelation. Are you familiar with that section?

Me: A little.

Olcult: In Revelation it speaks about an Antichrist, someone who assists the devil. This Antichrist wheels incredible powers and gains the trust of the world. Although, working with the devil, he gets the leaders of the world to believe he is there to save them. Sound at all familiar? I believe you have been in contact with the president, which now has your house completely safeguarded to protect you. Your neighbors have seen you shoot lightning bolts from your fingertips. The president has told many of the United Nations leaders you are a superman of sorts who can do all kinds of things and they should all put their full trust into you. The Antichrist derives his powers directly from the Beast himself. Any of this coming together for you, Thomas?

Once again, I wanted to have quick and witty comeback, but it was hard. Everything Olcult said was true. But I cannot cave. I must use my revamped brain and think logically.

Me: Okay, let's say I believe your ridiculous story. In Revelation, the Antichrist brings upon the end of the world. Seems to me the Pelusoians are going to try and do that, not me or the so-called devil.

Olcult: Okay, try to follow me, if you can. The universe is continuously expanding. As time goes by, it is not slowing down with its expansion, it's speeding up. All the galaxies are flying to farthest reaches of the known universe. At some point, sooner than most understand, galaxies will become so distant from each other that there will be no stars when you look into the sky. Farther and faster, all the galaxies are flying apart, separating themselves by great distances. Their speed is doubling and tripling and exponentially going faster as time goes by. At some point all galaxies, all everything will be so far from each other they will not be able to be seen. Then they will all begin to cool. The suns will burn out, and the universe will literally die. Everyone and everything in every galaxy everywhere will cease to exist. All life will cease to exist. This will be the true end.

Me: I've heard this theory before. I believe they call it the great freeze or something like that. That's not for a very long time, and there is nothing that can be done.

Olcult: What if I tell you the Pelusoians are on the verge of a solution to this, saving the universe from death, not planetary death, not the death of a galaxy, but saving the universe from the death of all that exists?

Me: You're getting close to the end of your ten minutes. If I was working with the devil— and I am not saying I am— how is destroying Earth and its inhabitants going to help stop the destruction of the universe?

Olcult: Because, as I said, they are very close to a way to slow down the effects of dark energy and maybe even stop it altogether. It's even possible they can reverse its effects. But they are starving. They are dying out by the trillions. They have tried to ration food for the top scientists who can make this happen, but even they are about to starve and die. Earth and its seven billion humans and trillions of other eatable resources will buy them just enough time to finish their work and initiate their theory to save the universe. Look at the pressure you have with the weight of the world on your shoulders. Your world is one planet of countless others in your galaxy in a universe with countless galaxies.

Me: If this is true, and that's a big *if* because you are a clever liar who manipulates facts and people to get your own end result, but if it is, there has to be countless other planets that you could feed the Pelusoians.

Olcult: Not true. There are planets with life, but none close enough for the Pelusoians to get to in time, even with their wormhole technology. The Pelusoian scientists who need to be alive to implement this reaction will be long gone, and so will any chance of saving the universe. There is also the fact that we humans are well fed and mostly disease free. We have been fruitful and multiplied. We are of the perfect size and have the proper nutrients needed to for the Pelusoians, who are very limited on what they can eat. You are an intelligent person, Thomas, I know that. I have been told that the Pelusoians will give you the same offer they have given to me—a planet of your own filled with just selected humans of your choice who will be completely obedient to you and you alone. They have discovered a way to reverse the aging process and literally stop death and any form of sickness. You will live lifetimes at your physical peak as the ruler of a planet inhabited by the most beautiful beings there are for the rest of time.

Wow, as far as offers go, that would be one for the history books. I would be lying if I said that there was not a part of me that did not give that idea at least some thought. But Olcult is untrustworthy. The Pelusoians may be no better.

Me: Well, I have to say, that is one hell of a pitch. But I cannot betray the human race as you have so obviously done. Also, I do not believe I am the Antichrist. The Bible is very clear the Antichrist helps usher in the destruction of mankind. I am working to save mankind. No 666 on me anywhere nor do I plan to initiate a law where people need to have it on their hand or forehead.

Olcult: Those are minor details of the story. I'm sure you realize much of the Bible was written or rewritten and translated over and over again and added to here and there. But the basics are sound. No one can tell the exact future. It does not work that way. But there are probability outcomes that can be 70–80 percent accurate. You have so far followed very closely the role of Antichrist without even trying or even knowing who you are portraying in this situation.

Me: No, too farfetched—all of it. But if it's true that the universe will eventually come to an end of its existence, then that's the nature of existence. Born or created, live or exist, and burn out or die, it's just the way.

Olcult: So you are telling me that if an asteroid is headed to Earth that you should not attempt to deflect it or change its course because that's nature and that's the way it's supposed to be? Bullshit! You would do everything you can to live as long as possible. It's called survival, and that's the true logic you are failing to recognize.

Me: Everything has a price or cost. You are asking me to give up Earth and the human race so your Pelusoian buddies can make a universe that will last forever and defy the natural order of things.

Olcult: So instead you will be the devil's bitch. Yeah, save the world, but somewhere along the story, things will change, and you will be the cause for the fall of mankind.

Me: You said it yourself, Olcult, the future cannot be told or read. Too many variables to be able to see the final product with 100 percent accuracy. Anyway, this destruction of the universe is quite some time away.

Olcult: Time is not a constant, Thomas. Your short period is another being's eternity. Some insects only live for twenty-four hours. Their whole life is a day and a night. That same concept is true with higher life forms. Your millions of years is another being's next morning.

Me: Either way, how do you know that the human race does not figure out this same equation given our leaps in technology? Or maybe that is the real reason. The Pelusoians fear us humans will eventually surpass them on the evolutionary scale and turn the tables on them.

Olcult: I hate to even give you the odds on that. You have an ability to sense what is right. Your favorite line in one of your favorite movies, "The needs of the many outweigh the needs of the few." Do the seven billion on Earth outweigh the countless lives that exist or are yet to exist or will never get a chance to exist because time runs out for them? Your loyalty to your fellow humans is admirable, even though you got the shaft in your life too, if not more than I have.

Me: That may be true about me having many reasons to not have faith or stick up for my fellow man, but that does not mean you abandon them all. By the way, you forgot the rest of the quote from my favorite movie, "The needs of the many outweigh the needs of the few or the one," the "one" being yourself, doing what is right because you need to do it, because to not do it would be impossible to live with yourself and that decision.

Olcult: So you are going to be the Antichrist?

Me: No, I am going to be Thomas Williams. I am going to believe in my fellow man and do what I know to be right.

Olcult: To be right? Your partner in crime is evil itself. It's the counterbalance to good, you idiot. Rationalize it all you want, but it still comes down to the same conclusion. You are working with the devil, the master of deception and evil, and you're using the power he gives you and doing what he wants you to do. But somehow that is the right thing to do?

Me: Or give up all my brothers and sisters as well as the creatures of Earth and their offspring so they never have a chance. Anyway, since when did you get all religious on me? What happened to all that pure logic and science? Now you believe in a story primitive man created to explain the unexplainable. That was a giant leap.

Olcult: The change occurred because of science and logic. The analysis of the things you are doing was not of science or machine, even with the concept that primitive man would see a cell phone or jet as godly or magical when it really is just technology beyond their understanding. But the power you wield has none of the properties to explain it as anything but real magic, a power from the essence of the beginning of time and creation itself. Even in the face of something I find hard or impossible to believe, I have to come to terms with what is the only explanation. When you do your thing, it leaves a fingerprint, the same fingerprint from two thousand years ago, except not quite the same. Thomas, I could sit here and explain the science, and it would take longer than we have. I am not fully convinced myself. The whole "God and devil" concept seems below my intelligence, but I have to weigh the empirical evidence. I know that ring on your finger has been given abilities that derive from the only real magic that exists. It's from God, but not directly. Even if you don't agree with me and this fight goes on, chances are you will lose. There will be a huge death toll, probably on both sides, and if the Pelusoians win, there may be too many casualties on Earth to feed them long enough to finish their research and save the universe. If you win, the universe loses by a slow death where it gradually fades into nothingness and no life at all exists. Please think this out.

Me: I think we are going in circles now, Olcult. I am not going to give up the earth to anyone or any race. Humans have a future and a destiny. You're right, we cannot see the future, but we have to give them the chance to have one. That is my final word.

Olcult: Okay, Thomas, you know who you are working for. You know what he stands for and what the Bible says about him. When you finally see the truth about him, it will be too late, and you will have not saved mankind. You will go down in history as the one that sent mankind to hell and allowed the universe

> and all life to go extinct by the greatest liar and deceiver that ever was. And you did this knowing all the facts. Don't forget that.

With that he hung up the cell. His last words rang in my ears over and over. I knew from the beginning I was working with the devil, but this is the first time I had someone say it to me no holds barred. The crisp reality of it being said out loud just hit harder than at any time I questioned the aspect myself. Olcult, with all his rottenness, was good at drilling home his point using a combination of logic and common sense. I am working with the devil. I am doing what he wants me to do. But I am doing it to save the world. This had to be the "lesser of two evils" scenario playing its way out. I was doing the right thing. I was doing it for the right reason, right?

The rest of the day I tried to keep myself busy with simple or normal things I have not been doing because of my new life. I did laundry, the dishes, vacuum, and whatever I could to keep my mind off the big picture. But no matter what I did, I kept hearing Olcult and what he said. When you're young, you always believed there was right and wrong, and it was as easy to determine which is which just by telling the color black from white. But it's not that way. The shades of grey are immense. Saving the world has got to be the right thing. Working with the devil has got to be the wrong thing. Saving the universe has got to be the right thing. This dilemma was best to be sorted out by the best scholars and philosophers. Once again I got that overwhelming feeling I was way out of my element and far out of my league.

The doctor had called from the hospital and said that they had no choice and could not wait for my call, that Justin was put into an induced coma without any problems so far. His vitals were strong, and he seemed to be holding his ground.

Every few hours I would collapse in my chair and cry. Toby would always seek me out during each breakdown and sit on my lap and lick my face. He was shaking as I was. He knew the stress and pressure I was under. In his own doggy way, he would do his best to comfort me. Toby used to do that with Shawn too. Toby loved us both unconditionally and showed it every chance he could.

CHAPTER 23

After hours of cleaning and doing busywork, I heard something outside, something I had never heard before. It was a loud siren but not like on a police car but more of a loud horn. I got up and went outside, where it was even louder. It was an ominous sound. It seemed to originate from more than one place. They would all go off at the same time but from multiple locations. It went on for five minutes and continued to off. I was unsure what it was. While outside, I looked down at Toby, who also was hearing it and turning his head in that way a dog does when he seems to be analyzing something. When I looked down, I saw my ring was glowing brightly. Its glowing was synchronized perfectly with the horn going off. Something is wrong. Something has happened.

I ran into the house and turned on the TV. The screen was black, yet I could hear the announcers talking. As I switched the channels, I noticed the same black picture was on every channel. I had turned the TV on mute last time I was watching it, so I turned up the volume.

The TV and all the channels were not showing a black screen; they were showing a live picture from the Hubble Telescope. It was a picture of space. But it showed on TV as just black. Then the picture showed something in the corner. The Hubble Telescope moved its angle to show the planet Jupiter. I was not a huge astronomy student, but Jupiter had a very distinct look to it.

The spinning eye, which was a hurricane the size of earth, made it obvious to any viewer which planet this was. Why are they focused on Jupiter? So I turned up the TV quite loudly to try and drown out the horn blasting outside. They were showing a full screen of what the telescope was focused on with half of Jupiter and half of the blackness of space.

> Broadcaster: The disturbance was just picked up within the last couple minutes. Although nothing can be seen in the spot Hubble has focused on next to Jupiter, scientists insist that other satellites are tracking unknown radioactivity coming from this same coordinate. At first it was believed that the planet Jupiter had been once again hit by a comet, but they have now ruled that out and say that these readings are coming from a distance of 350,000 miles to the side of the giant planet. But as you can see, when Hubble is directed to that position, nothing out of the ordinary can be seen. With recent events from the *Voyager* probe, any anomaly is being scrutinized by the world's top scientists. This just in, the *Voyager* probe, which almost a week ago sent us that terrifying message which had the world in a state of panic, has baffled scientists by stopping dead in space in contrast to all known scientific explanations and laws of physics. *Voyager* also just ceased communication by radio signal to NASA. We are currently trying to get confirmation of this from NASA, but we are yet to get any reply from them.

Just then I heard another strange sound from my room. Although I wanted to try to find out all I could about this event, the sound continued. As I got up to see what was making this strange sound, I discovered it was the cell phone Agent Brock had given to me. It was no wonder I did not recognize it; the ringtone was extremely unusual, like nothing I had heard before. I grabbed it and answered.

> Me: Hello

President: Mr. Williams?

Me: Yes?

President: I want to make you aware of these new events. I'm sure you have ways of knowing what's going on far beyond my resources, but I was not sure if you were updated on what is happening near Jupiter.

Me: Only from the TV and apparently some warning siren that's been going off here.

President: With the sirens, we were hoping the local division authorities were going to hold off on the emergency sirens, but anyway, one of our satellites picked up a radiation signal. We thought at first it was something from Earth, maybe a nuclear power plant or experiment, but we have determined it is coming from space. We then thought it was from our sun and possibly some unique form of solar flares. After further investigation, we ruled that out as well. It is coming from a position outside the orbit of Jupiter's moons.

Me: I was watching on TV and saw Hubble was pointed to a spot near the planet, but it does not appear that anything is happening in that location.

President: We agree. The exact spot we have tracked this radiation spike to does not appear to have any anomalies. But my best men are telling me there is, and it is not a natural phenomenon. Something is going on in that location. I wanted to know if you had any insight.

Me: Not yet, Mr. President, but as I said, I was just made aware of this situation. I am certainly going to further investigate it.

President: From our conversation, I was under the impression there was going to be more time. Was I mistaken?

Me: No, but this is not an exact science for any of us, Mr. President. I know the timetable was moved up, but I thought we still had much more preparation time. These Pelusoians are smart and very advanced, but I have recently discovered they are desperate as well. We all know what happens to a wild animal when it is cornered and becomes desperate.

President: Is there anything I should know, or any suggestions on what I should do?

Me: Just try to keep the public calm. Make up a story using some kind of a rational explanation. Eventually there will be no way to hide this. Until that time, we should just try our best to contain it.

President: Well, the cell phone Agent Brock gave you will connect us at any time. No information is too small. Anything you think I should know, do not delay in contacting me. Brock is also there to help you any way possible. Brock is one of my best men and will do whatever it takes to do what you ask of him.

Me: Yes, I have met Agent Brock. I want to thank you for him. His arrival came at the very best time possible. Let me see what I can find out and get back to you. I have to be honest, Mr. President, this could be an early warning of the wormhole formation.

President: If that's where the wormhole forms, our best and fastest would take years to get there. There will be little we can do. We were hoping, if the wormhole was closer, we might be able to—

Just then I could hear a commotion of voices on the other end of the cell phone, multiple people talking at once to the point where I could hear the president yell at them to talk one at a time.

President: Mr. Williams, we have just got some new intel. It's almost hard to believe.

Me: Okay, I'm ready for the unbelievable at this point.

President: Hubble has picked up an object at the coordinates very close to the center of where we are getting the energy readings.

Me: Okay, well, maybe we can get an idea of what is generating all this radiation.

President: The object is not what is generating the radiation signature. It's the *Voyager* probe. It is next to Jupiter. We have confirmed this visually. Its last known position was outside of our solar system when we lost track of its signal. It has gone from the Oort cloud to orbiting Jupiter millions of miles in minutes, possibly even seconds. There are several civilian telescopes that are going to see this. There will be no explaining this to the public.

I could hear the shakiness in his voice. My nerves were not much better, but I had to maintain my calm.

Me: Are they absolutely sure it is the *Voyager* probe?

President: Yes, it has resumed communication with NASA. We also have a full visual on it. It's the *Voyager* probe without any doubt.

Me: Why would they do that? I'm sorry, Mr. President, I was just thinking out loud. Let me see what I can do to get you some information.

President: Very good, Mr. Williams. I will await your call. Thank you and God bless us all.

He then disconnected, leaving me standing there, shaking internally and externally. I feel like a novice checkers player trying to play chess against a computer. I was out of my league. I felt like I was about to vomit. My head got very warm, and I even felt a bit dizzy.

This was not the posture of a man ready to save the world but more like a scrawny schoolboy about to get beat up by the neighborhood bully.

The president's voice was unlike how I am used to hearing him when he does speeches—with confidence in every word, just the opposite of the man's voice I just talked to.

It was time I spoke with the devil again. I had been putting it off. After my conversation with Olcult, I was really reluctant to talk with him. Olcult was a liar and a bastard, but I got a strong sense he was telling me what he truly believed. His perspective may be different than mine, but the facts (if true) are the facts. There was no way I was the Antichrist. But as I reviewed his words, what he said rang so accurate. Without even knowing it, I was following the path he described without even trying. The situation was unfolding in a way that made it look like I was the Antichrist.

I tried to put it in perspective: On one side I have Olcult, a human who has been raised and brainwashed from his first memories to hate mankind combined with the abuse in his childhood that helped in guiding him down this path. He was well educated by human schooling and also taught at a level far beyond the knowledge of our world. He was bribed with the ultimate idealist "happily ever after" ending to motivate his every desire. He was almost a Hitler type in some strange correlation.

On the other side was the devil. He is the one mankind has been conditioned to know as evil incarnate. The one who would ultimately bring the beings of Earth to the brink of disaster and throw them into the pit of hell. His intelligence and knowledge combined with thousands (or hundreds of thousands) of years' experience with all human history and everything they have ever done or thought at his disposal.

One thing is for sure, I cannot do a tightrope act. I need to pick a side and, no matter what, back that side without doubt or hesitation. I cannot let my personnel views or experience cloud my judgment. Olcult has tried to kill my nephew and me several times. Although he claims he is doing this for some honorable cause of saving the universe, he is doing this because he hates the human race and the way he was treated throughout his life. But most of all, he is doing this for his own benefit, that shiny reward at the end he is sure the Pelusoians are going to give him for a job well done.

I left the TV on in the other room and could hear all kinds of discussions and scientific talk, so I decided to go back out and catch what they were saying. The picture was now reruns of what I saw before of Jupiter and then panned back to the side of it and that spot in space.

> Broadcaster: We have lost our feed from NASA and with the Hubble Telescope and are told the government has stopped them from allowing us to view the images. But we have two other civilian satellites we are trying to access so we may continue to view the area in question. Before we lost Hubble's transmission, we caught this image. Although blurred, we have attempted to clear it up. It appears to be the *Voyager* probe that had left our solar system but somehow is now near Jupiter's orbit. Our own experts have now confirmed that this is the *Voyager* probe. We can distinctly see the golden album that was attached to it when it was launched back in the seventies.

At that point she was interrupted by someone on her earpiece.

> Broadcaster: We are being told that we now have an image from a land-based telescope and have confirmed it is the *Voyager* spacecraft. Its last known position was millions of miles from Jupiter. There also appears to be something happening at the site. Let's see if our uplink can show us what this new telescope is seeing.

The image started off very blurry, and you can tell there were television technicians franticly trying to zoom and focus and do their best to improve the picture and clarity. The image showed *Voyager* frozen in space with the golden album facing us, making it obvious it was exactly what they were claiming it to be.

> Broadcaster: As you can see, it clearly is *Voyager*. Maybe we can pan back a little to show its position with Jupiter.

The telescope/camera did pan back. As it did, it showed once again the corner of the giant planet. As the camera/telescope began to focus more on the probe, the craft began to glow, dim at first but steadily brighter and brighter. Then the tiny craft, which looked frozen in space, began to spin. Between the movement and the changing brightness of the probe, it was hard to keep it in focus.

> Broadcaster: Okay, we are going to split screen. We have another telescope from New Mexico that seems to have a better view of these events.

The screen split into two images. The first one still showed the little craft spinning like a kite in a tornado. But the second image was much clearer. This second telescope was obviously of a much higher quality. It showed Jupiter in the background but also a very good look at the *Voyager* probe, which was a good distance to the left of the planet. The probe was not only getting brighter, it started to emit all kinds of colors as it spun faster and faster, red, blue, and green and the colors were brighter and started changing so fast that it almost looked as if it was blending into one color.

Suddenly the small craft exploded into a brilliant bright light. This took the cameras off focus for a couple seconds, and then they came back. There was no more probe. In its place was a vortex of light spinning rapidly and expanding quickly. It was still very bright and still emitted multiple colors; although the colors began to fade to just a white light. With Jupiter in the background, it was hard to make a judgment of the scale size. It continued to increase in mass and then seemed to stop. Then the brightness of light began to dim. What was left was just a black spot with the flickering stars all around it where the *Voyager* probe was. You could easily see the outline of a circle because the stars were all around it except for that one area, a black circle of emptiness.

The broadcaster who was trying to keep up with describing the events had lost her words, and there was just silence with some mumbles from people in the newsroom where they were broadcasting from.

Then from the immense starless hole in space came the tip of a triangular ship, narrow in the front coming to a point, but as it came out farther from the hole, it began to show a thicker mass. It looked to be silver and shiny and not like any human creation. It took it at least a minute to fully exit the hole. The ship turned and left the area of the dark circle and maneuvered toward Jupiter and then stopped. Suddenly there was a bright light that came from the ship and shot at the planet, but it did not seem to hit or harm it. But the other view showed it did have some kind of impact because it lit up something close to Jupiter. Another bright light came out and hit something else in a different area.

At this point the broadcaster had been replaced because it appeared she had become too overwhelmed with what she was seeing and left her spot at the table, and a gentleman took her place.

> Broadcaster 2: It is hard to describe what we have seen here. But it seems the *Voyager* spacecraft appeared near Jupiter's orbit. Our telescopes had locked on to it and confirmed what it was. The craft began to spin and glow. It finally exploded and turned to a swirl of colors and debris. When it cleared, there appeared to be a giant hole in space which was void of stars. At which point, and we can only speculate, an alien spacecraft with dimensions we are unsure of came out of this hole in space. A ship triangular in shape and of a design like nothing this reporter or quite likely any human being has ever seen before exited the hole, turned sharply toward Jupiter, and shot a bright light from the front of the ship, and I am now being handed an update. The two beams of light

which came from the alien ship destroyed two of Jupiter's moons known as Ganymede and Europa. This has been confirmed by three other satellites from other places around the world.

In the midst of all this, my special cell phone rang. I did not have to be psychic to know who it was. I answered it in as calm a voice as I could manage.

Me: Hello, Mr. President.
President: I take it you saw what they did. There is no way to keep this from the public. Tell me you have some news for me.
Me: Not yet, but I think it's safe to say that it has begun. That's just the first ship of many.
President: Why blow up Jupiter's moons? Is there some inside information why they would do that?
Me: No, I believe they are just demonstrating their power and technology to us.
President: Ganymede is the size of Mercury. They blew it into pieces with one shot. One hit like that to us will be catastrophic. I am hoping you are ready to stop something like that weapon if it's used on Earth.
Me: Sadly, Mr. President, they won't use that on Earth. It would kill too many of us. They need us for food. So that won't be an issue.
President: You are sure of this?
Me: Yes. When they attack us, it will be with ground troops. So if you have any high-level secret weapons at Area 51 or somewhere, now would be the time to get our soldiers acquainted with using them. This fight will be hand to hand and not from a giant laser in the sky.

President: Well, thank God for that. At least it gives us a chance.

Me: I would not go that far. Their ground and portable weapons are no doubt just a smaller version of what they used to take out the two moons.

President: We may have some weapons that are not readily known to the public and are rather advanced, but nothing like people think we have. I am going to address the world. Anything you want me to say to them or add to my speech?

Me: Just confirm you have a secret weapon and it is very advanced and as powerful as our alien invaders have.

President: I was thinking more in the lines of being able to tell them about you. Something to give hope. With what everyone just witnessed on TV, hope is going to be our strongest weapon.

Me: Chances are they are monitoring everything, maybe even this call. Let's not give them anything more that could help them. I still need to consult with someone. I will get back to you soon. In the meantime, have your speech writer's do their best work ever. It's going to be needed.

President: I will, and they will. You are the only hope this planet has, Thomas. I know you don't need that pressure nor do you need to be told that, but I feel I had to say it anyway.

Me: I know. Try to keep the world calm. I will get back to you soon.

President: Very well, and may God guide your thoughts and actions.

Me: Thank you.

Why did he have to phrase it like that? Comments like that just make Olcult's claims and words speak louder in my mind and give me more doubts at a time I cannot afford them. Makes me wonder where God is at a time like this. There are billions of people scared out of their wits, who must be praying to him for help and intervention. I know he exists. Even the devil says that. But if we are his children, why does he not help us?

> TV/Devil: Because he has more important things to do than watch over Earth.

The TV which had the news footage of the events in space was now showing the devil in his chair in the mansion.

This is new. I thought he could not speak to me through my mind anymore?

> Devil: I'm not, I'm speaking through your TV.
>
> Me: I did not say that out loud. How did you know what I was thinking?
>
> Devil: I think the time to worry about the small details has come and gone. If you have not noticed, the game clock has started.
>
> Me: Yeah, I saw. When you said they moved up their timetable, you were not kidding.
>
> Devil: I have not been kidding with you at all about anything since the beginning. Better realize this is no game and what is on the line here, Thomas.

I could not sense him through the TV as I could when I am in the mansion with him. It was obvious he was talking and acting very raw and rough with me. Of course, it is, as he says, game time, and his worry meter might be bending off the gauge at this point.

> Me: Go easy there, Luke. It does not help to vent it all on me. I have a lot on my plate too.
>
> Devil: Oh am I being mean to you? Suck it up, soldier. This is no time to go soft. Thicken that greasy skin and realize this is it. What we

have been talking about and planning for is now happening.

Me: What's with all the insults? My skin is thick, but I don't need you or Olcult fucking with my head.

Devil: Yeah, I know all about the claims Olcult has made. I warned you that, with all his advanced toys and super knowledge, his most dangerous weapon is his manipulation and mind games. But you sucked it right up. Ever heard the term *divide and conquer*? It's one of the oldest and most effective strategies in war.

Me: I know all about it. But with all your insults and witty comments, you have danced right by the real question. Is it true?

Devil: The Pelusoians are now in this galaxy, my galaxy and yours. They are no longer out of range.

Me: You did not answer my question!

Devil: I am talking to you through the TV because we can't afford to have you away from your body. I hope you have some ideas and have dug deep into your revamped brain to come up with some good stuff, or this will be a quick war.

Me: Not going to answer me?

Devil: You have a lot more to worry about than that. I have one last bit of advice. Remember when I told you to keep it small and simple?

I was pissed off with the way he was acting and that he would not answer my question, so I did not answer his. I looked away from the TV and him. Just then, the room shook, and it darkened outside to almost night. His voice came roaring way louder than the speakers in the TV would have the capability to do. This caught me off guard, and I looked back at the TV to say something smart-ass back as we have both had done so many times in the past with our conversations. When I looked at the screen, I saw a very different-looking devil sitting in the throne. It was not the excessively good-looking skater/surfer dude in his early twenties; it was a red-skinned body connected to a face right out of a nightmare.

Devil: This is no time to have one of your hissy fits. I picked you to win this, and if you don't, you will have an eternity to realize how upset I am. Now I will ask you one last time, do you remember what I said about keeping it simple and small?

I was scared of him. For the first time, I was really scared of him.

Me: Yes.
Devil: Time to drop that way of thinking. You need to do whatever it takes to get the conclusion we have discussed. Are you hearing me?
Me: Yes.

As quickly as it went dark, the light of the sun came back through the window. It startled me, mostly because I was very fidgety at that point. When I looked back at the screen, the devil was back to the way I was used to seeing him, very handsome and drinking a martini.

Devil: Sorry if I was a little loud with you, Thomas, but there are no more simulations. This is the real deal. Don't doubt me. To doubt me is to doubt yourself. That will not help the cause at this point.
Me: I realize you are trying to motivate me, and you are doing what you feel will help in these upcoming events, but with all your years with humans and accumulated wisdom, don't you see I am at the breaking point. More pressure is the last thing I need.
Devil: Okay, maybe I let myself go a little too far. I just need you to know this is it. Time to do

> what we talked about. Loosing will kill everyone and will leave me and you in a terrible situation. Don't let that happen. Don't lose. Do what you must. You have heard my threats, so let me leave you with a more positive note. Win. Get them somehow to forget about Earth and this galaxy, and I will reward you, reward you in every way possible and some ways impossible for you to even comprehend. We will talk again soon.

With that he held up his martini glass and gave me a toast, and *poof*, the TV shut off. Once again, I sat in the chair wondering how someone like me could be put in a situation of this magnitude. Advanced beings have entered our solar system and want us for dinner. The time to back out or quit was long gone. Now that I look back, I'm not sure there ever was a time or option for that. I was drafted.

Maybe I did go along with this at first because I wanted to be the one who saves the world. Maybe I was also flattered that I was picked as the best choice. But I now see this was no reward or blessing. Being picked for this was not a great honor at all. It was a curse of the worst kind. Everything is up to me. Win or lose, death and destruction were on the menu. If the human race was going to have a chance to evolve any further and survive, it would be based on me and my actions from this point forward.

I looked down at the ring. I said out loud, "It's all up to you and me."

> Me: The world is depending on me to save it. I am the good guy, the hero, and I am not going to turn into the Antichrist. Am I?

With that I walked into my room, not noticing that, after I said that, the ring blinked once in the positive.

To be continued.

This is a Trilogy.

The Devil's Science Part 1
IN THE BEGINNING

The Devil's Science Part 2
DAVID AND GOLIATH

The invasion has started, and Thomas is faced with the impossible odds of going to war with an entire army of advanced aliens whose goal is to make all life on Earth food for their race. While battling for the safety of Earth and its occupants, he must also fight his own priorities and beliefs. How far will he go to protect Earth, and what will be the ultimate cost of attempting to save us all?

The Devil's Science Part 3
REVELATION

This is the incredible conclusion of this trilogy that will leave the reader sleepless and terrified. Is Thomas the savior of all mankind, or is he the one the Christians have been warned of thousands of years ago? This final book will tie up all loose ends and leave readers with deep philosophical and ethical questions to ponder the rest of their lives.

ABOUT THE AUTHOR

Jate Hemms was brought up in far upstate New York (20 minutes from the Canadian border) in a middle income family. A shy kid through much of high school, he gradually came out of his shell in college. Always good at communicating on paper, that ability sharpened and expanded in a way that he could verbally express himself to persuade others. Jate also discovered he had a knack for speaking to crowds or audiences and ultimately getting him on the college debate team. Although not much of an athlete, he has always enjoyed sports and commentating games during his college years. Always interested in Science and Astronomy, he took every class he could in those fields. Finding that many people were offended by some aspects of science and how it conflicted with religious and biblical beliefs. He also studied all forms of world religion, especially Christianity which allowed him to be able to try and see both sides of the argument in an educated way. Always being caught in the middle of these two ever clashing topics, he tried to create a way that would combine them both, so room for compromise could be made. Happy that our new Pope recently made the announcement that science was not the enemy of the church, he continues to try to bring both groups together and inspire others with his stories.

CPSIA information can be obtained at www.ICGtesting.com
Printed in the USA
LVOW11s1914060915

453069LV00002B/58/P